THE PERSUADER

Robert Pollock

THE PERSUADER

G. P. Putnam's Sons
New York

FIRST AMERICAN EDITION 1970

Copyright © 1970 by Robert Pollock

Library of Congress Catalog Card Number: 79-114402

PRINTED IN THE UNITED STATES OF AMERICA

For
Wynne, Adam and Ben

THE PERSUADER

There were times when he knew how to love,
Long ago when ideals were born,
But he learned how much they could hurt him;
Now he lives so he'll never be torn.

The Persuader was born to deceive, he's a man you should never believe.

It's tough and you've got to be strong,
Or they'll crush what you're trying to make.
You protect what you have of your own life
Though you know that to do it you'll fake.

The Persuader was born to deceive, he's a man you should never believe.

That's how it goes 'cause they make the rules:
No crossing the line or playing with fools,
To know them too well is a sin they can't bear,
Persuade them too far and they'll turn and say how could you dare?
They'll forget that they taught you to lie for a sham called success,
Then you'll end with your dreams on the heap and your life in a mess.

The Persuader was born to deceive, he's a man you should never believe.

And they say that he cheated to win
That he lived and to hell with the cost.
Well, he's paid and the price was his real self,
So now the Persuader is lost.

"The Persuader Song"
Music by Dudley Moore.
Words by Robert Pollock.
World Copyright.

NOTE

One of the problems of having real people in a novel is that time will not stand still, that between my writing and your reading fate will almost certainly have moved in and altered the situation. It does not help that fashion itself is wholly orientated to continual change, and in all probability this principle permeates through to the people reporting about it. So, rather than pander to the constant urge to be ahead, I must ask you to accept that, at the time, the real people written about did exist and worked for the newspapers and magazines stated.

The other characters, the fictionalized ones, are composites, taken and made up from personal experience and observation. If they appear to mirror actual persons, either in name or in description, then this is purely in the imagination of the reader and is not intended.

ROBERT POLLOCK

Putney Heath, London, 1969

Between the idea
And the reality
Between the motion
And the act
Falls the Shadow . . . of the Persuader

With acknowledgment and apologies
to T. S. Eliot and "The Hollow Men"

1

SINCLAIR hated press parties, particularly the ones he organized. It was eleven thirty, half an hour before the first journalist would sign in and start the expense-account champagne flowing. He told the white-coated waiter to pour him a Scotch, and then he walked onto the balcony. He stood eighteen floors above Sloane Street and looked out over London. It was late April, warm but slightly overcast, and he could see the trees in the square below and they were still. A perfect day for trout. On the Test, near Stockbridge, it was almost time for the noon rise. He could visualize the river and his favorite beat, and he saw the water ripple as if someone had thrown a pebble into it. His first cast fell short; he let the rod end dip, then whipped the line back, let out more line and watched it as it snaked and then fell with the light, pretty imitation fly settling last. That one was very good: He tensed as his heart beat with the special quiver that only a fisherman understands.

"Well, Sinclair, think we'll get a good turnout?"

He almost jerked, but as he turned to answer, his face showed its confident, easy smile. "I think so, Major Carter. It's a very pleasant day, there are plenty of taxis around, and after all we do have a good product."

The major laughed. He still looked like a major, which was what he had been a long time ago, but now he was a managing director—not perhaps a very different role, exept that instead of a company of trained fighting men he had a cosmetics company to control. Sinclair had often wondered how the hell a typecast army man came to be running a beauty organization. He always came back to the major's wife. She must have been about fifty, but she looked as if she'd been on a course of the Swiss doctor's cell shots. Her skin was very smooth, and the lines it carried were what you would expect to see on a well-cared-for forty-two-year-old. Sinclair never felt very secure with her: She always managed to show him just too much thigh when she sat in his office, and if she stood near him, her breasts inevitably ended up pressing against his arm. It was all too Hollywood; he knew that she expected him to react to her. He wished to Christ they'd all grow up and try screwing someone else. Probably she had done, and that was how the major came to be in the beauty business.

They went back into the suite together. The major was impatient: He liked the feeling of importance that talking to the press gave him. The questions they asked were always unloaded and innocuous enough to allow him to expound at length about the company and its achievements. Nobody ever asked him about the cost of the emotionally inviting jars and bottles that his company poured its beauty-promising creams into—whether they in fact cost more to produce than their contents and, if so, why. Sinclair —and an expensive and well-placed advertising budget—took care of that. He could stand away from the hard facts of his business life and chatter on about the scientific chaps who'd come up with yet another wonder for the age-hating public. And if you worked for a magazine whose existence depended on the advertising pages that Carnel Cosmetics and its competitors bought from you, then you too would shy from the awkward, misplaced inquiry. "It's the promise that sells," Sinclair had told him. "If they believe the promise, they'll make it come true—they have to, and to do it they'll even deceive themselves."

Two middle-aged women arrived at the reception table, and Sue Black, Sinclair's assistant, asked them to sign the visitors' book. Sinclair primed the major. "The tall one is Esther Grace; she's the editor of *Beauty Shop*. The other one's Doreen Spears. They travel as a pair. You just have to be polite; they're trade press, and they'll print whatever we send them."

He took Carter over to meet them.

"Esther, Doreen, you both know Major Carter, don't you?" They gushed, and Sinclair moved away before they could bore the arse off him as well as his client.

He stood back and looked at the room. It was the Tower Suite at the Carlton Tower. The partition between what was normally the lounge and the bedroom had been pushed back and the space cleared. Among the whole of one side were cloth-covered trestle tables, carrying the bar and a very lush buffet luncheon spread. Against the far wall was the presentation table. There "the product" and its advertising and sales literature gleamed in full glossy color. It was Carnel Cosmetics' launching pad for Hometan, the cream that gave you a painless tan in only four hours. The entire campaign right down to the wrapping on the jar was based on a split picture. One half showed an attractive but pale-skinned girl sitting at her makeup table applying the cream. The second half showed the same girl, beautiful and bronzed, running through the surf on an idyllic-looking beach. Sinclair had tried it out on himself. It had worked, but it made him look like a fag chorus boy from a second-rate touring company.

He wondered whether he should go into the adjoining suite to check the models but decided against it. If the gimmick hadn't worked, there was not much he could do about it now. The room was beginning to fill at last, and the dead quiet of the preparty lull, when everything was neat and tidy and the waiters nervously fidgeted with their carefully placed rows of empty glasses, was giving way to the hum of activity. The atmosphere had relaxed because the strain of not knowing whether the guests were going to come or not had been eased; now it was only a question of degree and numbers. In another five minutes the room would be crowded, and it would be difficult to find a waiter for a second or third drink. It was work time.

Sinclair checked the celebrity turnout. It looked very good. Ernestine Carter of the *Sunday Times* was sitting on the long sofa by the windows talking to Beatrix Miller, the editor of *Vogue*. Sinclair looked around for the major, but he was still holding an audience on the other side of the room with two dykes who were hanging on to every word, and since the man was obviously enjoying himself so much, Sinclair decided to postpone the introductions. The beauty girls from *Woman's Own* were swapping gossip with a randy photographer; as Sinclair wove through the crush, his eyes searched the faces and his mind eavesdropped. The trick was not to let them catch your gaze and so spark off recognition. If he thought a conversation worth listening to, he would stop with his back to them; his right ear was well trained.

He saw Brigid Keenan from *Nova* at the signing-in desk. He wanted to talk to her about a possible feature. But as he started to worm his way through the crush, he was stopped short, by the sound of his own name.

"For once it was Dan Sinclair who got dropped."

"What made Tessa do it? God, I'd give him a double-page spread just for the promise. In color."

"Darling, you'd give the magazine away if you had the chance."

That was a piece of gossip he could do without.

It was a quarter past one, and Sinclair's antennae told him the party was at its peak. He scanned the room, mentally rechecking the important names. Most of the newspaper girls were there, from the *Times* through to the *Daily Mirror* and the *Sketch*. They were the instantly important ones. Because of the publication time lag he could always pick up the magazine editors later, but even they seemed to have come out en masse.

"Hello, Dan."

He turned and saw Mary Steward, assistant to Tessa Drake on the *Perceptor*.

"Hello, Mary. How's Fleet Street's top column?"

"Circulation rising as usual. Have you seen my boss and your friend yet?"

"I didn't know Tessa was here. We haven't been in touch lately. Let's say we have a conflict of ideals. Your boss doesn't really approve of PR men. This particular PR man, anyway."

"Maybe you should change your image, give up PR and go legit."

"What, and miss all the fun? No, I don't think so, there's nothing wrong with Public Relations; we've all got it, you know."

"I suppose so. Maybe not everybody appreciates the message."

Sinclair was anxious to move on. "You're probably right. Well, I think it's time we showed you people what you've come to see. Take care, Mary."

He squeezed his way past the elegant backs and only paused to give brief hellos to Penny Graham from the *Evening News* and Judy Innes, the fashion editor of the *Daily Mail*. On his way to the major he mentally checked that enough of the photographers knocking back the booze had actually brought their equipment with them. The major had torn himself loose from the trade and had transferred his ego to the national daily press. He was talking to Tessa Drake, and for an instant Sinclair almost changed direction—almost, but not quite. He interrupted them.

"Hello, Tessa, how are you? I'm sorry, Major, but I'll have to prize you away from Miss Drake. It's time you handled the presentation."

"Yes, of course. Maybe we can continue after I've done my little piece, Miss Drake."

"I'm sure we can, Major Carter. I think we can rely on Dan to bring us back together again. He's very good at bringing people together, aren't you, Dan?"

"I think that depends on the people, Tessa. Some just don't jell, do they?"

Sinclair led the major to the presentation table. He felt like a toastmaster, but there was not much alternative, so he made it as curt as possible. He simply banged on the table, waited for the murmuring to subside and then gave a short, but *short,* introduction.

The major coughed and pushed his hands into the pockets of his double-breasted jacket. "Ladies and . . . ah"—he looked around the room—"yes, gentlemen. [*Pause for faint titter.*] I'm sure you all know Carnel Cosmetics." He inclined a grateful smile toward Sinclair. "As I've been telling some of your colleagues, we are about to launch the latest product in a long line of highly successful merchandise: Hometan. [*Further pause for scattered applause.*] Before you leave, you will of course be given a sample jar of Hometan to test for yourselves, together with all the relevant literature." Sinclair was praying he'd keep it short. "If by any unforeseen chance the name of your publication does not appear on the extensive advertising schedule, then don't despair; [*more laughter*] we haven't completed it yet, so there is still time." Very droll: In other words, play ball with the editorials and who knows? we might toss you some advertising revenue. "And now it is my extreme pleasure to present some of the cast from that scintillating West End smash hit musical, *Surfride.*"

The major stepped down, amid gasps of surprise and applause. The room rocked with the blast of music, the door to the adjoining suite burst open, and seven members of the *Surfride* cast irrupted into the room. As they formed up and went into an erotic go-go dance, the self-styled cynical journalists fell apart. They clapped and gave out with gasps of "Wonderful!" "Fantastic!" "What a knockout!" The scene had suddenly been converted from a very sedate and proper lunch party into the nearest the Tower Suite would ever see to a freak-out. It wasn't so much the music or the dancers themselves; it was the way they looked. They had been at the Hometan, and the effects were startling. The photographers, who up until then had considered the whole operation no more than an opportunity for some free booze, were going crazy. Motorized Nikons and Rolleiflexes burned and clicked as they yelled to the girls to pose and pout into their lenses. For starters the girls were nude from waist up—this in fact was in character with their stage parts—but by the grace of Hometan every other titty along the line was bronzed. One photographer was madly humming "Oh, what a pity" to himself. To get the right balance, Sinclair had had the girls cream the opposite sides of their faces, drawing a line from the forehead through the nose line and down to the chin. They looked like a group of painted witch doctors doing a frenzied fertility rite.

"What happens for their show tonight, Dan?"

This was Marion Cummings, fashion editor of *Impulse*.

"Hometan only takes four hours, Marion. The curtain doesn't go up until seven thirty, so they've got until three thirty to start balancing out."

"How many did you attend to yourself? I bet you took care of the third one from the end."

"Sweetheart, they all took care of themselves." But he picked up the cue and looked at the girl. Marion's perception was good; she had spotted the only one he would have bothered with. Her breasts were high and firm and the nipples full. He let it go at that and forced his way through the crowd.

"Well, Tessa, what did you think?"

"Oh, I still think you're a clever bastard, Dan. Always climbing on the backs of people already in the news."

"It's a sure way of making the papers. I'll take a bet we make every national daily tomorrow. Including yours."

"I wouldn't bet against a sure thing. Don't you ever get just a little sour with the hustling?"

"Why should I? The clients pay me to hustle, and it's what I do best. You're sounding sentimental—you're acting like a woman who's trying to do a conversion job. It's about time you realized we enjoy being on our side of the fence."

"I didn't know you were on the turn. Don't say the ram of Fleet Street is becoming ambidexterous?"

Neither of them had looked at the other while they cross-talked. Both had been watching the publicity stunt that would put the name of Hometan on every breakfast table in the country the following morning. Now Sinclair looked at her. She was tall and thin, like a model; but she was past a model's peak, and her face held more intelligence than those whose daily duty is to look into a piece of ground glass and act as if they loved it. Her hair was very dark, and her skin had the tough, sallow look that professional women journalists seem to acquire, or maybe are even born with.

"Tessa, why don't we have a meal tonight?"

"Don't tell me you want to eat with me, Sinclair. Say it's the paper you want, and I'll tell you I don't let PR men entertain me out of office hours. You should know by now that I'm one chick who's not obsessed with her own important status in life. We're nothing but the paper that's behind us; that's why fashion journalists don't retire early. The minute their names come off the by-line they cease to be important. There's a sudden chill, and the warmth only seeps back with a new job and a new way of doing favors for people like you and your publicity-seeking clients."

"Jesus, I only asked you out to dinner."

"Charm somebody else, Dan, and don't worry—I'll write up your Hometan story; I haven't any alternative. You're right, everyone else will cover it, and if I don't, then I'm out in the cold. You did a good job—you made something out of nothing and you created a national story."

"Come on, Tessa, the stuff's good enough to stand on its own. I just added the gloss."

"Maybe you did, but I don't like the way you go around fabricating your so-called gloss."

"If we're going to start moralizing . . ."

She came very close to him and the words came very taut. "Why don't you get stuffed?"

She turned and very quickly left the suite.

The room was quieter now. The journalists had drifted away; the music had been turned off; the dancers had gone, and with them the photographers. He had hardly noticed the change. The waiters were starting to clear away, and everything was suddenly finished very quickly. Sue Black came over to him.

"I really think that was a big success, Mr. Sinclair."

"Yes, I think it was, Sue. Did everyone sign in?"

"I think so. I'll type the list up when I get back to the office."

"I may not be in until after you've gone, so just leave it in my study and ask Freda to do a note for me on tomorrow's appointments."

"All right, then, I'll see you tomorrow, Mr. Sinclair."

"Good-bye, Sue, and thank you. Don't forget to take some Hometan for yourself."

He could see the major beaming at him as he wove his way across the room.

"Dan, that was superb, that really was." His voice had lost its clipped edge. "Brilliant idea, tying in those *Surfride* people, worth every penny. Must say you were absolutely right."

"I'll let you have a press-clipping layout and report on the magazine activity by lunchtime tomorrow, Major."

"Yes, very good, Dan. Well, can I give you a lift anywhere?"

"No, thanks, Major, I think I'll walk back. It'll do me good."

He went out through the swing doors into the weak afternoon sunlight and stood watching a party of Americans arrive. Then he went back into the hotel and crossed the foyer to the telephone desk. He made a short local call, looked at his watch and this time really left the hotel. But he didn't walk; he left in the taxi that had delivered the Americans.

They filtered through the West End traffic and then joined the slow stream traveling east. It was as if the entire City of London were returning to its warren from lunch. There were dark suits and bowler hats everywhere, and the girls hurrying along the streets had longer skirts than their contemporaries in the West End. He was only a couple of miles from where the whole "swinging London" bit started, yet it was as if he had suddenly come across a pocket of resistance.

The taxi pulled up at its destination, and Sinclair paid the fare, tipped without argument and went into the massive building. As he waited for the lift, he looked through the large glass windows into the general office of the insurance company. The rows of desks were filling up. Soon a calm would descend, and at each desk there would be a bowed head—some scrutinizing claims, others assessing medical reports—and the girls would be tapping out policy details on forms that looked like miniature Magna Cartas. He thought it was all very dull, but then these people were part of the great British mass, they were all consumers, and they could be influenced. Every day when they read their newspapers and magazines they were open to persuasion. They believed what they read as if there were a magic about the printed word. And this made them vulnerable to him, and to those like him.

The lift doors opened, and Sinclair told the disabled operator to take him to the eighth floor. They traveled alone and in silence. He stepped out onto carpet. Facing him was a heavy mahogany door. He opened it and went through to the reception room beyond. The woman at the desk smiled. "He's expecting you, Mr. Sinclair, please go straight in."

He opened the second mahogany door, but this time he knocked. The room was expensively furnished, and the fittings were genuine Louis Quinze. Cyril Mansfield was sitting at his desk, and in front of him was a single sheet of unheaded, typed foolscap paper.

"Thank you for being prompt, Sinclair. Please sit down."

Mansfield had been a client of Sinclair Enterprises for three years, and at no time during that period had Sinclair ever seen him outside his office. They never discussed the weather, their mutual well-being or any of the other topics of preamble. Mansfield issued instructions, accepted advice and rewarded results. Their meetings were kept strictly within the bounds of the matter in hand. Sinclair's main functions were to advise and to arrange the total avoidance of personal publicity. There wasn't a national newspaper with a photograph of Mansfield on its files that wasn't at least ten years out of date. Public knowledge of his name was restricted to the handful of people with whom he did business. The reference to him in *Who's Who* was limited to the data available at Somerset House and the fact that he had been educated at one of the better public schools.

He was one of the most powerful financiers in the City of London.

He pushed the typewritten paper across the desk.

"I would like a close approximation of this information to be published in tomorrow's financial papers. Do you consider that could be accomplished?"

Sinclair read the perfectly typed copy.

"Yes, I don't foresee any difficulties."

"Excellent. The matter has relative importance."

Sinclair folded the paper and stood up.

"Thank you, Sinclair, I am very grateful to you."

* * *

The receptionist smiled again. "Good afternoon, Mr. Sinclair. So nice to see you."

Sinclair reread the paper as the taxi took him back toward Ludgate Circus. It amounted to what would be called "a well-authenticated piece of intelligence from a usually reliable source." Succinctly put, it was a take-over rumor; its publication would ensure a rise in the value of the shares of the two companies named and might even precipitate an actual bid. Sinclair knew from experience that it need only be published in one city editor's column to generate the effect Mansfield wanted. The rival night editors would pick up the story as they read their competitors' early editions, and by lunchtime the London evening papers would be carrying guarded denials from the chairmen of the two companies. He guessed that by then Mansfield would have unloaded the shares he must have acquired some months ago and taken his profit.

He told the driver to stop outside St. Paul's and walked through to the telephone kiosks. The call was guarded; he simply asked his contact to meet him in the Old Kentucky in Fleet Street in twenty minutes. He arrived at the brightly lit, garish restaurant first and ordered a coffee and waited.

The city editor arrived looking flustered. He wasn't the glamorous financial journalist figure most people would have imagined; he wore what any commercial man would put on as weekend clothes, brown suede shoes, gray slacks and a slightly beat-up sports jacket that obviously had high sentimental value. He saw Sinclair almost immediately.

"Hello, Dan, what have you got?"

Sinclair gave him the folded paper. "What do you want to drink?"

The man hardly looked up. "I'll have a tea, thanks."

The tea arrived and he put three spoonfuls of white sugar in it. He drank some and then automatically reached for his cigarettes. "Do you want one?"

"No, thanks, I haven't smoked for over a year."

"Lucky bugger. Wish to hell I could give 'em up." He flourished the paper. "Where did this come from, Dan?"

"You know I can't tell you that, but it's accurate. I'd like it to run in tomorrow's column. You can cut it back, of course, provided the guts of it get through."

"I'll have to. We've done a piece on ICI and that's gone down, so we've only space enough for filler items."

Sinclair stood up. "A filler paragraph will be fine. Finish your tea. I'll take care of the other as usual. How's your family?"

"They're fine, thanks. It's the boy's tenth birthday next week. Christ, how the time flies."

"This will come in very useful, then?"

The man looked up; he was embarrassed.

"Yes, it will, just right. I'll see you, Dan."

It was after six by the time Sinclair got back to his office.

Sinclair Enterprises took up the whole of the fifth floor of a semimodern block in Hay Hill, Mayfair. Sinclair lived in a flat above the office, in what was comically called the penthouse. The general office and combined reception were laid out in what the architects and interior designers call *Bürolandschaft*, meaning in effect open plan with Kew Gardens added. Desks and functional lounging chairs were separated by well-placed groups of green vegetation; there were fresh flowers on every table and—what couldn't be seen by the uninitiated—closed-circuit television cameras to observe the waiting visitors. The only screens were in Sinclair's office study and in his flat.

He collected the messages and his appointment notes and walked the stairs to his flat above.

The first, rather overwhelming impression was of a miniature but decidedly more comfortable lending library. Books rose from floor to ceiling on three sides of the sitting room, broken only by spaces taken up with electronic equipment and objects carefully culled from the chic marketplaces. The flat had the sort of casual look that only very experienced and talented interior decorators seem able to achieve—casual, but to the perceptive totally deliberate. None of the furniture came from those very clever instant-design factories but had been custom-designed in Italy.

Sinclair swiveled the volume control on the hi-fi unit. Music permeated the entire flat, rather as if the angels had decided Hay Hill needed soothing. Its almost unobtrusive, cool effectiveness was a further well-calculated ploy in the total buildup that Sinclair had spent money and time in creating. He went through to the bedroom and stripped. He turned the sun-ray lamp on and, while it was warming, went into the adjoining bathroom to shower.

The phone rang before he was properly dry. He sat on the floor with his back to the lamp and took the call. It had come through on his unlisted number, which meant it had to be a client.

"Hello, Dan, this is Michael."

"How are you, Michael? And how is the dress business?"

"I don't run a business. I'm a designer, for Christ's sake."

"You may be a designer, but you're still in business. In case it slipped your mind, you are currently being promoted by my organization as Britain's leading ready-to-wear designer and your very efficient company happens to be well on the way to earning for itself a Queen's Award to Industry. So, my friend, how is the dress business?"

Slight pause.

"Actually, it's rather good. Lord and Taylor and Bloomingdale's both came in today—thank God, at different times—and between them just about bought me out. New York will shortly be subject to vast deliveries of designs by Michael Smith. By the way, how far apart are these stores? We can't go giving their buyers apoplexy."

"Lord and Taylor is at Fifth Avenue and Thirty-eighth Street. Bloomingdale's is a fair walk away by American standards, at Lexington and Fifty-ninth. It's all right, you won't cause a war. Did you show them anything from the new collection?"

"What? Between them they virtually bought across the board."

"Well, I think you should let me have, say, four personally executed and signed sketches in the morning, and we will send them round to the London Bureau of *Women's Wear Daily*, marked IN ADVANCE and EXCLUSIVE. Then be prepared with all the facts and figures when they ring. And, Michael, I think it might be rather a nice touch if you dropped the hint that you will be going to New York to carry out a series of promotions."

Sinclair reached for the sun lamp's protective glasses, slipped them on and turned round to face the ultraviolet rays.

"But, Dan, neither of them invited me to go to New York to promote the clothes."

"That's hardly the point. *Women's Wear* is the American fashion market's bible; everyone has to read it, and if they report you as saying you're going there to promote, then someone will pick it up, and before we know it, the first-class air ticket will be on your desk.''

"OK, if that's the way you think it should be done." He paused. "I was wondering whether we should throw a party this season— you know, the one we had last year was a real groovy smash."

Sinclair sighed and turned the lamp off.

"I think you can overdo the party bit. They're all right if you're launching something, or opening a new business, like last year. We'll spread this season's budget on separate showings. I'll arrange a series of special meetings at the showroom with individual magazine editors; we'll show the collection to them and then serve a champagne lunch. That way they're a totally captive audience and we can plan out what sort of coverage each of them can give us."

"Who shall we get in first, *Queen* or *Vogue?*"

"Neither. I have a possible deal with *Maintenant,* so we'll start off with Nanette Freberg and her entourage."

Sinclair cupped the receiver between his left ear and shoulder and paced the room, trying to dress and talk at the same time. "I've had a very good biography written on you—it accents your East End working-class beginnings and pushes the butch bit. I want to emphasize that you're not only not bent but very much the other way. I think maybe it would be a good idea if you started playing football again with your show-biz mates. Then we can get some pictures taken of you in action and contrast them with the brilliant designer at work in the fitting rooms. Perhaps we could even say you're being called the Steve McQueen of the fashion world."

Smith was obviously pleased with the suggestions. He was still green and had not yet reached the stage where he believed his own press clippings. *Give him time,* Sinclair thought; *another six months, and he'll be complaining about the coverage the* Daily Express *is giving his competitors.*

"That sounds great, Dan. You don't want to come over to Alvaro's tonight for a meal, do you? Then perhaps we could go on to the Revolution afterwards." Sinclair changed the phone to the other ear. God, they'd have his soul if he let them.

"I'm sorry, Michael, I've already got something fixed. Let's make it next week sometime."

"Yes, OK, then. Well, I'll drop the sketches in tomorrow morning."

"That will be fine. I'll see you, Michael."

He put the phone down without waiting to hear if there was any more.

It was a fine, clear night, and he thought of walking through the park to Knightsbridge and then picking up a cab, but decided to drive. He cut through Bruton Lane to the twenty-four-hour garage and picked up the six-cylinder Porsche 911S.

The club was in the Cromwell Road, near the Air Terminal. From the outside it could have been one of the many private hotels that in-season lived on tourists and off-season on students and sales representatives from out of town. He signed the members' book and squeezed his way to the bar. The tape recorder was playing, of all things, Paul Whiteman, and in the small clearing in the center of the dimly lit room couples were dancing very close together. It sometimes took guests or new members a minute or two to realize that the boys were dancing with the boys and the girls with the girls. Occasionally they would swap around, but everyone knew that was just for giggles.

It always surprised Sinclair to see familiar faces in the dark, smoky atmosphere; he supposed, though, that they felt safe in the company of their own. The clichéd rumors that sped with such malicious feeling about rising pop and film stars could often be confirmed by just propping up the bar any evening after the theaters were out.

If you watched closely, you could see the system at work. It would start with a deliberate stare, then a smile; then the one who would be doing the paying would casually drift over and buy the first set of drinks. It was rare for Sinclair to be propositioned—it was as if there were a sixth sense that told them not to bother with him. The only people who thought he was queer were women, the kind who had a passion for reforming by using what they thought of as their totally fatal charms, and the type of man who underneath the masculine shell had a latent urge that he couldn't admit to and so made vicious protestations against what he feared most in himself.

Sinclair remembered a time at a party in New York. The husband of one of the fashion editors had come over to him and, in that direct American way, had asked him straight out, "Pardon me for inquiring, but are you a homosexual?"

Sinclair had been very polite. "No, I'm not, actually. Why? Are you?"

The man had nearly choked on his drink.

"Good God, no. But you know, if I looked the way you do with your long hair and pink shirt an' all, then that would be good-bye to any promotion at the bank."

Sinclair remembered thinking that the American's overt masculine emphasis only served to strengthen the theory that the American male made such a deal out of pushing the good-clean-boy bit that there must be something to hide. What with the Mom fixation, maybe they were really a race of latent fags. . . .

"Two vodka-and-limes, please, Lesley."

The girl was blond and very soft, with the sort of bosom that wasn't appreciated in the rarefied strata of the glossy-magazine world. Her name was Nancy Trace. She was a free-lance fashion writer with a style that was slick and very postgraduate. Almost every editor in the business had used her work to put some life into her pages. There was always a chance that, like Sinclair, she was taking in the entertainment, but he doubted it: If she was there with a man, why wasn't he buying the drinks? Sinclair, in spite of his sophistication, was only a couple of degrees less surprised than the average man would have been.

The barman gave her the drinks, and she moved back into the crowd. Sinclair watched her go to one of the booths on the far side of the room. Since it wasn't considered unusual for people on their own to wander around acting as if they were looking for a so-called friend, Sinclair decided he would chance getting a pass made at him and slowly pushed through the dancing couples until he maneuvered himself to where he could see who the girl was with.

"Jesus."

They were holding hands like a couple of young lovers, and the older woman, with short straight dark hair cropping the sides of her narrow, pointed face, was kissing the girl's cheek. She looked up and into Sinclair's stare, and she recognized him. She suddenly looked very ill. It was enough. He didn't feel so very good himself, like a wronged husband who had just caught his wife out with her lover.

He put all the windows down in the car and drove very fast. It was the only thing he could think of doing that might get rid of the feeling of decay. Why the hell hadn't he gone to Alvaro's with Michael Smith? As he slowed the car down, he knew why, and he pressed the control that operated the specially installed electric windows. One of Sinclair's greatest assets was that he never felt sorrow, pity or remorse for long. At the most he needed only seven hours' sleep to remove any trace of guilt or even good intentions from his mind. He could think clearly now, and as the realization of what he had seen came to him, he smiled. He had often wondered about Nanette Freberg, if only because she had never reacted to him as most women did and because she almost seemed to resent his familiarity with her staff. The more he thought about it, the more the recollections slotted into place. Her husband had been a couturier of the old school, suave and too well cared for. It was almost common knowledge that he was gay, and the general reaction had been pity for Nanette. Sinclair could look at this situation without emotion or sentimentality now, and of course it was all suddenly very simple. He operated on his side of the fence and she on hers, and between them they kept the façade of a professionally successful relationship. The only really surprising element was Nancy Trace. Sinclair was better informed than most, but even his grapevine hadn't picked up a hint of a clue in that direction.

As he locked the car away, he knew that he now had an edge. Nanette Freberg was holding down one of the top fashion jobs in the country. An affair with a male photographer, that could be tolerated, even understood in the so-called permissive society, but with another woman—and one whose work *Maintenant* used frequently on its pages—not a hope. The all-male, conservative board would go out of its pseudosophisticated mind.

It wouldn't be blackmail or anything as crude, but there would be a new understanding between them, and if there was one relationship which Sinclair knew how to cherish and exploit better than anyone else, it was one where a special understanding existed. He added an item to his reminder list: cancel appointment with *Maintenant*. Timing, as the man said, was of the essence. Particularly if it could be controlled by Sinclair.

2

IT took Sinclair about three minutes to come to and focus properly. He lay nude from the waist up under the Finnish eiderdown and enjoyed the sensuous, warm pleasure of its texture against his skin as he contracted, then relaxed the muscles of his body.

He could hear Mrs. Pond in the kitchen as she prepared his breakfast: fresh orange juice, muesli, eggs and whole-meal toast. Only when he had eaten his way through the health-kick diet and finished the first cup of dandelion coffee and honey would he consider himself functional.

She knocked on the door and came in, carrying the tray. Under her arm were copies of all the national newspapers.

She knew never to expect more than a grunt or moan, depending on the previous night's excursions, in response to her well-practiced soft "Good morning, Mr. Sinclair." She left the room in the same hushed manner and went about the business of clearing and organizing Sinclair's personal way of living.

She was of the old school, and she enjoyed the mother feeling that four years of taking care of Sinclair had given her. Her own children were grown and in their turn had become parents. Next to them and her grandchildren her greatest concern was that her latest charge had nearly reached thirty-six without, to her knowledge, the prospect of settling down with a nice young girl appearing in any way imminent.

As he poured his second cup of coffee, he reached for the papers. He hardly glanced at the front-page pictures of half-nude dancers modeling Carnel Cosmetics' sensational new product, Hometan. There had been no doubt in his mind that they wouldn't have been there in the first place, and he was long past the point of any feelings of satisfaction for having produced the situation that made their publication possible. His office staff would produce the accurately computed readership summary—by social strata, naturally, that would impress the client with their expertise. Sinclair's only stimulation would have come if any of the papers had neglected to cover the story: That would have been a challenge.

He sifted the editions until he found the financial column he wanted. It was there, a paragraph under the ICI story. It read well and was virtually a verbatim version of the copy he had passed. He gave a self-satisfied sigh, and then his nerves jumped as the television screen set between yet another range of bookshelves blinked into a picture. The vision had been triggered by Freda's key as she opened the main door to the office a floor below. She had at first glanced very quickly toward the hidden camera but then seemed oblivious of its watching eye as she went through her routine. She put her coat away and changed her Jourdan boots for town shoes; the covers came off the typewriter and the Sony Solax desk calculator; she connected the coffee percolator and started opening the mail. By then both Sue and Ann—their second secretary—had arrived, and the office was beginning to assume an air of activity. It only needed Doris, the switchboard operator and junior, to walk in for Sinclair Enterprises to be under way.

Freda didn't come through on the intercom until he had showered and shaved and was knotting his tie. She always had very good timing.

"Good morning, Mr. Sinclair."

"Morning, Freda. Everything all right?"

"Yes, perfectly. I just thought you might like to know that Major Carter telephoned to say how very pleased he and the board members were about the party and the coverage in this morning's press. Also a messenger came from Michael Smith with some sketches for *Women's Wear Daily*."

"Christ, he didn't waste much time!"

"What was that, Mr. Sinclair?"

"Nothing, Freda. I'll be down in a minute."

As he was walking out the door, the unlisted phone rang. It was Mansfield. "Very satisfactory, Sinclair." It was unusual for him to ring through with congratulations so soon.

"Sinclair, I have recommended your services to a valuable business acquaintance. His name is Ernest Stokes; he is from the north." *Not the bloody Pole, I hope,* Sinclair thought. "He could prove a valuable acquaintance. I believe he will telephone you for an appointment later this afternoon."

"I'll be very happy to see him, Mr. Mansfield."

"Yes, I should be grateful if you can see your way clear to giving him every possible assistance. Thank you, Sinclair."

The phone was producing the dialing tone, and Sinclair replaced the receiver.

He went straight to the general office and gave the daily greeting, in spite of the fact that it was pouring with rain outside. He told Freda about the call from Mansfield, and gave her the written check list to run through. There were ten items.

(1) Send flowers to each of the seven dancers from *Surfride* with a card and his name.

(2) Telephone every paper that ran the Hometan story and thank them for being so generous.

(3) Alert *Women's Wear Daily* to the exclusive on Smith.

(4) Have Ann type a letter on my personal notepaper thanking everyone who signed the visitors' book at the press party for attending.

(5) Make an appointment for 6 P.M. this evening with Keith for a haircut.

(6) Send a check to the home of the city editor, the usual amount.

(7) Ring Prudence Glynn's secretary on the *Times* and ask if she can lunch later in the week at the Terrazza.

(8) Check with Mr. Fish to see if my shirts are ready.

(9) Make lunch reservation for two at the Westbury for 1 P.M.

(10) Cancel appointment Nanette Freberg, editor *Maintenant*.

He added one final item:

(11) Carry out immediate routine background check on one Ernest Stokes.

The canceled appointment left Sinclair free to go through with Sue the report she was preparing for Major Carter. He had the ability to close his mind to all other problems and concentrate solely on one specific project at a time. The result was a superbly detailed follow-up program on the initial Hometan success. Once that was completed, he immediately switched his mind to Michael Smith and dictated an eight-page proposal to Ann that illustrated step by step exactly how he intended creating the events that would advance Smith's reputation to the point where the fashion journalist would be so sold on the message that they would inject their own enthusiasm and complete the job for him. Sinclair's basic ploy was to create an idea which was presented in such a way that it excited and impressed. Once that was accepted, the journalists themselves would take it up, expand it, and the snowball would start to roll.

He left the office at twelve fifty. The rain had stopped, and the weak sun was trying to dry the wet pavements. It was warm enough to bring the birds out in spring shifts; *nowhere in the world,* he thought, *do you see so many great-looking chicks as in Bond Street on a spring day.* He turned at Conduit Street and went into the Westbury. He told the headwaiter whom he was expecting and then went in to his table, relaxed into the shiny black patent couch and waited for his date to arrive.

Most businessmen, in public relations or otherwise, have offices. Sinclair had a study.

He sat back and relaxed in the comfort of the chair that its designer, Miës van der Rohe, had called the Barcelona. Now *he* would have made a superb client. Sinclair visualized the double-page spread in the *Sunday Times Colour Magazine.* Real talent, no need to hustle. "If a man make a better mousetrap than his neighbor, though he build his house in the woods, the world will make a beaten path to his door." Emerson was right.

The screen on the internal television console flickered and strobed into a picture. A well-built man of about fifty was pushing the lift bell.

Sinclair looked around the room, checking the details that made up the total impression. At one end banks of white louvers concealed his changing room; one door was just ajar, showing enough of the shower unit to make the point. The inevitable bookshelves lined the long wall ahead of him. Behind stretched eight yards of Pilkington double glazing. The fourth wall held the television controls, tape recorders and hi-fi equipment. He glanced at the floor, Spanish rugs from Casa Pupo over flush-laid disused railway sleepers. (He had borrowed that idea from the Swiss Center.) There was no desk, only a low glass and steel coffee table, surrounded on three sides by a continuous black button-back hide sofa.

The reception-area camera took over and exposed the visitor. He was taller than he had appeared at the lift doors, and well dressed by business establishment standards. Blue SB3 with a single vent, turnups on the twenty-inch bottoms, white shirt, plain blue tie and highly polished Bally lace-up town shoes. He carried a brown leather briefcase, on which his initials were stamped in gold.

The intercom spoke: "Mr. Ernest Stokes is here, Mr. Sinclair." Sinclair stood up, had a last glance at the room, flicked off the television screen and walked over to the door. He opened it and came out with open hand and smile. If the late President John F. Kennedy could make the effort, so could he.

"How do you do, Mr. Stokes." He held the door back and allowed the man to walk ahead. He could always judge the first reaction; the ears usually moved. Sinclair smiled again.

"Do sit down, Mr. Stokes." The man sank into the black hide, not yet totally oriented in his surroundings.

"You don't believe in desks then?" The voice was thick, northern and direct.

Sinclair eased into his sitting pose. "I don't believe a creative executive needs a desk. I have staff who use them; all I need is a battery of those"—he pointed to the telephone installations—"and a tape recorder. Really, all I do is think, talk and act. In fact, I could operate just as well from a field."

"Oh, I see." The voice was slower, as if Stokes accepted the explanation without understanding a word. "You come highly recommended, Mr. Sinclair."

The door opened, and Sue walked through on cue. She was carrying a tray, and the ice in the two tall glasses made wonderful bell sounds in the upper register as she moved. She bent over and carefully placed the glasses on the low table. Stokes tried to keep his eyes away from the back of her thighs. She stood up. "Teacher's, Canada Dry and ice. I hope that's all right, Mr. Stokes."

He cleared his throat. "My goodness, why, yes, that's absolutely right." He just managed to avoid watching every movement as she left the room.

Sinclair broke the reverie. "What can we do for you, Mr. Stokes?" He felt totally in control.

Stokes reached for the briefcase. He put a large folder on the table and gently took from it a set of photographs. "Take a look at these, Sinclair."

Sinclair studied them. They showed a dark, long-haired girl

posing in what she thought were prime Jean Shrimpton positions. She was pretty, even sexy in a provincial way, and there was a filial likeness to Stokes. She was obviously the man's daughter, and Sinclair knew he should tread carefully.

"She's very attractive." He tried not to have a "so what?" expression on his face when he said it.

"She's going to be the next Twiggy, only more so."

Sinclair's back muscles tensed. "How is she going to do it?" He knew what the answer was before it came.

"Not how, Sinclair. Who? Who is going to do it? That's the question."

"It can't happen overnight, Mr. Stokes. It takes time, money and an awful lot of the right kind of effort."

Stokes stood up and carried his drink over to the windows. It was dusk, and small oblongs of yellow and blue light were appearing in the dull, uneven slabs of concrete below. He spoke with his back to Sinclair. "You don't have to sales talk me, Sinclair. I know what's involved, I wouldn't be here if I didn't." He took a long, hard drink and sighed. "I'll pay you a flat fee of ten thousand pounds for the first year, plus expenses, plus twenty-five percent of her total income for the next three years. No bargaining, yes or no?"

It was Sinclair's turn. The Bacardi and lime tasted good.

"What happens at the end of three years?"

Stokes turned and walked back to the table. He looked at what was left of the Scotch. "You've done a bit of background on me, lad, and if you've been thorough, you should know I'm straight. If you do it right, you won't suffer."

"Fifty percent of the fee in advance."

"You'll get it quarterly in advance, and I'll pay the expenses on the dot."

Sinclair knew he was past playing the I'll-consider-it bit. "All right, you've got a deal."

Stokes sat down, took out his wallet and handed Sinclair a check for £2,500. It was signed, made out to Sinclair Enterprises and carried the current date. "What now?"

Sinclair glanced at the check as if it happened every day.

"First I have to meet her. What's her full name?"

"Maureen, Maureen Stokes."

"We'll have to change that. She'll need a permanent flat in London."

"I've already arranged the flat. It's in Cadogan Square, between Knightsbridge and King's Road. Do you think that will do?"

"The Portobello Road or down by the river at Limehouse might have been better, but it's not too bad. I hope you've taken a decent lease, because we'll have to completely redo the decor."

Stokes looked puzzled.

"It will give us wider exposure—*House and Garden, Good Housekeeping, Jardin du Mode*—broadens the image. Mr. Stokes, you'll have to agree to let me do this my way, because I will have to change her: She will acquire a new image, a new look, a new attitude. And you may not like the result. Publicity has a peculiar effect, and not only on the person directly involved. Up to now you've been the dominant force in her life; that ceased the minute you signed the check."

Stokes stood up and looked at Sinclair. He was the father figure and the tough businessman. "Christ knows but she wants all this badly, Sinclair, and I'm just fool enough to give it to her. But, my God, if you go beyond what I'm paying you to do"—his voice was rough, and the words rasped up from his chest—"if you touch her, I'll finish you, understand that."

"Stokes, we have a rule here: Never screw the staff or the clients, it's bad for business."

"It'll be more than bad for business if you cross the line, lad." Stokes finished his drink and started to pack up the pictures. Sinclair interrupted him.

"I'd rather keep those, they might come in useful when we do a before-and-after feature."

Stokes relaxed into a smile. "That's all right, lad, good thinking. How do you think you'll start?"

It was Sinclair's turn to walk over to the window. He pulled the curtains aside and stared out over the dark Mayfair roofs. It was almost as if he were talking to himself.

"The most important thing is to get the product right before anyone sees it. The right packaging and the right message. Then we work on the photographers and the press; they'll sell her to the public for us. The vital factor is the first major newspaper articles."

Stokes stared at him, taking in every word.

"Those articles will form the fact sheets for everything else that's ever written. Newspaper people are busy and overworked, and they are tired, Mr. Stokes. They work to deadlines, and they work for superiors who are only interested in speed and results. That's how PR's exist: They take the slog away by creating ideas, facts, sympathy and largess. The story is the big thing, and if it's provided for them, neatly packaged, it won't matter if the truth bends a little here and there. But it is the sum of that bending repeated and repeated that makes a reputation. When a journalist has to write a feature, the first thing he does is check the clippings library. I've known some who've put out a fifteen-hundred-word personal interview on the strength of one short telephone call and a rewrite of everything that's already been published."

Sinclair turned from the window. "That's the way it is. If your company only exports twenty-seven percent of its output, we don't have to say so. We would say you export to eighteen countries. It's true, but it's not the truth. The fact that you only sell an average one and a half percent to each of these eighteen countries is incidental."

He walked Stokes to the door and opened it for him. In the open-plan office only Freda was left, clearing up for the start of the next day.

"When do I meet her?"

"She'll arrive on the four twenty at Euston tomorrow afternoon. I don't see why we should waste time."

"Well, here's to success." Sinclair held out his hand. Stokes took it, thought for a second of repeating the Masonic pressure, but decided it would be a waste of time.

"I'll confirm the contract by letter, just so we both have it on record. Nothing like knowing who to sue."

As the outer door closed, Sinclair turned to Freda. "Call it a day, love, and in the morning open a new file. Head it"—he paused—"head it THE PROPERTY."

3

THE Manchester-London Intercity Express was on schedule. Maureen Stokes settled back in her first-class seat and tried to pick up the storyline in *Honey* magazine at the point where she'd left off to sample the British Rail luncheon. It was no good; it didn't mean anything to her. While her eyes scanned the words, her mind was on London and what lay ahead. She threw the magazine onto the vacant seat next to her and stared out the window. She caught the reflection of the only other person in the compartment and automatically adjusted her short skirt; the man turned back to his *Financial Times*.

She checked her watch; another hour and they'd be in. She wondered what Sinclair was like. Her father always missed the most important parts. "Oh, he's very smooth, got all the smart trappings, but I think he'll do the job. It won't take long to find out, anyway."

You could run a check on a man's financial status and on the way he ran his business, but there was only one way to find out what he was like as a man and that was to be with him.

For the next few months Sinclair was going to be the most important person in her life, more important even than her father. What was it like, she wondered, to be paid to turn a dream into a reality? How would he do it? She closed her eyes and rocked to the rhythm of the train. It had taken a long time to convince her father that what she wanted most was more than the romantic yearnings of a dreamy teen-ager. It was the business angle as much as anything that had swayed him. A top model earns more than ten thousand a year, she had told him, more than his MP friends, more than the general manager of his factory. Modeling is a legitimate business, she had argued; it's accepted; to be a top model is to be part of the in crowd. She had reeled off the standard names: Barbara Goalen, Fiona Campbell Walter, Jean Shrimpton and now Twiggy. They had all been nobodies before modeling shot them into prominence, so why not her, why not Maureen Stokes from Chester?

It wasn't as if she were entirely without experience. The local newspaper photographer might not be Norman Parkinson, but at least he was a professional, and the pictures they had made together had been good enough to get her a job modeling at lunchtime sessions in Manchester's top department store. Everything she had read in magazines and books about modeling had pinpointed the one vital turning point in almost every successful model's career: the time she had met the man who molded her. With Suzy Parker it was Richard Avedon, Shrimpton had Bailey, and Twiggy Justine. When they wrote about her then, maybe it would be Sinclair.

Once her father had been sold the idea that she was determined to make it, the same techniques that had made him one of the largest plastics manufacturers in the country were brought into operation. "Invest in talent; find and get the best; it always pays." When he wanted a research chemist, he found out which of his competitors had the top man; then he got him. It was the same with Sinclair. He had sent out the instruction to draw up a short list of the most successful and influential men in the world of fashion. As a double check he had his London office and an independent consultancy work on the project separately. They both came up with the same answer: Sinclair.

She remembered the glowing reports. "It would appear that without doubt the subject mentioned has a considerable reputation with members of the fashion press as being consistently successful in all known endeavors. Discreet inquiries with subject's clients past and present elicited a highly satisfactory response from all quarters."

The precise and guarded phrases had laid bare his history in cold, unemotional terminology. To her, the odd but significant coincidence that one of her father's financial friends also employed Sinclair clinched the decision and made it part of fate; for her father it was a confirmation that the information gathered could be relied on.

She opened her eyes with a start as the train ignored the waiting passengers on Luton station and roared on toward its destination. There was always something grand about being in a fast nonstop express—it made you feel as if they had cleared the line just for you and that once your train had been checked out, the people in charge could relax and get on with the business of transporting the lesser passengers.

The excitement was beginning to rise in her now as they neared London: What would he think of her? In Chester she was treated like local royalty, used to being sought after. There she was the girl the women envied and the men admired; what she did, where she went and with whom were hot gossip; she was the girl the boutique owners rang first when their new stock arrived—what Maureen Stokes bought and how she looked were the image the rest modeled themselves on. In Chester Maureen Stokes was high society. In London she was nothing, and to Sinclair maybe just another client.

She knew that one of the hallmarks of a provincial was the very effort to be unprovincial, the assumption of an experienced air of big-city sophistication that the local senses as a try-on. There was still a grudging mystique about London that was never admitted, and however hard you tried, you were copying. Only Liverpool and the pop-music explosion had taken away the capital's leadership for a time, but even that had now diminished, and London was always where you had to go to succeed, to achieve the real rewards and recognition. You had to become part of its rat race, to be absorbed in its ways, and only then could you assume its superiority.

Maureen Stokes had taken her first big step toward cutting the bonds of her background with this realization. To Sinclair she would be a hick from the sticks; well, that was fine, she needed him, he was the means to where she wanted to be, and he was being well paid to help her get there. The trick would be to make her as necessary to him as, at that point in time, he was to her. She was looking forward to the process of dual metamorphosis.

Freda Drayton hated railway stations, so she waited in the back of the chauffeur-driven hired limousine and killed time studying the photographs of Maureen Stokes. She thought that maybe Sinclair had taken on too much: It was all very well promoting financiers, beauty products and dress designers, but quite a different set of problems was involved in taking a presumably no-talent though pretty provincial broad and turning her into a top model and a high-ceiling fee-earning commercial property.

In Freda's second year as Sinclair's secretary he had given her a present of a course at Lucie Clayton's School of Modeling. Not, he had said, so that she could suddenly take off, but just to give her a little extra confidence and polish. She remembered going to her interview with the half thought in her mind that perhaps Clayton's would perceive her hidden photogenic beauty and rush her into stardom in the same way they had done with Jean Shrimpton and Celia Hammond. The rather chic and direct Miss Clayton had killed that idea the instant Freda sat down. The approach was practiced but refreshing. "If you're less than five foot six, you haven't much hope of becoming a model. It's a generalization, but, to be fair to you, if you've come here with any soft dreams and pink illusions, forget them. For every twenty girls who come through that door, maybe one stands a chance of becoming a model." Freda took, with gratitude, the grooming course, and decided that if she was going to be a secretary, then she'd settle for being a damned good one, with the added virtues of confidence and polish.

It was four thirty, and for once the train was on schedule. Freda stood at the ticket barrier feeling like a private detective looking for the subject. Every now and then she would sneak another look at the photograph, just to check herself. The flood of arrivals had dwindled dramatically; it seemed as if either she had missed spotting the girl or else she hadn't been on the train in the first place.

She was about to start looking for dark-haired station strays when she saw her. She was halfway down the platform, heading a trolley of luggage; the photograph was a good resemblance. She was about five eight, her hair was still dark, but in spite of trying to follow *Vogue* and *Honey*'s advice, she wore too much makeup. Her black boots disappeared under the hem of the maxi topcoat, and to give a final touch of provincialism she wore a hat. Why, Freda wondered, did they always dress up so? She felt for Sinclair.

"Hello, Miss Stokes, I'm Freda Drayton, Mr. Sinclair's secretary."

"Hello. Couldn't Mr. Sinclair come, then?" Her response was edged with something more than disappointment.

Freda hoped the smile wasn't too icy. "He thought you'd rather go straight to the flat and settle in. He's asked me to take care of you, and if you're not too tired, perhaps you would like to meet him for dinner this evening."

The girl returned the smile. "Why, of course, I expect he's very busy."

The chauffeur helped the porter to load up and eventually they drove off into the heavy stream of rush-hour traffic.

"What's Mr. Sinclair like, Miss Drayton?"

She was prepared for the quizzing. "He is the best public relations man in London, and I would judge that he's possibly the only man who could take on and succeed with the sort of brief your father gave."

"What brief was that exactly?"

"That you would become the next top model, eclipsing Twiggy."

The girl was staring out at the shopwindows. "Yes, that's right." She turned to look straight at Freda. "Do you think he'll do it, Miss Drayton?"

"As I said, if anyone can do it he can."

They didn't talk again until they were in the Cadogan Square flat.

"I'll ring Mr. Sinclair and let him know you've arrived safely."

The girl didn't seem too concerned. She went into the bedroom and started unpacking the mountain of suitcases. It was then that she noticed the flowers. The card read: "Welcome to your new city—Dan Sinclair." She thought that very smooth and forgave him for not meeting her in. . . .

"It's Freda, Mr. Sinclair."

"Well, how is it?"

"Very well."

"What does that mean, Freda? Do we have a dog on our hands, or what?"

"No, I don't think so. I think everything is fine."

"I'm sorry, I guess you can't talk. OK, love. Well, tell madam we're all dying to meet her and let her get on with the unpacking. Take the car back to your place, tell the driver to hang about while you change, then go back and pick up Miss Stokes and bring her on to Claridge's by eight thirty."

"Right, I'll take care of that. We'll see you later, Mr. Sinclair."

Sinclair put the receiver down and went over to the refrigerated drinks cabinet. He made himself a tall Americano, and as he added the vermouth to the Campari and squeezed the lemon rind he wondered whether the Stokes-Sinclair mixture would be as cool. He gave the lemon an extra squeeze.

The Palm-Court-type orchestra was playing as Sinclair sat down amid the potted greenery. He had chosen Claridge's for the first meeting because, one, it was expensive, two, the food was good, and, three, there was almost no likelihood of bumping into any press girls or photographers. He wanted to keep the girl out of sight until he thought she was ready to be shown off.

They were only fifteen minutes late, and considering the circumstances, that wasn't too bad.

He had sat well back in the huge room so that he could watch her entrance. Freda was leading her over and, Sinclair thought, looking a bloody sight more interesting than Stokes. God knew whose dress she was wearing, it looked like a Carnaby Street knock-off from a John Bates original. It had probably been a smash in Chester or wherever she came from, but at eight forty-five in Claridge's it didn't quite make it. He went forward and held out his hand.

"Well, how are you, Miss Stokes? I'm sorry I couldn't meet you in myself." She was giving him her best look—slight smile and wide-open eyes from under her long dark lashes.

"That's quite all right, Mr. Sinclair, Freda was very helpful and efficient." She paused, it was supposed to have significance. "Thank you—the flowers, they're lovely."

"Good. Shall we go straight in and have drinks at the table?"

As the drinks waiter came over, Sinclair hoped to God she wouldn't order a bubbly pseudo. She surprised him and asked for a vodka and tomato juice. The small talk over the drinks and the menu reading was naturally stilted and uninspiring. After all, Sinclair thought, it was a pretty highly charged first off: the girl from the sticks being entertained by the man whom her father had hired to turn her into a fairy princess with no midnight problems.

They were halfway through the *carré d'agneau* when Sinclair decided it was time they got down to cases. During the afternoon, while the girl was being carried closer and closer to London, he had drafted out his opening gambit. It was essential that he establish right from the beginning that he had total control over her and that he develop in her an attitude of professionalism. There must be no halfhearted amateur little-girl embarrassments; unless he could create an immediate discipline and dedication, they would be dead before they started.

He took a large swallow of the St.-Émilion.

"Maureen, I think we should talk business."

She looked up from her plate, first to Sinclair, then to Freda, then back again, giving him all her attention. "Yes, Daniel." Her smile was fixed.

"If this operation is to be successful, you have to understand and remember a number of basic but very important factors." He waited and sipped the wine. "Whatever may happen between us, you are our client, and that means that my organization is working for you and backing you in total. No matter what I say or do, even if it appears that I am tearing you to pieces, always remember that."

"Goodness, you sound dreadfully severe."

She turned and laughed to Freda, but she got the message and cut it short. "I'll remember that."

"Good. Maureen, look at that woman on the other side of the room, the one in the green cocktail dress. Tell me what you think about her, what impression you get."

She looked across at the woman and studied her; she kept looking at her while she answered Sinclair.

"I think she looks like a rich spoiled bitch. She's mean, she's showing off her jewelry, and she's showing too much bosom for a woman of her age. I think I would dislike her very much indeed."

"You're right, she's most of those things, and her husband doesn't care much for her either. He's a property developer; they're well known in their own little circle. Now, think on this: Do you believe that woman wants to create the impression you have of her? Of course not. In fact, she probably thinks she looks very good—most people, and particularly people with money, cling to the belief that they know best how they look. Mostly it doesn't matter too much, but in the image business it's vital. Everyone forms instant visual opinions. That same woman with a different makeup and dress and without the flash jewelry could actually look quite stunning."

The girl stared hard at the woman. "You're probably right. Are you trying to say that I look wrong, too?"

"Not really. I'm saying that once you realize what messages your look is giving to other people, then you can set about controlling those reactions. And when you have complete confidence in the way you intend others to assess you, then you have a built-in success syndrome."

Freda had never heard him talk that way; she had always

known he was good, but she accepted it like any other accomplishment. Hearing him analyze what she had taken for granted was something new and fascinating.

"What I'm really getting at is that first we decide on the perfect image for the product that is to be our ultimate. Then we dissect it, break it down and see how you are to be molded into that image. But it's much more than just a physical façade. The attitude, the innerness of you, has to be molded too, and there's the danger."

She was eager now and excited. The food on her plate was cold and unfinished, and the waiter took it away and brought them coffee.

"How do we start?"

He stirred the brown sugar in the neat cup, then drank some of the black coffee. "We will give you a new name, a name that has force, a name that is simple to utter but different enough to never slip the memory. To you the name will be more than a new sound; it will be your other self. You will grow to stand outside it and be Maureen Stokes looking at the product. So we will be able to discuss our product without becoming entangled in emotions; that new person will be a third party, a joint creation."

He wondered if he was laying it on too strong. He didn't want to sound like a complete Svengali.

Her laugh was nervous and full of emotion. Freda sat there trying to appear cool and efficient. The name had suddenly taken on vast importance. Sinclair realized this and hoped to hell it wouldn't turn out an anticlimax.

"Let's have some champagne. You should always have champagne at a christening."

The sound of the cork popping broke the tension.

Sinclair raised his glass.

"Here's to . . . Jackson."

The girls mumbled the name in unison and then sipped the champagne.

"I like it, I think it has a ring. It's not too tough, is it, Daniel?"

Freda answered for him. "I think it's excellent. I really think it's marvelous."

The girls repeated the name to each other over and over, using different emphasis and tone. They sounded like a soft-shoe-shuffle team going into a curtain number. Sinclair laughed at them and thought that the girl really was very pretty; she was beginning to unwind, and as she giggled, he could see through the makeup to what she could become.

"Oh, Daniel, I didn't think it would be like this." She was still laughing. "I thought you'd be a rotten old fat lecher who'd have me running round the office desk."

"Watch out. It could still happen."

"I think you're too nice, and I bet you don't have to chase girls anyway."

The waiter smiled at them as he refilled the glasses. He enjoyed hearing the young girls laughing.

Sinclair wondered whether it was the drink. He blinked his eyes and looked a second time.

"What's the matter, Daniel?"

He was right the first time; it was just that he hadn't noticed it at first.

"What was it, Daniel?"

"It's your neck—I've only just seen it properly."

"Why, what's wrong with it?"

"Nothing, nothing at all; in fact, it's rather beautiful. Not many women have such a neck. Nefertiti had one. Yours is long and slender and looks as if it might have been made to carry your head high above the clouds."

He stopped himself. It must be the drink; he never became that lyrical without some help. But he knew nevertheless that it was true; it was only that he needn't have said so.

She liked him for his attention. The three of them talked of London and people, and Freda and Sinclair gossiped to her.

At last Sinclair motioned to the waiter for his bill.

They left the hotel arm in arm, with Sinclair in the middle. The car was opulent enough to take the three of them on the back seat, and they collapsed into its wide expanse.

"Do you know London well, Jackson? Have you been many times before?"

"No, I haven't. I really don't know my way around at all."

"That, young lady, is the next item on the schedule," said Sinclair. "I'd like you to be ready at ten tomorrow morning—well, let's say eleven as it's your first day. Sue, my assistant, will pick you up and take you on a tour. Not Buckingham Palace and the Houses of Parliament either. I want you to start breathing the atmosphere."

"Does that mean Carnaby Street?"

"No, it doesn't. Apart from Foale and Tuffin, that scene is passé. I've arranged for you to see some of the best wholesale collections on the market—it will give you an eye, a standard. The one thing you'll never do is model trash, even if it means working only one day a week. Learn from what you'll see; try some decent clothes on; get the feel of the cloth on your body; sense how to make the garments work for you."

She took in every word, considered, memorized and then stored his instructions away to be used as the time came.

She was eager. "Whose designs will I see?"

"John Bates at Jean Varon, Gina Fratini, Ossie Clarke, Jean Muir, Michael Smith. That will take you right through until after lunch. Then you can see some boutiques—Biba's, Brown's, Annacat, Adele Davis."

They waited for the traffic lights at Sloane Street, crossed into Pont Street, and then they were in Cadogan Square. Sinclair waited while the chauffeur helped her from the car, then walked her up the steps and opened the front door.

He handed her the key. "I don't need this now you're installed." He took her hand. "Well, Jackson, tomorrow you start. Just don't be too impatient; we'll make it happen. Good night, and sleep well. And that's not a wish; it's an instruction."

She laughed again and watched him return to the car. She thought he moved very well; his body was coordinated; there was nothing awkward about it. He smiled back at her through the window, and then the car moved away.

"What do you think of her, Dan?" Freda was perfect. In the office she always called him Mr. Sinclair, but alone it was different.

He sank into the upholstery. His face was carrying a frown, and when he answered, he didn't move his head or his eyes but stared straight in front.

"I think she is probably very cunning. She needs us, and she knows we know it. So she'll stay in line and cooperate. But to want what she wants, you have to be very single-minded and very tough. We'll see."

The car stopped again, and the driver opened the door for Freda.

"Good night, Dan. It was a marvelous evening—I think you handled her very well, just the right degree of firmness."

"Thanks, Freda. And thanks for coming along. See you in the morning."

The chauffeur half turned his head. "Shall I take you home now, sir?"

"No, just drive for a bit. Go down to the bridge and along the Embankment."

As they drove through the dark streets, he thought about what he had said to her father: *The most important thing to get the product right before anyone sees it.* He reckoned it would take an intensive month, and then he might be ready. Underneath the makeup her face was good, her skin was clear, the eyes were wide and dark and bright, and the bone structure looked as if the planes and cavities would absorb and bounce the light. Her hair was bad, but he knew that could be fixed like all the rest.

Maybe she had it.

As he watched the lights on the river, he sensed a tremor of excitement and he knew that it could happen.

The car slowed down as it approached Chelsea Bridge. "Shall I keep going, sir?"

"No, you can take me back to Hay Hill now."

She lay on the bed in the flat and felt very good; she repeated the new name to herself, over and over again. It was clever, a man's name for the girl he was grooming to go all the way. It was right for the unisex thing, and it was also in keeping with the others with the solo names: Verushka, Twiggy and the Shrimp. The dinner and the liquor let her shed her own private inhibitions as she thought of Sinclair. He really was divine; he was coordinated and in control; it was going to be easy to take the passive part and let him take her and change her. It was what she wanted. All the times before with men she had always felt superior, and what had frustrated her most was that they had let her feel that way, but with Sinclair it was different right from the start. The bastard had sent his secretary but cushioned the insult with flowers; none of the others would have dared to play it that way. That made her think of David and what she had left behind.

It would have read like a story out of a back number of *Woman*. He was tall and slim with thick, dark hair and a quizzical smile that made the corners of his eyes crinkle. He was very proper: a doctor, driving the new red Triumph convertible that was supposed to add the dash of spice. He was part of the great young middle class which put devotion, security and right thinking before everything else, whose hypocritical foundations were appalled and shaken by new attitudes and new ideas. The future would have been mapped out before her: a new house in the proper area, holidays in Spain, two children, a daily maid. And a growing boredom that would eventually force her to join the married party games. The men throw their front-door keys in the middle, mix them up, and you take your pick and everyone gets a new sleeping partner for the night. For the night—it was always sex at night; even that had to be put in its right compartment, everything neat and tidy: Saturday night was performance night. She thought of all the thousands of couples copulating between the hours of ten and midnight on the great traditional Saturday night. Up would go the nighties, out would come the big men, and the women would close their eyes and pretend it was Steve McQueen or Paul Newman. She wondered who the men visualized; it certainly wouldn't be their wives.

She bet even money Sinclair wasn't like that. If he wanted it across the ironing board at three thirty in the afternoon, then he'd get it. Her body flexed at the thought, and she wondered what he was like stripped. He looked powerful, and his hands were strong, and she thought of his body on her. She drifted into sleep, and for the first time in a long while it was with an anticipation and an excitement for the day ahead.

4

"**T**HE first appointment is at the Coat House." The early-morning rush-hour traffic was still heavy, and the car crawled. "They make fantastic coats, so they're not cheap, and it's all a very cool operation. They were one of the first wholesale houses to put a caution on for American buyers, caused something of a wild sensation when they did it."

"Sue, you'll have to talk down to me for a while. I'm not up on your trade vernacular yet. What the hell is a caution?"

"Oh, of course . . . well, in Paris you have to pay to see a new couture collection; the price is usually the cost of one design. If you buy, then the money you've paid—the caution—is marked off against the sales. It's to stop people knocking off ideas for nothing."

The car made a right turn and then drew over to the curb.

"Well, here we are."

Jackson looked at the façade, a smoked-glass window you couldn't see through and, at the side, a wall of mat aluminum with a door shape cut into it. They pushed it open and waited in front of the desk, which was shaped like a capital *J* that had fallen on its side. The reception area was small; the beige tufted carpet continued up the wall to make its own skirting. The girl took them through a low-ceilinged black-and-white tunnel, and at the end was the total and brilliant white of the bare showroom. There wasn't a coat in view.

They sat in the white chairs and stared at the white panels in front of them that rose from the white carpet to the ceiling; that was white too. The music started, and seemed to come from what looked like a square-headed miniature Martian standing on guard in one corner of the room; it was a hi-fi loudspeaker unit. The inset overhead lights dimmed, and one of the panels slid back; spotlights suddenly hit the open space. Standing in the glare was a tall, very thin model. She was wearing a honey-colored fox coat, to the floor. As she moved into the room, the spots went out as the ceiling lights became brighter. She showed the coat as though it were hers, and as she disappeared into the tunnel, the lighting did tricks again and there was another model waiting to come on.

"Don't think all the showrooms are like this; some are like spare attics tarted up."

The showing took thirty minutes—it was perfectly timed, a coat a minute. Jackson couldn't help whispering; she felt as if someone would suddenly appear and tell her to keep quiet if she talked properly.

"Why haven't I seen any of these coats in the shops? I think they're marvelous."

"We're only seeing what they show to the press. Every design house makes about fifteen percent of its collection basically for the fashion journalists. Simple fashion desn't make interesting photographs; clothes like these do."

"But, Sue, I like the clothes. If I saw them in a shop, I'd want to buy them."

"Well, that's the other end of the game—the deadheads of the business, the shop buyers. I guess there are only about a couple of dozen outlets in the country who really know enough to buy fashion like this; everybody else is too scared. All they think about is last year's sales figures; they work on the premise that if you take what sold well last season and put it in a different fabric, you must do as well again. It's not that good fashion wouldn't sell to the public, but it's got to get past those outdated matrons in their funny hats. Most times, after a magazine photographs new fashion, the wholesale house has to beg a store to stock the design, and then probably on a sale-or-return basis. That's why it often seems impossible to actually go out and buy what you see on the fashion pages. Firms like this one sell their top merchandise to stores like Fortnum's and Harrod's. But the bulk of it goes into Europe, where they understand what it's all about."

They moved on to sit through four more shows that covered the best of the market, from the sexy and pretty designs of John Bates to the floating lightness of Gina Fratini. They lunched off bagels and lemon tea at one house and then picked up the car to take them over to Biba's in Kensington.

"This is the swingers' paradise: The whole concept is to be a jump ahead of the pack. If you want to know what's coming, this is where it's at: here or at Ossie Clarke's place, Quorum; or if you want to pay more, Marrian McDonnell, Annacat; or Brown's for the imported French gear."

Jackson followed her into the dark of what had once been a pub and got lost in the growth of Victorian coat stands that were used as display racks. The statutory boutique pop music was blaring out, and girls dressed as if they were waiting for the fancy-dress party to start wove between open-eyed, miniskirted and wide-culotted nymphets that would have sent Humbert Humbert screaming.

"I'm going to try some on. Where do I change?"

Sue took her through to the communal changing room that looked like a strippers' rehearsal hall. Standing by the entrance was a boy wearing very dark sunglasses, a sleeveless leather jacket which looked like a copy of a coal heaver's topcoat and a sharply pressed pair of ordinary seaman's trousers that were so tight they must have been part of a "tiddly-up-the-line suit." None of the girls took the slightest notice of him.

Jackson pushed through the crush of half-naked girls to the long mirror by the wall and looked at herself. The dress was like a white cotton vest, and it wasn't designed to be worn with underwear.

"What do you think, Sue?"

"Maybe it's just a little way out; why not try something else?"

Jackson left Sue holding the dress she had come in and went off into the semidarkness of the shopping area. Five minutes later she was back with an armful. They spent an hour and a half in the boutique, and when they left, they were loaded down with carrier bags that advertised where they had spent their money. As they sank back into the car, Sue checked the time; it was nearly six o'clock.

"I think that's enough for today. God, I don't know about you, Jackson, but I've had it."

"Oh, it was great! I could spend all week doing this—it's lovely looking at so many new clothes."

"Well, I think that's just what Mr. Sinclair has in mind. He asked me to take you back to the office—he's worked out a training schedule, I think."

The car dropped them at Hay Hill. Sinclair's door was open, and they went straight through to the study. He was watching an

early-evening television program; he didn't look up or say anything but motioned to them to sit and watch with him.

It was an outside-broadcast coverage of a fashion parade. The
announcer was trying to describe the clothes without sounding
coy about it, and he was failing dismally.

"Christ, they don't know what time of day it is!" Sinclair was
livid. "I've never in my bloody life seen so much crap as when
they try to do fashion on TV. All they think they have to do is
stick a model up in front of a camera and have some idiot who'd
be better off announcing the weather talk about what we're going
to see the girlfriend in this season, and that's their contribution to
a business that's done more than the Beatles to change the lives of
half the women in this country."

He stabbed the remote-control button and erased the picture
from the screen. "Well, how did you two get on?"

It was his brown day: The single-breasted, slightly waisted suit
jacket had been cut and made by Tom Gilbey; the pale coffee-
colored silk shirt was by Turnbull and Asser; and as he crossed his
legs, they could see, to great effect, the ankle-high shoes reminis-
cent of spats that Cavalli of Bologna had had made for him in
brown and beige mottled toadskin. His close fair hair was thick at
the sides and ran down the back of his neck to curl on the shirt
collar. Keith was always very careful when he cut Sinclair's hair:
Any longer or thicker and they would be in Campsville. The image
was of an affluent trendy, confident enough to be able to forget
what was being worn that day but knowing that it was totally
right.

Jackson answered him. "Fabulous! I didn't know there were
that many good things to see; it makes you realize how much
you've missed."

"Well, you've seen them at their best, before the stores get their
hands on them and stick them on the rails along with the tat. This
is why people like Susan Small and Jaeger take their own depart-
ments within the store—if their merchandise got mixed in with
everyone else's, half the people would never know they existed or
what their designs were like."

"What do you want us to cover from now on, Mr. Sinclair?"
said Sue.

"I fixed with Michael Smith for him to design a personal range for Jackson, so tomorrow she can spend most of the day at the salon and fitting rooms."

He looked over at Jackson. "I don't think you need Sue with you, and she can be getting on with working out the rest of the schedule. Sue, Ann has typed a list; pick it up on the way out, and in the morning you can start putting things together."

He could see they were both dead beat. "OK, Sue, that'll do for today. I just want to run over some details with Jackson. You needn't hang around anymore."

She was grateful for the hint. "Fine. All right, then, I'll see you in the morning. Good night, Jackson, good luck with the fittings."

She closed the door behind her, and Sinclair stood up. "It's drink time—what'll you have, love?"

Jackson asked him for a gin and french, and when the drinks were made, he sat back and studied her. She had been in London only a day, and already he thought he could see a slight change— nothing obvious or dramatic, but there was something, maybe just a shift in attitude brought about by the environment and the new people she was meeting.

"What's the verdict, Daniel?"

"Nothing, I was just thinking, I've seen girls change before. You have a new young girl in the office straight from secretarial school, and as the weeks go by, the little things begin to add up. She alters her hairstyle; her skirts get shorter; even her language takes on a new edge. But with you the whole process is deliberate and highly concentrated—it's like taking a problem and feeding it through a computer. You get the result in seconds, instead of the days it would take if a string of accountants worked at it. I was wondering how you'd stand up to the pressure."

"I'll stand up to it, Daniel; don't worry about that. I made up my mind a long time ago what it was I wanted—well, this is it, this is the start, I don't care how tough you make it. I learned a lot from my father, you know; he wasn't always rich, but he decided early on that was what he wanted to be, and for years there was nothing else. You can't have it both ways: If you want something, then nothing must be allowed to sidetrack you. People play at it, and then they wonder why the others are at the top; they forget that while they took time out to enjoy themselves, to ease off, the others were still working, and the investment paid off. Well, it's the same with me: The time is right; that's why we found you. I didn't just get on a train, you know—we looked at the market, and when we checked, yours was the name that kept coming up. I've got a lot to learn, Daniel, I know that, but you've never had a more dedicated pupil. I know I don't look right, dress right or maybe even think right, but I've got the need and the drive. If it wasn't you, then there would be somebody else."

She suddenly smiled at him. "But then it is you, so that's all right, isn't it?"

It was a switch for Sinclair; he was the one who usually delivered the lectures. The determination on her face as she spoke was something he hadn't expected, and for the first time he really knew that it wasn't a game for her. She wasn't like the yearly run of debs who announced via the gossip columns that they were going to become models or boutique owners, and you knew all the time that they were shooting off their rich pampered little mouths and that the next item to hit the pages would be the announcement of their engagement to some the-game's-the-thing idiot from the City. This girl meant it. She wasn't one of the group; she was a loner; other people were unnecessary to her unless they formed a link in the upward chain of events. It made what he had to do that much easier. There would be no need to explain away the scheming, there would be no question about whether or not a thing was right and proper but only what it accomplished. This gave them power: In a society where the majority conforms to rules of conduct, the immoral have the edge; their actions are never inhibited by the guilt of conscience.

"Right, now there are two important people for you to learn from. First, Smith. Forget the publicity, he's one designer who really does know what he's doing. He came up the hard way, not the College of Art and a diploma; he was cutting patterns in a shmutter sweatshop while the others were buying their fabric retail instead of from the wholesalers because they didn't know any better. The press make a virtue out of that by writing it up as a charming anecdote, instead of blasting the crass amateurs for their complete lack of common business sense."

She loved it when he let his feelings go, and she drew on his prejudice because she knew it was what made him vital. He had the sort of command that only comes with real knowledge, colored by an instinctive hate of the amateur.

"Talk to him, draw him out, learn what makes a dress collection work. By the time he's made your wardrobe you should know more about the fashion business than most of the so-called fashion press you'll ever meet. They'll rabbit on about 'cut' and 'line' and 'chic' as if they think they know what they're talking about—forget it, half of them don't know the difference between yarned and piece-dyed. They read each other's columns and follow the pack. In Paris they've got more idea, because they take fashion seriously there, but here there are maybe half a dozen: Ernestine Carter, Pru Glynn of the *Times,* Jean Rook on the *Sketch*, Marion Cummings on *Impulse,* Sheila Wetton on *Vogue* and a few others. The important thing for us, though, is not what they know but what they say in print. If a journalist has two million readers, it doesn't matter if she's soft in the head, provided she writes what I want. After Smith, I want you to meet the Countess and her boyfriend."

He got up to renew the drinks, and she was laughing.

"Don't tell me you've got royalty on the payroll?"

Sinclair gave her the glass. "Well, in a way maybe they are royalty. You'll think they're a couple of nuts when you first meet them, but I'll tell you—between them, they know more about beauty and hair and makeup than anyone else in this town. They won't even talk to the press—not that many have ever heard of them—and if they did, the press wouldn't print what they had to say: It would crucify their beauty advertising; that's one subject where the truth really hurts. They're in semiretirement now, and for laughs they read the beauty pages of the magazines. I want you to use their house like a second home. If you learn only part of what they can teach you, then no commercial makeup artist in the business will ever be able to tell you how to look. You'll do the telling—they'll be there to do the running about."

It was nearly dark when Sinclair walked her across the square to the waiting car. He hadn't realized how long he had been talking. He stood back while the driver opened the door for her.

"Oh, I forgot to tell you, Jackson, we had a pile of old magazines delivered to the flat. They're worth reading, if only to see how the looks have changed over the years. You'll see how the top girls developed as the issues went by. That won't happen to you: When you appear in print for the first time, that's the way you'll look, perfect; the only development will be in status."

She wound down the window.

"Thanks, Daniel. I thought maybe you'd given me the rest of the day off, but I see it's dinner alone and bone up on the opposition."

She wheeled the window up and waved at him as the car drew away.

5

MICHAEL Smith's ready-to-wear showroom was off Bond Street, in the area that used to be the domain of the couturier when there was a London couture business worth talking about. What there was left of it struggled on with the pretense of creating each season a collection that had something to say. But the lack of money, a clientele whose numbers diminished weekly with notices in the *Times* obituary columns and a minimum of any real creative talent had demoted the couturiers into high-class dressmakers. Only the type of woman who wanted to pay for the fading cachet of their label on shapes even the vast size range of the ready-to-wear market couldn't match continued to patronize them in any numbers.

Unlike the Coat House showroom, Smith's was large, with rails of dresses arranged in an open square. Orange chairs lined the free side, and in front of each pair there was a matching table.

The color scheme throughout was beige and orange and was even carried through to the note pads and specially made slim orange pencils set sharpened for use. Most wholesale houses showed their collections a season ahead of the one that was current; in April, for instance, they would show the autumn designs. The advance timing was necessary for physical reasons: first taking sufficient orders from the buyers to be able to judge which designs would sell, and then manufacturing for delivery immediately after the summer sales. Nobody could afford to take the chance of making large stocks of designs that might not sell, and the operation and its timing were calculated to reduce the risk to the minimum. Sinclair's pet hobbyhorse was that if the wholesale houses invited the public to their shows instead of the store buyers, there would be a revolution. If the public once found out what was originally available that was passed up by the trade and never saw the light of a price tag or swing ticket, they'd lynch the buyers en masse for the mealymouthed, frightened incompetents most of them were.

The reason boutiques had become an overnight success was that for the first time the designers could show off what they were doing without first having to have their wares vetted by people buying for others. Michael Smith had heard Sinclair sound off time and time again, and because he was a designer, he agreed with him and passed the message on, with the proviso, of course, that there was a new generation of buyers whose authority was growing.

When Jackson arrived, Smith showed her the range hanging on the rails in the showroom and then took her through the back and past the tables where the pattern cutters and the machine hands were making the specials and the models that would come together as his next collection. They went into a smaller room that had just one long cutting table and two high stools. Hanging like dusty hides on the walls were brown-paper dress patterns that looked discarded but could be taken down and revamped and updated to whatever subtle alteration the current vagaries of fashion were dictating. At the far end of the room was a short and slightly built man in a soiled white coat, making tea from an electric kettle.

"Jackson," said Smith, "this is Albert. He's a wonder, the backbone of the business, aren't you, Albert?"

"You'd never bleedin' know it. How many specials d'you want by yesterday, then?"

Smith laughed at him. "Don't take any notice. Underneath it all he's a fourth-generation tailor; he reckons making women's clothes is beneath his dignity."

"Too true, mate. I suppose you want a cup of tea? . . . Who's the bird you got, then?"

"She isn't a bird, you silly old sod; this is Jackson."

The little man croaked a laugh. "Jackson, that's a feller's name. If you can't tell the difference by now, mate, I reckon you need seeing to."

He turned, and for the first time he spoke to Jackson. "I'd have him put down if I had my way—calls himself a bleedin' dress designer, he does, and he can't even tell the difference between an Adam and Eve."

"I'm sure he can, Albert; it's just my funny name. Can I help make the tea?"

"There you are now, a proper bird, knows how to make a cup of tea." He sidled up to her. "More than he does. Now, what'll be your pleasure?"

"Albert, stop flirting with the customers and get on with it. I am going to design, and you are going to help make, a superb collection of dresses for this splendid young lady. She's going to be a top model."

Albert looked disgusted. Then he turned to Jackson with a professional eye.

"She ain't bloody skinny enough, too much tit. You don't know what you're talking about."

"Well, that's where you're wrong, because we're going to change all that. Everybody's fed up with the flat-chested birds. Jackson's going to knock 'em cold."

Albert looked her over again, walked around her, muttering to himself. When he had finished, he turned back to the cups, poured spoonfuls of white sugar into each and handed one to Jackson and one to Smith.

"I'll say this, you're very nicely built, miss, a basic tall size twelve, and you're good-looking, so maybe he's right. Be a pleasant change, it will."

While he drank the sweet tea, Smith told Albert about the collection they were going to make for Jackson. They discussed her as if she were in another room. She sat on one of the high stools and listened to them with obvious enjoyment. They were no longer sending each other up; their language was their own and showed a mutual respect. They were like an old music-hall double act, insulting each other on cue but finishing in harmony on the curtain number.

"All right, then, so that's it started," Smith said, and Jackson was back into the conversation.

"What comes next, Michael?"

"Well, Albert will just take your measurements. Usually we'd just get you into one of our standard twelves and do a bit of pinning, but for this kind of operation we'll go the whole hog and start from scratch. I'll leave you with him. If the old bastard tries anything, just yell."

Smith put the cup back and then left them alone. Albert took his tape measure and had her stand in front of him. There was a note pad and a pencil on the table, and he took a long time and great care as he measured her.

"What do you think, Albert? Will I do?"

"Oh, well, it's very good really. We'll have to raise your left forepart a bit, of course."

Jackson fell apart. "Raise my *what*?"

"Your left forepart—your left tit's a bit higher than the right, so we have to take a larger clam, don't we? . . . Yeah, very funny, I know, very sexy."

"What's a clam?"

"Eh? Oh, that means a dart; I got to increase the bust allowance, so I got to have a bigger dart, haven't I? Right, now. Just hop on the virgin's altar and we'll have your rising difference."

He was enjoying the conversation, too, and she could sense that although what he was saying was probably the real thing, his delivery was carrying innuendos.

"Go on then, Albert, you'd better tell me. It's all part of my education."

"You see, when you measure a feller for a pair of trousers, you got to take the outside and the inside leg measurements. So you ask him very politely which side he dresses, and you pop the old tape up the other side. Now you can't go shoving a measure up a bird's skirt, so you sit her on a tabletop and take the distance from her hipbone to the table; then she stands up and you measure from the hip to the length, take one from the other, and you've got your inside-leg measurement without embarrassing the poor little lady."

"Albert, we don't have to go through all that palaver. You can do what you like. I won't mind a bit."

He gathered himself, looked over at the closed door and then sniffed.

"It would make it a lot easier if you just slipped off that dress, so I can see what I'm doing, like."

She reached both arms behind her neck and opened the zip, and then she stepped out of the cotton shift.

"Hadn't you better lock the door just in case? Someone might think I was trying to seduce you."

"Don't be daft, what would you want to have me for? Nobody would bother, anyway—I seen enough birds stripped off in my time, gets so it don't mean a thing."

She was wearing tights over briefs and a small half-cup transparent bra.

"Well, I must say, love, you got a lovely pair there, very nice indeed. Now just open your legs a bit and we'll get on with it. No, not so wide."

He knelt in front of her and took the measurement of the outside leg; then he took the tape with its flat brass end and put it on the inside of her thigh. He held it there but was careful that his hand did not touch her.

"Right, that's that then. You can put the old dress back on now."

As she zipped the back up, the door opened and Smith came in.

"How are you doing, Albert?"

"All finished, mate."

"Good. OK then, Jackson, I'll give Dan a ring when we need you in again for the first fitting. Actually he's just been on the phone; he asked me to tell you to hop a cab over to the Countess' place. You're going to have quite a day—special dress collection in the morning and afternoon with the beauty queen."

She gathered her things together and gave Albert a quick peck kiss.

After Smith had seen her off, he went back into Albert's room.

"Well, what do you think, Albert?"

"Give her a couple of months and she'll be a bleedin' raver, I reckon. Tried to get me going, she did. But I think you might just be right—she's a beauty and she comes over, and that's something nobody can't teach 'em."

The Countess wasn't a real countess, but somehow the demeanor and authority that had earned the nickname she had once been given stuck and became as real as her talent. She had met Norman professionally, soon after her husband had died. They were both past middle age, and it had seemed logical that they should join their talents in business. A fondness had grown up but had not developed into anything more emotional. Norman was queer, and although his excursions had become less and less frequent, he still occasionally ventured up to the West End and, if nothing else, took a Turkish bath and paid for the pleasures that when he was a younger man had come very easily to him. He considered himself very lucky: Sex as a physical thing was relatively unimportant to him now, and unlike too many of his contemporaries, he hadn't become the pathetic figure that haunted Victoria Station and the lavatories of Piccadilly. He had the Countess, and they gave each other the companionship they would not have found alone in their own avenues of normality.

They shared an utter contempt for the commercial worlds they had once been part of, where the glittering pots and labels were what they were paid to front for. They had retired comfortably to Wimbledon, where they could enjoy Sunday walks to the windmill on the common and watch the young married people and their children play at the pond and take riding lessons from the school in the village. As Norman had never affected the vanities of the camp homosexual, he was never obviously queer, either to their neighbors or to the local shopkeepers, and so their image could very easily have been that of an elderly married couple who might, at one time, perhaps have been on the stage. The Countess still had her bearing, and this made her seem a large woman who overshadowed Norman. But at night, when they were alone, she became smaller, and the beauty of her clear skin and the still-bright eyes made Norman feel very warm and secure, as if he were back with his mother, whom no woman had been able to replace.

Jackson was surprised as the taxi took the bend off Wimbledon Parkside: She had not thought that a country look could remain so close to the center of London. They pulled up outside a row of shops interrupted by the entrance to a backwater of neat, clean cottages that would have seemed more in place in the heart of Surrey.

The door was opened by the Countess.

"Ah, you must be Jackson, come along in. Let's see, what's the time? Don't suppose you've had your lunch, have you? No? Well, you must have some fruit and camomile tea—learn to make camomile, very good for the skin, insomnia and colds. That's it, leave your things on the stand and come through to the workshop. Norman, Dan's young protégée's here! Come along, jump to it."

Where the cottage had formerly finished, they had built on a corridor which led to what the Countess had called the workshop. It was a large room with a glass roof, and it had been divided up into partitioned sections.

"I didn't imagine anything like this," Jackson said to her.

"Oh? What did you think—that we ran one of those pampering salons for the flabby idle?"

"Well, yes, I suppose I did, really . . . but this is so organized and efficient-looking."

"It has what we need, dear; this is where we do our work. Ah, here's Norman."

He was wearing a navy blue silk roll-neck sweater over slim navy trousers, and on his feet were the sort of rough weave pumps that people buy to wear on holiday in Spain.

"Hello, love, how nice to meet you. Has Emily made you something to eat yet? . . . It's all right, Emily, you carry on. I'll do it."

He went away again, and the Countess took her over to a makeup table built in a black-covered recess. The mirror had lightbulbs studded around its border, like a mirror in a theater dressing room, and above were sets of small spotlights.

"The best light in the world is daylight, but you'll probably spend most of your professional life indoors, so this is where you'll learn how to paint yourself."

Jackson sat on the swivel stool and waited nervously. It was like being at the doctor's: She wasn't quite sure whether she was supposed to take any clothes off or not.

"While we're waiting for Norman, let's get you cleaned up; then we can all see what we've got to work with."

She gave her a smock and then put a white bandage over her dull brown hair, which she pulled back behind her ears until it was flat against her skull. She took one of the large pots from the table and started to rub the contents over Jackson's face.

"Don't worry, it's only butter, very good for cleansing the skin."

As she wiped the butter away with tissues, and with it the cosmetics and makeup that Jackson had arrived wearing, she talked.

"Before you leave today, I'll give you some papers to read. Study them and carry out the instructions to the letter; that's very important. And I'll give you a supply of creams and oils. From now on, don't buy any of the expensive beauty creams or cleansers; they're a waste of money. When you get up in the morning, wash your face in milk; then cleanse with almond oil—don't use water, particularly London water. There now, that's better. What a pretty skin you had hidden away under that muck."

Norman came back into the room carrying a tray. He cleared a space on the makeup table and put it in front of Jackson.

"Ah, I see madam's been at work already. Let's have a look. Do eat, don't mind us."

While she ate the chopped fruit, they stood behind her and looked at her face in the lighted mirror.

"I do the hair, you know. Emily's the face expert."

He paused to smile warmly at the Countess; then he took Jackson's head in his hands. He looked away as his long fingers pressed and then gently combed through the thick hair.

"Yes, well, you shouldn't let a hair salon shampoo your hair with what most of them use—detergent, that's all it is, terrible stuff. Until Dan arranges your own top man, arrive washed and wet. I'll give you some marrowbone and yolk of egg to use."

When she had finished the food and the tea, they took her over to a steam tub.

"Just slip out of your clothes, dear, and pop into that."

She did what the Countess told her and was not embarrassed as they watched her. When she was nude, she sat in the tub, and the Countess zipped up the cover until she was enclosed up to her neck. They pulled two chairs over and sat looking at her again.

"This is the best sort of steam bath; only your body sweats, not your face."

Her nose began to itch, and she wondered what she could do about it. The situation had suddenly become Kafkaesque: She felt imprisoned and unable to move.

"Excuse me, you wouldn't have a tissue by any chance? I can't get at my nose."

Norman laughed at her. "Try the slits in the front, love."

She found them and felt relieved as her hands went through into the cool air and it was all right again.

"Now then," said the Countess. "While you're sitting there, just listen and take this in. The way you look is separated into two distinct compartments, and they should never at any time blend into each other. One is the care of your looks, and the other is the alteration of your looks. The care means the right diet—I'll be giving you a paper on that—the right potions, exercise and health. Alteration means makeup. The fact that most women use either too much makeup or the wrong kind means they don't like what they start out with; they want to improve on it. You must be more subtle."

Norman interrupted, or rather added to what she was saying. "Always subtle and always natural, even if it takes you hours of preparation—nothing must look deliberate."

The Countess went on as if she had only taken a breath. "First the eyes: A woman's eyes, ultimately, are the most important thing about her face; more than any other feature they dictate whether she looks beautiful or not. You're lucky, you have large, almond-shaped eyes to start with. We'll show you how to make them look deeper and even longer."

As she went on, Jackson sat intently. When it was time to leave the steam bath, she had heard how almost every part of her body should be treated and cared for and what could be done to improve it. They broke for tea and afterward started another session, this time with Norman leading, about hair. He produced wig after wig, each in a different style or color. It was to decide her basic new color and look.

"That's it," he said at last and looked at the Countess for confirmation. "Copper-bronze, no doubt about it."

"You're right, Norman, it gives life to the skin tones and brightens the green content of the hazel eyes—perfect."

He combed out the long, loose, slightly curled style, and then he and the Countess stood back and inspected the image of Jackson in the mirror. They were pleased with what they saw.

"Yes," said Norman, "I think we're well on the way."

The Countess looked fondly at him. "You'll make her some matching pieces, won't you, dear?"

"A whole wardrobe of them. Switches, falls, fringes, everything."

He rested his hands on Jackson's shoulders and looked over the top of her head at her face in the mirror.

"Next time you come everything will be ready. You're going to be very lovely, you know."

When she left them for the first time, laden with literature and jars and beauty recipes, she was a new color, and she had left behind the old look that had been Maureen Stokes. It was the beginning of an education that was to produce the person who would be known as Jackson.

The days passed very quickly for her. Sinclair immersed her in fashion, design and journalism; she was taken to the right places at the right times. The personal files on the press that Sinclair had compiled over the years were opened to her, and it seemed that she sat endlessly in his study memorizing the foibles and indiscretions of every fashion editor she was ever likely to come across. She learned which journalists could be bought, not with money but with flattery, and which were inviolate. Without noticing it herself, she was changing almost daily; the confidence that the knowledge she was absorbing gave her began to show through, and in it all her feelings for Sinclair deepened. His cynicism and contempt for what she had held in awe mesmerized her. He could analyze a fashion article in a leading newspaper and almost tell her paragraph by paragraph how it came to be written the way it was. To her, that was power, and power of that kind in a man like Sinclair was irresistible.

"You like him, don't you?" Sue Black asked her once. They were sitting at a pavement table at the Sands in Bond Street, and the question interrupted her daydreaming.

"What? Well, yes, I suppose I do. Why?"

Sue laughed. "It happens to us all, particularly at first. It's the sheer efficiency of the man; he always seems to be so damned right."

She wasn't so sure she liked the personal implication. Sue Black was a great girl, but she was an employee of Sinclair's, not another client.

"I imagine one grows out of that sort of thing fairly soon."

Sue Black took the hint. "Yes, of course."

But it was true. For Jackson, Sinclair was a hunter: He went out and brought back the goods; he fulfilled a purpose that went back through centuries of evolution. If they had still been living in caves, he would have been the pack leader. What she had yet to learn was how to break through the barrier. He treated her well and took care of everything she could want, but there was still a professional façade between them that excluded anything close or warm. It was a new experience for her. She had never gone after a man before in her life, there had never been any need, they had always come to her . . . but then none of them had been like Sinclair.

"I think we'd better go, Jackson. Mr. Sinclair expects us at four sharp."

They paid the bill and joined the passing crowd of birds and pretty young men and tourists. If the man expected them at four, then four it must be.

SINCLAIR ENTERPRISES, LTD.

CONFIDENTIAL PROGRESS REPORT

CLIENT: *Ernest Stokes*   SUBJECT: *Jackson (Maureen Stokes)*
REFERENCE: DS/P/70/1   DATE: June 21, 1970

Your daughter has been under our direction for approximately four weeks. She has been assigned the professional working name of Jackson and will in future be referred to by this name only.

The object of the program thus far (Phase 1) has been: (a) to familiarize Jackson with the environment in which she will eventually operate; (b) to sophisticate her outlook; (c) to improve her physical capabilities; (d) to provide her with a wardrobe in keeping with her proposed profession; (e) to create personal living conditions to match her future image.

The results, in our view, are highly satisfactory. We give as follows precise details relative to headings (a) - (e).

(a) *Environment*

i. Jackson has toured the fashion market and is familiar with the leading fashion houses and designers. She is knowledgeable about the way in which this section of the industry operates and can now evaluate the status of the individuals concerned. A similar situation has evolved in the allied fields of beauty and cosmetics, accessories, interior design, boutiques and stores.

ii. She has been introduced, in name and theory only, to the magazine and newspaper staff.

iii. She has been provided with and read all available newspaper clippings on Jean Shrimpton, Penelope Tree and Twiggy.

iv. She has been introduced, again in name and theory only, to the foremost fashion photographers, and is aware of their specialized and often limiting capabilities. She has received basic training in how to react to a camera and how to work on photographic sessions.

v. She now has a working knowledge of the rudiments of photographic techniques, including lighting.

(b) *Outlook*

The information and experience gained in (a) i-v has aided the reappraisal of Jackson's outlook.

i. She no longer views the people with whom she will come into contact with anywhere near her previous awe.

ii. She has been escorted to and where desirable made a member of the following establishments: Club dell'Aretusa, Burkes, the Revolution, Annabel's, Étoile, the White House, Chez Moi, The French Pub, Terrazza, etc., etc.

iii. She has seen the best of the current theater and cinema offerings and subsequently read reviews of these plays and films by the leading critics.

iv. She has been taken to the leading art galleries by an expert and received a critical analysis on the merits of contemporary artists.

v. She has attended an advanced course in French cooking at the Cordon Bleu School. This, incidentally, not necessarily to improve her own cooking but to give her a greater appreciation and knowledge of what is served.

vi. She has attended an advanced driving course with the British School of Motoring.

vii. She has attended recording sessions made by leading pop artists and groups. She has been made fully aware of the hierarchical strata of the musical world.

(c) *Physical Capabilities*

i. She has attended regular sessions at a private health and beauty center, where, under the supervision of the principals, she has been fully instructed in makeup and beauty care. She also has regular health baths and massage.

ii. She has undergone a complete medical examination and been made fully aware of the dietary prerequisites for maintaining a top physical condition.

iii. Her teeth have received the attention of a Harley Street dentist, and where necessary, cosmetic dentistry has corrected any defects.

iv. Following exhaustive wig and color tests, her hair has been completely restyled and colored. She now possesses a full complement of handmade wigs and hairpieces and is fully conversant with their styling techniques.

v. Her hands and feet receive regular attention from leading practitioners.

(d) *Wardrobe*

A basic wardrobe has been exclusively designed and made for her by Michael Smith. Additional items such as coats, shoes and all other accessories have been obtained from the leading sources.

(e) *Living Conditions*

Since May 3 Jackson has been living at the Basil Street Hotel. This has been arranged in order that interior designer Michael Anderson and his company can completely redecorate and furnish the apartment in Cadogan Square. This work has now virtually been completed, and Jackson will resume residence on June 25.

Summary

To all intents and purposes Jackson would now be considered a sophisticated and intelligent young woman of exceptional physical attraction. The program of training will continue, but in a less intensive form, and will basically be aimed at maintaining the newly created image.

Phase 2: Future Planning and Action

i. Jackson is now ready for a series of black-and-white and color photographs to be taken. We will commission Harvey Reading, and specimens will be forwarded to you in due course.

ii. As planned, Jackson has remained completely unknown. We will now proceed to give her exposure. This will be accomplished by social activity in the company of the photographer Reading. Through association with Reading Jackson will be introduced to *Vogue, Queen* and leading advertising-agency executives. Reading will be permitted and encouraged to consider Jackson his discovery.

iii. Until this time the care and styling of Jackson's hair have been carried out privately; this will cease. As of now she will attend the salon of Philippe Groves. Groves is currently the hairstylist most in demand by fashion and beauty editors for creative work on their photographic sessions. A high percentage of these women also go to his salon to have their hair styled. Jackson's appointments at the salon will be made to coincide with those of the most influential of these journalists. Groves will be permitted and encouraged to consider Jackson his discovery.

iv. The results of ii and iii will be that a number of people will want to book Jackson for photographic sittings. All such requests will be routed through this office. The proposed sittings will be vetted and approved; a number will be deliberately rejected. Jackson's fee scale will from the outset be on the same high level as the existing top London models, *i.e.*, twelve guineas an hour.

v. Arrangements are being made for the attached feature to be published in the *Perceptor* (circulation 3,070,594); it will be accompanied by suitable black-and-white illustrations (*see* Phase 2, Para. i). Other sets of suitable color illustrations will be discussed with *Maintenant* and the weekend color supplement *Impulse*.

Summary

It is considered that the above activity will take approximately three weeks to accomplish. A further report will be submitted at the end of that time.

Sinclair finished reading the report and signed it. He had been deliberate in the way he had drafted it. The style was completely factual—well, almost—it was the type of report a businessman would understand and appreciate.

In fact, he was almost surprised himself at the progress Jackson had made. She had taken and absorbed everything she had been taught, and she had changed. Practically all traces of her provincial background had been erased, and what had emerged was a cool London chick.

The only missing link was her sex education. Sinclair had put that in the background, and she had never given any indication either of what had been before or of what she wanted now. He knew that it had to come and that it was an essential part of making her into the image. He had seen the change come about with other models. Their pictures began to emote and take on an earthy quality, and one discovered that they had taken up a new man and that his influence was permeating through to the camera.

hint of curve, and I have never seen a fraction so beautifully distributed before. We got out the tape measure to record for posterity the very vital statistics, and here they are: 36-23-35.

For those of you who are unaccustomed to visualizing figures on paper, let me explain that Jackson has a real bust on a long and wonderfully proportioned, slim-hipped body. Topping the frame is a head of shoulder-tipping hair the color, as they say, of barbecued copper. As if all of this were not surprise enough, Jackson as a personality is not exactly the usual type of rising model girl.

"Modeling," she says, "is purely a means to an end, and in fact, it is a rather boring means. One's interest lies more in the area of a new integration of women into society that is male-dominated but female-financed."

What, you may ask, do we have here?

What we have is a very bright young lady who is not a mite shy about expounding her thoughts on the way we are living or not living. Jackson, incidentally, is not her real name; as she says, "What my birth name was is unimportant; what I am, that is vital." I can hear the murmurs of agreement on that point.

She also preferred not to dwell on her background, but I did learn that her father is a very successful north-country businessman and that Jackson has accomplishments in other if less apparent fields.

She is an expert driver and is considering taking up racing; she is a very knowledgeable fashion pundit and gave us a wickedly funny dissertation on the relative merits of our leading designers; naturally she cooks—"to perfection," offered Mr. Reading—but has dim views about marriage. "It does not appear to be the most satisfactory or lasting of human relations."

Not given to making wild predictions, I will just put the Drake view on record for all to see. Jackson is about to happen to us, and we may not be quite the same again.

ENDS

He liked it: It had Tessa Drake's racy, not too in-depth style, and there were enough background details and reported quotes to titillate the rest of Fleet Street. It would provide the springboard. Tessa Drake's weekly column was highly read, and what was more important, it was used as an ideas page by other journalists.

Perhaps Reading would provide that part of Jackson's education —he had the reputation, and Sinclair figured that the time was ripe for her. She had been like an athlete in training, except that sex was not a forbidden item on her schedule.

He picked up the stapled sheaf of papers and started to read.

DRAFT FEATURE FOR PUBLICATION IN
THE *PERCEPTOR*

Anyone Here Seen Jackson?
by
Tessa Drake

"The days of the fragile bean posts are numbered."

This is what photographer Harvey Reading said when he presented me with his folio of exclusive pictures over lunch in his studio just off the calm of Regent's Park yesterday.

Now, I've heard this one before, as those of you who follow the Drake saga will know. Not a week goes by but some young—or, come to think of it, not so young—Romeo pleads and complains that the dames that smile out from these pages have little in common with real women.

Real women, they muse, are curvy and have a shape that undulates in the right areas, but look at our crop of top models: Not only are they *sans* the necessary protuberances, but some are positively concave. What's the point, they cry, of making a swing to see-through fashion when there's hardly anything to see?

Well, being a not-too-skinny example myself, I think that maybe the men have something. One consolation, of course, would be that we could all start telling the boys from the girls again.

So as the first nail in that little old coffin the Drake Page reveals Jackson, and the first pictures ever published of a newcomer who, according to our very in and with-it young office lad, is a dolly. The young lady in question was dutifully introduced by her protector over the coffee, and it became very obvious what his enthusiasm was all about.

Jackson is certainly a stunner of a new kind—or maybe it would be more accurate to say, of an old kind, but totally updated.

She is tall—five feet eight—and has just a fraction more than a

The slight problem was, of course, that not only had Miss Drake not written the article, or seen or met Jackson, but neither had Jackson as yet met Reading. The story as it was written was at best semidocumentary. Sinclair was not too concerned; he accomplished his aims by carefully planned stages. Convincing Drake that she should publish his draft under her own byline, that came later; first he established an objective and then set about achieving it.

He checked the wall-mounted Piaget. It was five fifteen, time he left for Reading's studio, for the session that should produce the first set of photographs, some of which would illustrate the feature already written and scheduled for possible publication.

The studio would have overlooked Regent's Park, except that the windows had heavy black blinds closing out all the light. The walls, ceiling and floor had been painted black, to absorb the light from the units of electronic flash equipment. Reading used a series of white painted boards set on pivots to bounce the light to his order. His assistants moved carefully, arranging the battery of cameras that were attached to a crossbar set into a heavy wheeled tripod. Reading would decide which of the cameras he would use when he looked at the set through the viewfinders. The decision would be a subjective one, regulated by how he felt at the time.

Sinclair called to the assistant. "Is the girl here yet?"

"Yeah, she's in the dressing room, having her barnet combed out."

"Where's Harvey?"

"He's in there with her, doing a bit of chatting up."

Sinclair sat at the back of the studio, in the shadows and out of everybody's way.

"He's coming out now."

A beam of light appeared on the far side as Reading came from the changing room. It was cut off as he closed the door behind him.

"How yer doing, man?"

Reading was very slim, almost frail-looking; he had unkempt hair to his shoulders and a frilled shirt open to the waist. The bell-bottomed trousers were so tight that you could see his bulge and outline at the crotch. He had a habit of touching himself there; maybe it was for reassurance.

"I'm great, thanks, Harvey. What do you think of her?"

"Fantastic, just fan-fucking-tastic. Where did you get her, man? Is she yours?"

Sinclair's reply was partially unheard as the blast from the recorder disrupted the quiet.

"—I'm handling her."

Reading yelled back at him, "That's just about what I had in mind. Turn that bleeding thing down! Christ, all this commotion, it freaks me. Look, Dan, I'm going to clean everybody; it's just going to be me an' her. Just check me out: You want some black and white full-length in the clobber, then a load of color in Smith's knitwear gear and then a real groovy beauty head, right?"

"Right. Make 'em great, Harvey."

"What else, man?"

He called to the assistant. "Peter, tell the crimper and the makeup queen they can blow when they've finished with the bird. An' when you've done setting up, you can get lost too. I'll use the Hasselblad for the lot."

"Tell her I came by, will you?"

"Sure. I'll send the pix over on Thursday. See you, man."

Sinclair walked out into the warm evening. He wouldn't bother to ring Jackson until the morning. Late in the morning.

The hairdresser finished the comb-out and stood back to check her reflection in the mirror. He thought she looked bloody marvelous. Jackson smiled back at him and told him what a great job he had done. She didn't forget to thank the makeup boy—he would have had hysterics, and anyway, even by the Countess' standards, he'd done pretty well too.

"Tell Harvey I'm ready as you go out, will you, please, fellows?"

They got the message and quickly finished packing their brushes and combs and pins into the black bags that looked like doctor's visiting bags, except that neither of them looked very much like doctors.

When they had gone, she slipped off the loose overall and sat in her underwear and thought about Harvey Reading. She knew his reputation. It was inevitable that he'd try something—the point was, would she want to do anything about it? It had been a long time, and the schedule that Sinclair had set hadn't included much socializing. Harvey's theory, continually expounded at great length around the business, was based on a Stanislavsky principle that all feeling must come from within and that if you wanted to produce beautiful pictures of birds, then they had got to be feeling good inside. Naturally, he had the magic formula for making birds feel good inside. It was at least a fairly original and entertaining ploy for trying to have it off with as many models as he could swing over to his way of thinking.

Sinclair had preached priorities to her enough times for her to be able to evaluate exactly the purpose of her being in the studio: It was to make a superb set of pictures. There were occasions, she thought, when one's personal ethics had to be surrendered to progress. And in spite of what she might feel toward her mentor, all so far unreciprocated, advancement was the thing.

The studio was very quiet now. Reading had changed the record, and the sound of Donovan was soothing the atmosphere. Before he had left, the assistant had drawn down the continuous sheet of white background paper suspended from the ceiling. It hung in a long, gentle curve to the floor and then spread itself forward until it reached the leg of the tripod. The assistant had placed a large, clear inflatable plastic sofa on the white paper and set the lens of the Hasselblad camera toward it. Stalks of electronic flashbulbs with silver-painted umbrellas stood like giant insects, and the single modeling lamp gave a soft yellow light that seemed to insulate the setting from its black surroundings. The only other light came from the dressing room as the door was opened by Jackson.

"Over here, darlin'."

"Yes, I can see."

"Mind the cables, you can't see them."

She began picking her way slowly toward the set, trying not to trip on the cables that snaked from the feet of the lightstalks to the two Balcar packs by the wall. Reading sat on a high stool, behind the camera. He watched her come into the light, and he thought she was a crazy knockout. She was wearing a pale pink-and-brown-printed Macclesfield-silk shift with a loose pajama-cord-type belt. The fabric was soft and creamy; it stayed close to her body and rippled and twisted as she moved. She slipped her shoes off as she stepped onto the very heavy paper, and he could see that her legs were bare and brown and very smooth. She sat on an arm of the sofa and dangled them, and then she looked straight into the lens of the camera.

"Will this do to start with?"

"Holy bastards, it can't be true—she's too much!"

"What did you say, Harvey? . . . Harvey?"

"I said it's great, that's very good."

He looked into the viewfinder and squeezed the shutter release. The lights flashed their blue-white light, and then it was yellow again. He kept squeezing the release and shouting at her, "That's great . . . hold that . . . fantastic . . . again . . . again . . . more . . . don't move . . . look at me . . . shit!" He had exposed the twelve frames of film. He changed the magazine and was ready again.

"Jackson, sit on the sofa, lie along it."

She took up the pose as if she had been modeling all her life, and as she drew her legs up, the short skirt of the dress moved up her thighs.

"Is that too much leg, Harvey?"

"Yeah, just a little, kid, lower your knees a bit."

He was squeezing the release again, and he continued until he had used up the second roll of film.

"I'll do some thirty-five mm now; just stay as you are."

He connected the flash sync lead to the Nikon, moved in closer and started to take pictures. With each exposure he changed position and stance; sometimes he would be low, then above her. All the time he repeated the short sharp commands: "That's great . . . more . . . crazy . . . come on . . . you're beautiful, you're fantastic . . . Jesus, come on . . . come on. . . ." There were thirty-six exposures on the roll of film, and so his shooting wasn't interrupted until he had had enough. He stood very close to her. He was short of breath.

"You love it, don't you? You really switch on."

She smiled at him; her voice was thick and very lazy. "Harvey, you're showing."

He looked down, and her hand was on his leg, and then she touched him, and then she pulled at the zip.

The first time was a waste. Later, when they had made more pictures and taken a rest and had some drink, he watched her change. They only had the beauty shot to do. She sat in front of the wall mirror and combed out her hair, and he just sat by her and looked at her nude body. He thought that she was the only woman he had even seen about whom the word "beautiful" was a total accuracy and not even in part flattery.

Because he could not say it to her, all he could do was use his four-letter words and the overworked clichés that he applied to any happening or object. His hand moved to touch and feel her breast, and he kissed her shoulder, and as he went to hold her, his face was on her flesh and then down to her breasts. His nostrils moved quickly at the short intakes of the smell of her skin. That time it was complete and good. It was so good that afterward he knew that there would not be another time for him when with her everything would be so right. He knew he could not re-create what had created itself, because she had been part of that, and it was as if she had taken all he was capable of offering in the only place where he was total with his other self, his studio and his camera.

It took two days of darkroom technicalities and administration to produce the series of still photographs that had been recorded on the emulsion of the rolls of film.

Sinclair sat and sifted through the prints and color transparencies. He picked one of the color shots, fed it into the Leitz Autofocus and projected it onto the screen. It was like no other beauty head he had ever seen. Her look was warm and earthy, and because he knew, he could confirm what others who would see it would only like to suspect. Reading had shot her to the waist, and she was nude. The picture showed what had become her beauty. It wasn't pathetic, as most model nudes were, or teasing, like the girlie magazines. It amazed Sinclair what the weeks of training and education had done; it made him wonder how many other women there were whose potential would remain hidden because there was no one to take and mold them. Or maybe it was only Jackson who, as Maureen Stokes, had known that she had a potential that was dormant. He flipped the switch on the intercom.

"Freda, get me Nanette Freberg at *Maintenant,* please."

He stared at the picture until the phone rang. Freberg was on the line, and her voice was low and almost off-key.

"Hello, Sinclair. I expected you to phone before now."

"Nanette, how are you? I'm sorry I couldn't keep our date a few weeks ago."

There was no response.

"Nanette, I have some color beauty shots here of a new girl. Her name's Jackson; you've never seen her before."

"Yes?"

"I think when you see the pictures, you'll want to use one of them on a full page."

"I don't think we have the space available, Sinclair."

He waited. "She is the sort of girl you'd like." He was talking very slowly, choosing his words. "Reading took the pictures. I did think at one time I'd have a really zippy feature written to go with them. Maybe you could suggest a writer?"

There was another long pause.

"Send them over. If they are that good, I'll see."

"Thanks, Nanette. I'm sure you'll love her. The photographs, I mean."

He put the phone down and switched off the projector. It cost seven hundred pounds to buy a color page of advertising in *Maintenant*; PR's reckoned a color page of editorial put together by the magazine staff was worth three times as much. He knew Freberg would have to use the pictures; it would be the price of being caught out.

He called Freda again. "Try to get me Marion Cummings on *Impulse,* will you?"

When she came on the line, he started selling her the idea of using the color knitwear shots. He told her that Jackson would be picking up personality stories in the papers and that this would be Marion's chance to use a new face before all the other magazines moved in. She started to argue back that *Impulse* never used handout pictures, particularly in color, but shot their own, but when he said that Reading had taken them, she began to warm to the idea. Harvey Reading was too expensive for most PR men to use; he normally only did prestige work for the top magazines, which would credit his name, and for advertising agencies, which paid him £400 for a day's work.

When Sinclair finished by telling her that the knitwear Jackson was modeling was from the new collection designed by Michael Smith, she was virtually sold. Smith had status as a newsy designer whose work was also bought by the major stores. So she knew she could give her readers not only a good fashion story but one which would feature clothes they would actually be able to buy, a state of affairs that seldom happened in the high reaches of the fashion-magazine world, where one-off specials made for photography seldom went into production. This ability to create features which worked and which took the drudge away was one reason why Sinclair was not only tolerated but successful; there were other reasons, too.

He called Sue in and told her what was to be done for *Maintenant* and *Impulse*. He kept back a selection of the pictures for the files and for Stokes; they would be needed to accompany the next report.

He decided it was time for his lunch, left the office and walked down Hay Hill, past the glass and metallic coffee shop called Mindy's and into the restaurant of the Mayfair Hotel. Over the Italian specialty of the day he put his mind to the problem of how to persuade Tessa Drake that she should use the story on Jackson that he had written.

He remembered there was a saying in the fashion business: "Never kick the office girl in the arse; she may be your editor tomorrow." He always made a point of being charming to secretaries and assistants. It had paid off. At least four of the current crop of top fashion and beauty editors had started at the bottom, and when they were in that lowly state, Sinclair was around to charm and encourage them. Mary Steward might only be Tessa Drake's assistant, but she had already merited the Sinclair treatment. He was the living proof of the success of Dale Carnegie's teachings. He knew that if Drake found out that the Jackson material came from him, he was dead before he started. The trick would be to persuade Mary to take the story and pictures as if she had originated them herself. Once the feature was in print, he didn't give a damn what Tessa would say or do.

He telephoned Mary Steward immediately after lunch. She sounded very pleased about it and said she would be at the office around half-past five.

He spent the afternoon going through the reports on the Carnel and Smith accounts that Sue and Ann had written up. Because Jackson was new and was absorbing most of his interest, he had given more and more of the established work over to the office. He justified this by telling himself that it was the original ideas and his special touch that the clients really wanted; all the rest was routine. As the thought went through his mind he knew that he was fooling himself: The clients wanted him, and if they could have afforded the fee, they would have had him at their sides night and day. He was almost a status symbol that they liked to show off—"Yes, this is our public relations consultant, fine chap." Except at Christmastime. He remembered one client who rang to check through the champagne list. The client called the names, and Sinclair rated them by bottles.

"*Sunday Times*?"

"Three."

"*Daily Mirror*?"

"Two."

"The *Sketch*?"

"One."

"The *Evening Standard*?"

"One."

"*Vogue*?"

"Three."

"*Harper's*?"

"One."

And so it went on, until every fashion editor had been covered. A lot of champagne bottles were delivered that Christmas, but none to the offices of Hay Hill. At the time Sinclair had almost felt hurt; now he knew better.

He started setting up at five o'clock. He cleared the glass table of its papers, turned the hi-fi units on and adjusted the sound level. Then he took the black-and-white blowups of the pictures Reading had shot of Jackson and threw them faceup on the floor near the bookshelves. He moved them slightly, just enough for a couple to be seen properly, not so much that they looked deliberately positioned. The article was in the roll-fronted expanse of the teak sideboard that stood under the television monitor; it would stay there until he knew the time was right to bring it out. He knew that the best method of getting something—whatever kind of persuader you were, business, PR man or politician—was first to arouse in the other person an eager need; if this simple want could be created, you could get or persuade anybody. But first the approach, the presentation, had to be right.

She was almost on time. He had arranged that the girls should leave early, and it was Freda's last function of the day to show Mary Steward into Sinclair's study.

"Hello, Dan. What a super office."

"Thank you. You look rather spry yourself."

Sinclair sat her on the black sofa and went to mix the drinks. He poured her a gin and french—not too strong; he wanted her to be able to remember and take back what was accomplished. The situation was a delicate one, and sentimental recriminations with getting pissed as an excuse were something he could do without. Mary knew enough of his background to be aware that he and Tessa Drake had been somehow together at one time; he reckoned that she was loyal to her boss, and a wrong nuance could wreck the whole operation.

"How do you like working with Tessa?"

He gave her the drink and then sat in his chair, opposite her.

"I think she's super; she's so professional."

"Your column is the best in Fleet Street, you know. Apart from the circulation, everybody in the business reads it too; it gives them ideas."

She chatted on about her work. Sinclair listened intently and watched her. He thought she was attractive, in spite of the dark wavy hair that was currently unchic. Her figure was what the *Lady* would call "neat, with a firm, well-shaped, high bosom," and she was dressed to type, a droopy white crepe shirt belted into a short dark-brown wrap-over skirt. He looked at her legs; she was sitting with them crossed, and the skirt was high enough for him to see that she was wearing cling-top stockings instead of the regulation tights; that was unusual enough to be exciting. He let her see that he was beginning to stare, but she didn't adjust the skirt; instead, she leaned back and turned her head to look at the bank of equipment on the wall behind her.

"That all looks terribly efficient and complicated."

The result was that the wrap-over skirt opened and Sinclair was given even more to stare at.

"It all makes the system go round."

He adjusted his thinking; he had decided that it would not be a good ploy to try to seduce her, but she was presenting him with the signs so necessary to an Englishman—she must have learned that they were poor at taking the initiative.

"Does Tessa let you write much of the column yourself?"

She turned back.

"Oh, yes, she's marvelous. It's almost a team job now. She does all the really in stuff, of course, but if I come up with something new, she lets me write it up. Why, Dan, what have you got?"

He pointed to the pictures on the floor. "What do you think of those?"

She was slow and careless in uncrossing her legs; she went across to sit on her heels to look at the photographs. Sinclair went and stood above her, and though she was turning the prints and concentrating on them, she sensed that he was looking at her and dropped one knee so that it rested on the heavy rug. He could see right up her leg now. He bent down and took her glass. "Let me get you a fill-up."

She didn't move, and from the way she looked at him he knew she wanted him.

"Dan, these are fantastic. Who is she?"

"Her name is Jackson; she's a client. She's going to be very big."

"She's lovely, and different. Where does she come from?"

He brought the fresh drinks back to the table, and this time he sat on the sofa. She came and sat by him, and as she leaned across the table for her drink, the shirt opened and he could see the shape of her breasts beneath the see-through bra.

"You've got a story, haven't you?"

"Yes, I have, but I'm afraid your boss wouldn't take it if she knew it came from me."

She smiled at him, and he knew that she too had become a professional journalist. The story, and getting it, had become more important than friendship or loyalty. He went to the sideboard and brought the papers.

"I've written it in the style of the column. It's true, but it reads as if the writer had had lunch with Reading at the studio."

She read it through.

"I think it's perfect. With the pictures it would make a super lead."

"You'd have to say that Reading called you, that he originated the piece."

She looked at him for a long time before she answered; when she did, her voice was lower and she said the words slowly.

"That's all right, Dan, I know how it should be handled. I'll ring Reading and fill in with a couple more direct quotes. That nearly makes it genuinely mine, then."

He collected the pictures and brought them over to the table to pack them in a photographic envelope. While he was doing it, she stood up and came next to him. Her hand rested lightly on his shoulder while she watched him.

"Good. Well, that's that done then. I've got a super story; you've got a great piece of free publicity for your client."

He took the typed article and put it in the envelope with the pictures; then he sealed it. They were both acting deliberately, their movements measured, almost as if they were going through the rehearsed motions of a ritual.

Sinclair broke the ice. While he played at sipping his drink, he put his hand on the inside of her leg, the touch on his shoulder became firmer, and so his hand went higher until he felt her flesh above the stocking. She moved her legs apart, and he went as high as he could go. She only bent her body as she leaned down to put her glass on the table. Then she undid the waistband of the skirt, and it fell open. Sinclair held her, and waited while she took off the skirt and then the bra. He finished undressing her.

She lay on the sofa for him, and he flipped the remote control that activated the electrically operated curtains.

The article appeared in Tessa Drake's Tuesday column. It was the lead, and they had used one of Reading's pictures, very big. Mary had added the extra quotes and changed a few words; if anything, it was even more of a plug than Sinclair's original.

7

IT was Saturday night, and it was raining, Sinclair told the cabby to keep the motor running and wait. He knew he'd never raise an answer on the Pont Street rank at that time on a wet play night. He pushed the service bell marked JACKSON and waited. Her voice crackled back, identified him, and then the door buzzed and he pushed it open.

By the time he had climbed to Jackson's top-floor landing he was very much out of breath. "Jesus, I'm getting old." He coughed. He was going to wait and recover before pressing the second bell, but there was no excuse; she had left the door open. He went into the square hall that doubled as a dining room.

"Jackson, it's me."

"I won't be a sec, Daniel. Make yourself a drink and I'll be out."

He dumped his wet Mr. Fish topcoat on one of the pine chairs and went into the sitting room. She was the only one who ever called him Daniel; everyone else used Dan. He thought that must be very significant, and poured himself a J & B and ice from the dough chest that doubled as a drinks cabinet. Everything in this damn flat was serving a double purpose; maybe that was very symptomatic of something.

He looked around the room and decided that the interior designer had done a good job, that when the time was right, it would look very splendid in *House and Garden*. He made a mental note to invest in some modern paintings; maybe a series of Underlecht nudes would add the right touch of mod culture. The green-and-yellow-flowered Gallery Five wallpaper coordinated well with the dark-green carpet, white lamb's-wool rugs and bright-yellow chairs.

Yes, very chic, he thought.

Taste, they'll say, a perfect combination of the old with the modern, blending together to create an atmosphere of relaxed but now sensuality. Perhaps he should write the story himself. She suddenly appeared in the doorway.

"Jackson, you'll have to stop trying to make entrances. It's so out of date."

She sighed and walked over and stood in front of him. Her legs were apart and her hands on her hips. "Well? You got it—what do you think?"

He stood back and looked at her. It wasn't the look that a man usually gives a woman. It was cold and searching and critical. Especially critical. He sipped his drink and slowly walked around her until he was back facing her again.

She was only just getting used to Sinclair inspecting her in this way. She thought it was unnatural that a man, any man, could be so objective about her.

"Your underwear contours show."

"Well, what do you expect? Everything's so tight."

"It's supposed to be tight. Go and put a bodystocking on."

She looked at him in triumph. "I haven't got a bodystocking, Daniel."

He slumped into one of the heavy chairs and stared straight back at her.

"Then take off your bra and your knickers and your tights. You're not going to Chow's looking like a Knightsbridge deb dressed up for dinner with Mummy and Daddy. You're supposed to be a switched-on chick; go and get plugged in, Jackson."

She told him to piss off, under her breath. But she went back to the bedroom to change.

As she pulled the black silk crepe over her nude body, she felt her flesh tingle as it reacted to the cold material, and in the mirror she could see her nipples erect. She zipped up what there was of the low-cut back and twisted to admire her reflection. She looked like a bronzed version of a 1930's blond bombshell; the wide-bottomed pajama trousers of the culottes swirled, and the crepe clung to the soft, rounded cheeks of her buttocks. She almost waltzed back to the sitting room and Sinclair.

He finished the drink, stood up and repeated the inspection. "That's better, Jackson, that looks very good." For an instant his eyes stopped where her thighs met. The fabric was drawn tight there, and he could discern, quite easily, the shape of her. The instant passed. "You should photograph like a dream."

"Daniel"—she stepped closer to him, and the movement made her free breasts gently bounce beneath the crepe—"what do you really think about me? I mean, not when we're working, but like now when we're together, just like this?"

He stared steadily at a point just above her head, as if he were going into a yoga exercise. "You're always a client, Jackson, a very special client, and that puts you in a different category. What you do, how you look and what happens to you are largely the result of my thoughts, my plans. You're going to be a success, Jackson, because I say so; you're going to be the biggest model commodity this town has ever produced, and right now that is the only thing I think or care about."

He moved around her and walked toward the hall. "It's time we were going; there'll be a fortune on that meter." She gave her second sigh of the evening, switched moods and went back to the bedroom to find a coat. As they walked down the dim wide stairs of the house, he talked to her. It was like briefing a pilot for his next op.

"The whole purpose of this little outing is to make next Monday's diary columns. It will be a perfect follow-up to the piece in Drake's column. Veronica Duval's parties draw everyone; all the right and semiright glory hunters will be there clamoring for some sort of instant recognition. But she's the high priestess, and tonight you'll bathe in her reflected glory because I've tampered with the future a little. That very chic number you're wearing happens to be exactly what Duval will have on; the only difference, sweetness, is that she's old enough to know a bloody sight better, and in comparison to you she'll look like she's trying to make a comeback from the fashion grave. It's a piece of chemistry that ought to keep the King's Road mob twittering for a weekend or two."

They were at the door.

"Daniel—if it works, what then?"

He put his hand on her shoulder and almost softened. "It'll work, sweetness, and then you're free for the evening. There'll be people there to know—maybe even Reading. Just have a good time, look beautiful, and take care."

The rain was making the traffic even worse than usual, and the taxi crawled its way up Sloane Street toward Knightsbridge. Sinclair had switched off. He had the ability to do this even at a dinner party. If the people around were boring or if he just wanted to retreat, then his mind would leave them and wander among his own thoughts. He wasn't daydreaming; he was working, thinking and planning, and when they wanted him again, he could snap back into their small-talk reality.

Jackson studied him; the display lights from the closed shop-windows flickered across his still, almost sullen face. Right from their first meeting she had thought how attractive he was. She didn't usually find fair-haired men interesting, but Sinclair had a dynamism that you could feel burning. Even with him slumped beside her in the semidarkness of the cab she could sense his quiet, controlled vibrancy.

The taxi negotiated a red light opposite Bowater House and then shuddered to a stop outside Mr. Chow's.

Sinclair took the invitation from his inside jacket pocket. It was a simple but expensive black card with a sixteen-point silver typeface: "Veronica Duval's Chic-Out, bring a bird." The gimmick—everything Duval was concerned with had to have a gimmick—was that the invitations had been sent only to men.

The Duval—an endearment only her closest disciples could use —clung to the reputation of being the chic-est fashion body in the social firmament. She was also known, although not, of course, to her admirers, as the oldest hippie in the world. A founder, but now retired, member of the fashion Mafia, she gave parties guaranteed to be covered by Hickey, Greville and the diary columnists of every other national newspaper. They would take the pictures and write the magic words that fed the insatiable appetites of the ever-hungry reflected-glory fringe.

Sinclair helped Jackson from the cab and paid off the driver. People were already spilling out from the restaurant and slugging their drinks under the dripping awning of the neighboring shop. A few yards down the street a very sober policeman, hidden by the dry darkness of the arcade, leaned forward into the elements and pondered the situation. He decided that the £5 advance was worth a little more discretion and retreated out of sight.

They left their coats with the microskirted Eurasian and pushed toward the drinks table and the hostess. The restaurant walls were covered with personally signed photographs from the elite. Sinclair had arranged for one of Reading's shots of Jackson to be framed and hung for the occasion, and he saw with some satisfaction that it had been placed between those of Vidal Sassoon and Mary Quant. *Excellent company,* he thought. As he maneuvered Jackson through the jabbering, elbow-bending mass, his eyes moved quickly, recording, recognizing and dismissing. Every now and then he gave his smile, dropped his lids fifty percent and inclined the blond head a millimeter. That meant, OK, I see you, so you're at the right party too.

He always worked on the principle that it was they and not he who had to be seen. He double-checked, almost nervously, that neither Tessa Drake nor Mary Steward had yet arrived. The columnist and photographer he'd fixed were standing five feet from Duval, but in that crowd they might just as well have been halfway to Hyde Park Corner. He whispered in Jackson's ear and steered her over.

He gave them the confidant's elbow squeeze. "Having a freak chic-out, fellows?" They brought their drinks around and smiled with recognition.

Then they paused to take in Jackson. "Very nice." Jackson preened professionally.

The journalist put his lips to Sinclair's ear. "You're a bastard, Dan, do you know that? It'll crucify the old dame."

"Yeah, but think of the story it'll make." He took a neatly folded piece of paper from his wallet and gave it to the journalist. "There's your copy, Peter. All you have to do is get the right pictures."

The journalist read the double-spaced type:

JACKSON'S DOUBLE CHIC

Saturday night at Mr. Chow's will go down in party-giving history as the night when Veronica Duval was outchic'd. She was holding her guests enraptured wearing the latest little exclusive creation of pet designer Adrian Baseher when what every socialite fears actually happened. And it happened in the fantastic shape of Jackson, the new, new girl tipped as most likely to succeed Twiggy. Looking as if she had stepped straight from the pages of *Vogue,* Jackson advanced to deliver the customary cheek-kissing greeting— wearing exactly the *same* outfit! What went through Veronica Duval's mind one can only guess. But she certainly carried off what could have been a disaster with aplomb. Jackson was overheard murmuring that she would leave immediately and change. But fortunately for everyone at the party she stayed on.

He finished reading and looked up at Sinclair. "Christ . . . we might have to sub it a bit."

"As long as it's printed in substance, I'll be happy, Peter, and so, I'm sure, will you. Come on, let's get it over."

The two journalists lost their drinks and moved into position. Jackson and Sinclair advanced on Duval.

"Veronica."

She turned. "Dan, my pet—" Her eyes moved across to assess Jackson and froze. Jackson lunged on cue as the motorized Nikon whirred. It was over with less overt trauma than Sinclair had expected. The Duval certainly had control, if nothing else.

But he remembered the look she gave him as he gently steered Jackson away into the crowd that pressed around them, providing the excuse to move on and cut the cocktail conversations.

Harold Carstairs was trying to look casual as he propped up the foot of the openwork spiral staircase that led to the first floor. He wasn't being very successful. As each new bird slowly and carefully climbed the steps, his eyes wandered skyward. He was beginning to drool. "What color's the blonde got on, Harold?"

"Eh? What say, old boy? Oh, it's you, Dan." He smiled with relief and then whispered in confidence, "She wasn't wearing any, forward little bitch, and cling-top stockings to boot."

Sinclair tried not to wince. "Harold, I want you to meet Jackson. She is going to be a very successful young lady. In fact, I think you should talk very seriously with that editor of yours; you never know, if you play it right, I might let the magazine launch her." They guffawed at the joke that they both knew wasn't really for laughs.

Jackson was standing back drinking her champagne and trying not to look too bored. Sinclair turned to her and whispered, "This is worth some time, sweetness." Then: "Jackson, meet Harry Carstairs. He's the publisher of *Vogue*'s biggest rival, *Maintenant*."

Carstairs beamed and tried to keep his eyes off her breasts. "I say, rather splendid, my dear."

Christ, thought Sinclair, *he's the bleeding end with his phony British bit.*

Carstairs drained his glass and then did his coy look. "I say, do you two know what they say about champagne glasses and tits?"

Sinclair tried not to look too uninterested.

"Yes, well, they do say that the perfectly shaped little titty will fill a champers glass to the brim." With that nugget he scooped up

Jackson's left charley in the glass. "There, you see, Dan me boy, perfect." Jackson giggled.

"I'm sure you two are in for a real chic-out tonight; if you'll excuse me, I'll do a wee bit of circulating." Sinclair squeezed himself away from them and headed for the door. He knew Carstairs; he would try very hard to make Jackson, if he remained capable, and maybe he'd make it, if Reading didn't show first.

He cornered a waiter and supplied himself with a new Scotch. It didn't take him very long to decide that work was over for the day. There was nobody within striking distance that merited any excitement, and the sight of everyone on some kind of make or other had lost its interest. It was if his kicks were over and he needed time for his libido to recover its drive. He also didn't need to bump into the staff from the *Perceptor* just then.

As he reached that decision, he felt a warm hand slowly caressing the inside of his left leg; it was someone from behind him, and he rather hoped it was a woman. He took another swallow of the drink and stayed there, hardly moving. A woman's voice softly crooned in his ear. At least, that was the intention; to Sinclair it sounded like a sugar-coated rasp. But he knew it and was able to relax. "Marion, you silly bitch. You shouldn't go around touching up gauche young men at parties."

"Ooh, look who's talking, darling—give you half a chance and you'd have me standing up behind the bar."

She was about thirty-five, almost as tall as he was, and attractive in a kind of horsy way. She was the sort of woman who became more desirable as the evening and the drinks wore on. For Sinclair, it was a very early evening, and he was still quite sober. But she was the fashion editor of the *Impulse* color supplement, whose circulation and authority were now beginning to rival those of the *Sunday Times* and *Observer*.

"How's your little protégée, darling Dan? Don't think I didn't notice that very cute flanking maneuver you pulled on the hippie."

He ignored the dig. "Talking of my protégée, Marion, what did you think of the color transparencies?"

"Well, darling, that's really what I wanted to talk to you about."

"I'm disappointed, Marion; here was I thinking it was my body you were after."

She gave him her lecherous smile. "Darling, I think we should discuss the possibilities of your body, the young lady and my fashion pages in rather more detail. Why don't we leave this quiet soiree and adjourn, as the man says, to my pad?"

"Marion, where the hell are you getting that pseudo hip talk? Don't tell me you've got another East End boy wonder for an art editor."

"Now, don't knock your betters, dearie."

Sinclair was trying to decide whether the offer was likely to pay off or not when she interrupted his thoughts for the second time. "I don't think you have to worry about your Jackson's welfare for the rest of the evening, Dan."

He followed her stare back to the foot of the staircase. He could see that Carstairs was doing very well. His hand was under the low-cut back of Jackson's culotte dress, and he could see its impression as it moved over the roundness of her cheeks. He suddenly felt the urgent possessive protectiveness of a parent.

"Yeah, you're right, Marion, so why don't we go?"

It was cool outside, and the rain, for once, wasn't an objection. He managed to trap a taxi as it delivered a fresh supply of yakking humanity for the chic-out.

"What's the address, Marion?"

"Darling, it hasn't changed."

His mind flipped through the card index and came up with Notting Hill Gate.

As the cab slipped into the mainstream of traffic, he hoped Carstairs was getting good and pissed.

He remembered the flat as he followed her down the dingy hallway. She had put together a party to celebrate her appointment to the color supplement. He had arrived at nine o'clock, ready to eat, and had been forced to wade through what seemed like gallons of whiskey until at eleven thirty she had produced cold chicken legs and dry salad. *Thank God she's not the cookery editor,* he had thought.

She turned on the lights and the electric fan heater. "Give us your coat, love, and I'll get some booze out."

He thought he had seen the last of bed-sitter flats, but at least this one was clean.

In one corner there was the divan-*cum*-bed, and on the walls she had mounted the posters *Vogue* had put out to celebrate its centenary, a definite step up from Spanish bullfighters. Three rugs from a Liberty's sale lay on dark-brown carpet, and the dressing-table top, by the window, was covered with makeup and scent samples. Above the blocked fireplace was a black-and-white blowup taken from *Impulse*'s first cover.

He remembered the model; she looked so prim and pure and beautiful. She had married a queer photographer, who had got his kicks from photographing her making love to his second-best friends. Sinclair did not really have anything to say about that himself. What people did for kicks was only a matter of interest to him. If they were, in his view, scheduled for importance, then he would note the event so that when the time came, as it always came, he could remind them of his knowledge. As people gained in the status race, so they preferred the indiscretions of the past to be forgotten. They became more vulnerable as they moved upward, and this trait suited Sinclair very well.

There was only one chair in the room that he could choose without playing too hard to get. As he went to sit down, Marion came back into the room. She was carrying two very large glasses, filled to the brim.

"Darling, don't be formal, relax on the divan."

She sat beside him, looking like a private nurse attending an improving patient, and handed him his drink.

"There we are now, isn't this cozy? And much better than that noisy, crowded party."

"Marion"—he took a long swallow of the drink—"what do you really think of Jackson's pictures?"

"They're very sweet, Dan. . . ." She paused for full dramatic effect. "We might use them in the August issue."

Over the rim of the glass he projected his sincere and quizzically romantic look to the exact *Woman's Own* specification. "That would be absolutely marvelous. Marion, I think you deserve something rather special."

She put her drink on the floor and nudged herself closer. "Well, Danny boy, I don't see any reason to wait." She had uncrossed her legs, and he could see under the skirt and up her thighs to where it became very dark. "Why not give it to me now?"

The alcohol was beginning to work, and the thought of the

color fashion feature had taken the tenseness from him. "Well, baby, if you want it now, then I guess you'll have to have it."

She ran her hands over his legs, touched him, felt the hardness there, and then moved higher to pull his tie free, then slowly began to unbutton his shirt. He watched her and knew that there would no longer be a need to talk until it was over.

Her hands were on his body now, and as she worked to loosen his trousers, she kissed him on the chest and downward.

Sinclair was still an observer, a nonparticipant, and this seemed to make her movements all the more urgent.

He stroked the back of her neck because he knew it would please her, and then he slipped from under her to put his glass on the floor and finish the process of stripping.

She watched him as he carefully folded his clothes. He was still well built and tight, and all she could think of was his body.

"I can see why they call you Big Dan."

He smiled back at her and thought it was a hell of a way to do business. It was becoming a qualification, like having a degree or belonging to the right club. How would you word a *Times* Personal Column ad? They were very particular what they accepted; it hadn't taken them long to catch on to the innuendo of "musical tastes," and the queers had to find another code phrase. "Knowledge of the bedding trade"—maybe that would pass. He was nude now, except for his light-blue Shetland socks and his wristwatch. He was always knocked up by the prospect of making love with socks and a wristwatch on. It must look utterly ludicrous, but it was that kind of situation; some men did it for money; he did it for clients. For him it was a symbolic gesture of independence, a postscript that hinted at a time limit.

Her dress had a front zip running down to the hem, and as he opened its teeth he could see that she had done more than just prepare the drinks. Her breasts were full and loose, and her belly showed a deep pink line where her pants had cut into the flesh. The eyes were half-closed now, but mesmerized by his excitement. She reached up and touched him again and then gently guided him down toward her.

Her legs were wide and the knees high as she clutched at his buttocks and moved with the motion. He caught a glimpse of the blowup on the wall and the thick black lettering that spelled *Impulse*.

8

HER father was always on time—it was part of his makeup—and so it was no surprise to her to find him waiting at the luncheon table in the Étoile in Charlotte Street.

"I'm sorry I'm late, Dad. I was on a photo session."

"That's all right, love." He took her shoulders in his broad hands and kissed her warmly on the cheek. She was the only woman in the restaurant, and he felt very proud at the way the men had admired her as she walked down the carpeted space between the tables.

He ordered her a drink, and the waiter brought the menu to them to read.

"Let's get this over with, shall we? Then we can talk."

He told the waiter what they would eat, then settled back to look at her. "My, you've changed. I didn't recognize you from the photos, you know. It's amazing, really amazing."

She was embarrassed and laughed at him. "Come on, Dad, it's not that bad, surely."

"I didn't mean it that way, Maureen. You're different, that's all. I have to get used to my new glamorous daughter."

It was strange to hear her name used again. She had taken special care that day with what she would wear; she had got very used to dragging around looking as if she couldn't afford a decent wardrobe. It was a model girl's insignia, and although apparently perverse, it really was the right gear for the job. She might be booked in at *Queen* all morning to wear the new and expensive clothes their fashion editors had picked to feature, and in them she would be chic and elegant. But lunch could be taken on the run in the back of a taxi because she had to cross town to check in at Bill King's studio in Chelsea by two. Leading that sort of life, you dressed for comfort and not for fashion. But that day it was different because there would be enough that he would not understand without adding to his confusion. And because she loved him and respected him and was secure, there was no need for her to set out deliberately to shock him. There was no protest between them, only a deepness that spanned the generation gap which with others was a chasm.

"You know, nobody's used that name for such a time, it's nice to hear you say it."

He coughed. "Yes . . . well, here's the food, love. I hope you're hungry."

While they ate, each tried to snatch glances of examination without the other's noticing. She thought his hair was a little grayer at the sides, but he looked well—perhaps a little overweight; that was the business lunches. She remembered when there had been no time for lunch, and his meal of the day was at night, and they didn't live in the best part of Chester, and her mother was there to cook for them.

She's at home here, he thought; *at ease.* The rough, unsure edges that had made her taut and sometimes brittle had been smoothed away; in a way, she was lush, and her look was one of being well cared for.

"They were very impressed with that article in Tessa Drake's column, created quite a stir. And—er—the story in the diary column was a stunner." He paused. "David asked me to give you his love."

"How is he, Dad, got a new girl yet? I bet he has. He's going to do the marriage scene, is that one."

Her father smiled. "No, he hasn't gone that far yet. I think he's hoping you'll maybe change your mind and give it all up."

She wondered whether that was what David had really thought or whether it was her father's way of getting over a question on his own account.

"It's all going too well. I'd be a fool to chuck it now. You were right to get Sinclair, Dad. I mean, he really is great."

They had eaten their way through the poached Scotch salmon, and she had tasted the red strawberries from the trolley. He asked for a brandy for himself, and she had more black coffee poured into her cup. He picked a cigar from the stack of boxes the waiter offered, and when the end had been cut and he had got it smoking well, he leaned back and sighed.

"Oh, they do a damned good meal here. Now, how's Sinclair treating you?"

"Do you mean has he made a pass yet?"

"No, of course not." He drew on the cigar. "I mean, is he taking care of you; what do you do with yourself in your free time?"

She laughed. "Dad, you must be joking! I don't get any free time. If I'm not actually booked working, then there's his special indoctrination course. I know nearly as much about the people in this business now as the great man himself."

She leaned across the table, glanced over her shoulder and then in a stage whisper said, "Did you know that the editor of"—her voice was so low that he hardly caught the name of the newspaper —"has turned queer?" She held up her hands in mock defense. "It's true—left his wife and kids and gone to live with a lover boy. I bet that little tidbit would shock 'em back at the club."

He tried to look stern and made a pretty good job of it. "I don't know about back at the club, but it's not exactly what I expected to hear, I must say."

"Oh, come on, Dad, you don't take that sort of thing seriously."

"I see. What about this Harvey Reading that was in the article? Is he another of your queers?"

She thought that was very funny. "No, Dad, far from it. He's a very normal boy." The next line was a try at a casual throwaway remark. "We go out together occasionally."

Her father knew the technique and wasn't fooled. "Well, I'm glad at least you've got somebody other than Sinclair to talk to. You'll be careful, though, won't you, love? I mean, it is all happening rather fast."

"Don't believe all you read in the papers, Dad. They always have to blow everything up to twice the size. You know what Sinclair says? Well, he says that we all know the real facts behind at least one story that we've read in the newspapers, and ten to one these facts have been mixed up, twisted or exaggerated, right?"

He nodded his head thoughtfully. "Yes, I think he's probably right."

"So," she said, "how many inaccurate reports does that make? Thousands—and don't say, 'where there's smoke,' because you know what, that brings it down to gossip."

His smile was warm and full of love. "I know you're loving every minute of it, Maureen, but—er—you wouldn't forget to let me know if you needed me, would you?"

With a rush of fullness she realized how generous he was and how easy it was to be selfish. She knew that was probably the way with all children, that they mostly took and never really gave back. Why was it that way? she thought. It would be too late one day, and then you must feel guilty for all the good intentions that you never got around to. It was the way of things; only maybe too few remembered that, and when they in turn became parents, they forgot not to expect a profit on their investment. You could never repay your parents, and it was unfair of them to expect it, because how do you repay what they paid out in care and worry? The only way was to complete the cycle yourself and give to your own children.

She went with him to the station, and he hugged her, and they kissed good-bye in the train. She didn't tell him she was going to Paris with Sinclair, to be introduced to the French fashion press; he would worry, and she didn't want that to happen.

"Daniel, what do you do when you're not working?"

"I think."

"Oh, come on, you can't be thinking about PR and all that all the time."

"Why not? Anyway, that's what I tell the tax inspector."

They were at the bar in the hotel, and it was the end of the day. He ordered a crème de menthe for Jackson and a brandy for himself.

"Do you like Paris?"

"Of course I do. Doesn't everybody?"

"No, I don't think so. The French can be very boring until you know some of them well enough."

"Well, I think it's always the way it is in the books and songs; it's romantic. My father used to bring me with him when he came on business, and when I was old enough, I used to walk around on my own. You know, last year when we came, I went and walked along all the streets that Hemingway wrote about in his book. Mustn't that have been a good time to be in Paris?"

"It sounded very good, the way he wrote about it, but then he was a very good writer. What was your mother doing while you and your father were cruising round Paris?"

"She'd left a long time before that. Daddy divorced her when I was ten. Apart from being away at school I've been with him all the time. She's never written or anything; we don't even know where she is."

"Maybe she'll see your pictures in the papers and magazines and turn up to claim her famous daughter."

"Daniel, she wouldn't recognize me. Why, even Dad said he hardly knew me from that piece on the diary page."

He felt very satisfied. He had taken her to L'Hôtel in the rue des Beaux-Arts in St. Germain-des-Prés. It was a very in place he had been introduced to by a couple of American designer girls who now lived and worked in Paris. They had a very successful boutique just a few minutes' walk from L'Hôtel, and they were famous because their clientele were famous.

A party walked past their table, and the men gave Jackson a look, then checked to see who she was with and whether she was up to standard. But they were very good together. She was wearing a maxi-length Liberty printed-silk evening dress, with long sleeves and a scooped-out neckline, which Michael Smith had designed for her. Her makeup was very pale, and she wore no jewelry, not even a watch. There was nothing to distract the eyes from her face. Sinclair had on his dark-brown velvet jacket with wide lapels, and the handmade shirt and tie from Turnbull and Asser were a very pale pink. His face was tanned, and this, with the short, thick blond hair and sharp blue eyes, made him look very handsome. Together they were the perfect image of the new London people.

"What did you think about those people on the magazines today?"

"I thought some of them were fine. But my French isn't as good as it should be—every time I leave here I feel uneducated because I didn't bother to learn the language well enough, and I always say to myself that I'll brush up when I get back home, but I never do."

"Well, they were very impressed. When we get back, I'll fix up the details, and then you'll have to come over again to shoot some covers for *Elle* and *Jardin de Mode*."

"That'll be great. But what about *Nova* and *Harper's*? You know Harvey took my pictures in, and he said they were knocked out by them."

"You don't have to worry. We were talking to them about dates before I left. What's the situation with you and Harvey?"

"What do you mean, situation? We just see each other; he's been very nice, and he's a good photographer, that's all."

Sinclair held the Dupont under her cigarette. Its sudden flame and the way she pouted to draw it to the end of the Gauloise made her look very delicious.

"Did he turn up the other night at Duval's?"

"Oh, Christ, yes, he did. That man Carstairs was very put out, but Harvey gave him a few more drinks, and when he was just about flat, we propped him back up against the staircase and blew. Anyway, what happened to you? That girl Tessa Drake was there asking for you."

"I had some business to do, that's all. What did the Drake girl say?"

"She was quite funny, really; she said how nice it was to meet me after running such a big interview in the paper. I think maybe I made just a little boob."

Sinclair put a hand to his face and, with the thumb and forefinger, gently massaged his closed eyes. His teeth clenched, and the impression was of a man who had been expecting the bad news he knew he was about to get.

"What did you say, Jackson?"

"Well, she asked me how I got on with Mary Steward, and I said that I didn't actually know her, that you had sort of handled that part."

"Hmm. She didn't have hysterics or anything right on the spot, I suppose?"

"No, of course she didn't. She just said something about not knowing you had anything to do with it. It's nothing really serious, is it?"

"Don't worry, it can be handled. I suppose I should have told you the background, but it doesn't really matter. Would you like a nightcap?"

The waiter brought two more drinks, and she smoked another cigarette. Sinclair could sense what was coming. She leaned closer to him, and her voice was soft and slightly offhand.

"Daniel, how old are you? Thirty-three? Thirty-four?"

"You're flattering me."

"Well, I don't think you can tell people's ages anymore from looks; it's the way they think—you think now, that makes you now age." She laughed, but he knew that she wouldn't let it go there. He had been through the same kind of feminine third degree many times before.

"Haven't you ever been married or anything?"

"I've been anything a few times, and once almost more, but I've never actually taken the legal walk."

"Oh, you've disappointed me! I thought you were the sort of man who had a real first love away in the misty background that turned sour because she cheated on you and you've never trusted again." Her eyes were moist. She gave a deep sigh, then sipped the green liquid in the glass.

He knew that part of it was the soft light, the good food and the smooth liquor and that she had become sentimental, but it was a side of the relationship that he could not afford to develop. It didn't matter what he felt or thought about her in personal terms —she was a product, a means of cleaning up. To allow an involvement could be disastersville.

She wondered what the hell it would take to loosen him up. Of all the places in the world, surely Paris and the ambience of the evening should do it. She reasoned that the only thing he could possibly be worried about was that she was a fee-paying client. He was an Englishman, of course, and that didn't help; if he had been French or Italian, they wouldn't be wasting their time drinking in the downstairs bar of the hotel. Surely by now he must have decided that what she felt for him was more than just client professionalism.

"You know, Daniel, I think that you are rather special. No, don't smile at me like that, I mean it. You have things all your own way, don't you? It was like that for me too, back home, and now because of you, it is getting like that again; only this time it's the big city. Do you think we're making a good pair, you and I?"

"Could I have one of those cigarettes?"

She reached for the packet. "Why, sure. I didn't know you ever smoked, Daniel."

He looked over the flame at her. "Only in times of stress." Then he blew the smoke away and gave her his older-man-and-much-more-experienced-than-you look.

"Don't tell me the great Sinclair ever suffers from stress. I bet you're nervous."

He combed his fingers through his hair and flipped the loose ash from the end of the cigarette.

"Now, why should I be nervous? Here I am, in the most romantic city in the world, having taken a beautiful girl to dinner, drinking nightcaps only a few floors below where we'll both spend the night. That is not a nerve-racking situation. Provocative, maybe, but not nerve-racking."

He warned himself not to go too far too fast; the idea was gently to ease out of a situation, not to rush into it.

We're home, she thought, *and nearly dry.*

"Daniel, you're always reminding me that I'm a client. Don't you think of me any other way? I'm terribly grateful to you, you know. None of this would have happened without you, but it's not only that; it's . . . well, let me through, let me in to whatever it is that goes on behind that smooth, constant PR front you've built up to protect yourself with. I don't want to smash it down, just to be in on a small part of it."

He ignored the probing, because he knew there was only one answer that she'd want and that was something he wouldn't give her.

"Come on, Jackson, we should go up. We've an early plane back in the morning, and I have London appointments fixed for before lunch."

She nearly took his arm as they walked across the thick carpet.

"Am I getting too close to home?"

He looked down at her. "Yeah, maybe."

In the lift he held the key to her suite; she looked at the back of the liftman and smiled at Sinclair, as if it were part of a secret pact. Her suite was only a few steps down the quiet, carpeted corridor, and as they reached it, he opened the door for her; then he put the key into her hand.

"I promised your father two things when I agreed to help you. One of them was to make you the best, the most; the other was to watch out for you. It would be too easy for us to cheat, Jackson, and I don't think you'd like yourself or me for it. Sure, tonight you think I'm mad, but in the morning it'll be different."

He tried not to sound patronizing, more like a warm father figure; he doubted if it came off. He deliberately didn't kiss her cheek, because it would have been adding insult to injury. Instead, he put his arm around her shoulders and hugged her.

She moved away from him. "Watch out, Mr. Persuader, or you might crack. Good night, Daniel."

She clenched the door handle very tightly, and slowly, and very deliberately, she pushed it until she heard it click shut. Then she turned the internal safety lock.

It was a controlled white heat of temper; anything less and she would have slammed the door in his face. She wanted to smash and scream; instead, she sat in front of the mirror at the makeup table and took up a brush and pulled it viciously through her long bronze hair. Her face was without color, and her breathing deep and fast. As the physical reactions to her bruised ego played themselves out, the color returned to her face, and the strokes of the brush became slower until the tantrum was exhausted. She was calm now, and she looked at herself in the mirror and spoke to the reflection.

"You stupid bloody fool, why didn't you get the message? Jesus, he laid it on the line enough times—why did you have to go and throw it at him? You should have known; he's not real, he doesn't exist as a man."

She turned away from the mirror and the image of herself, and as she stripped off her clothes and climbed into the bed, her mind became cool and objective. Without her fully realizing it, the final vestiges of her provincialism had been swept away. The idealized romanticism she had brought with her, the dreams of a girl who came to the big city with ambition and the burning need to succeed, had all revolved around Sinclair as the person who could make them come true. It was like the new girl at school who fell in love with the prefect in her first term, only to find that with time, experience and achievement she surpassed her heroine and went on to become a heroine herself. When you enter an unknown environment, unheralded and without status, you are by the very nature of the situation unsure and passive. If you are clever and have the shrewdness of a potential woman, you wait and you learn. When you know enough, the time will come, and as if your beacon had suddenly been switched on, you will, at that instant, be independent, confident and ahead.

As she lay on the bed, she knew this had happened and that she had overtaken him. She no longer needed the emotional crutch he had supplied; she was almost grateful to him for rejecting her. She thought that was a laugh; the only time she'd even gone after a man, and when he turned her down, she was grateful.

He'd been so right when he'd said it would all seem different in the morning; only it wouldn't be the way he thought. She still needed him, but not like before; now she needed him only for his practical value and his expertise. She was the client, the boss, and he was being paid to serve her, and as long as he fulfilled his function efficiently, she would treat him well. It was like having a load taken off her back; she was free.

The Trident was on its approach run, and Sinclair looked out of the window to pick up the landmarks. He always took a seat on the starboard side so that he could play the game of pinpointing his office building. The morning was fine, and through the wisps of light cloud he saw the GPO tower. He related this to the Hilton and Queenie's rather large back garden, and before the plane moved over the river again, he had located what looked like Berkeley Square. The sudden open expanse of Richmond Park reminded him of the African veldt. Then they were down among the buildings, and the stewardess' voice was telling them to keep their seat belts fastened until the plane came to a complete standstill and please to check that they had all their hand luggage. In the case of Jackson this was something to think about; she had raided the duty-free shops at Orly and was loaded with loot.

The customs man must have decided that she was trying it on, or else he preferred her company to that of the rest of the plane's passengers; whichever way it was, Jackson lounged against the counter while he went through her bags, carrying out a calm but questioning conversation. In the end he regretfully let her go, and without a penalty.

They picked up the Porsche from the multistory garage, and in slightly more time than it had taken to fly in from Paris Sinclair dropped Jackson off at the Cadogan Square flat and then went on to Hay Hill.

He was showered, changed and in his study going through the accumulated messages and post by eleven. Mansfield had rung, and Sinclair told Freda to get him on the line immediately.

"Did you enjoy Paris, Sinclair?"

"Yes, I did, thank you. I took your colleague's daughter with me, on business."

"Good, yes, I hear that is going rather well. Sinclair, I would not usually ask you to obtain inside specialized information, but on this occasion it so happens that the subject is rather in your field." Sinclair didn't interrupt him. "There is a fiber company, Associated Vicose Chemicals (AVC), and I am reliably informed that they intend a take-over operation of a particular fabric-manufacturing company. It would be very valuable if I knew which company and how much AVC is prepared to go to. Do you think this could be obtained?"

"Yes, I think so, Mr. Mansfield. You wouldn't be able to tell me when the next board meeting might be, would you?"

"Yes, I can. It's in two days' time, at four P.M., in their Portman Square offices."

"I'll telephone you when I have the information."

"Very good, Sinclair. Good morning."

The line went dead, and Sinclair buzzed Freda.

"Freda, get on to Hart; ask him to come up at three this afternoon."

Sinclair had a working lunch and went through the reports. He saw that Tessa Drake had run once and Mary Steward twice. The bookings were coming in on Jackson, from *Vogue* and *Queen* through to *Honey, Woman* and the *Sunday Times*. It was straight modeling work, but the clothes and photographers they used were good and the exposure valuable. He knew that it was essential for her to get top photographic model bookings; the one flaw in the scheme would have been the starlet syndrome—personal publicity, and then fade-out because nothing concrete materialized. But the training and background work had been thorough, and everything was to plan, so far.

He made a note to look for a personal executive to handle Jackson's bookings. He wanted a tough, experienced woman who knew the model and magazine business. Maybe he should try to persuade one of Clayton's or Peter Lumley's girls to come over.

He looked at the telephone notes on Drake and Steward again and decided they could be ignored.

Hart was on time. He was about forty-five, thickset, and neatly dressed in a nondescript brown suit. He was the kind of man you would never notice; he blended into anonymity. Hart ran the best private detective agency in Europe. Outside the profession and the legal world he was virtually unknown, and whenever the supplements ran features on private eyes, he was the one they never mentioned. The company he had built up after the war now handled the European work for the top American agencies and occasionally made discreet private inquiries on behalf of the CIA.

"What is it, son?"

He moved around the study, adjusting anything he thought out of place. Every now and then he would stop, hitch up his trouser leg and pull on his black socks.

Sinclair told him the problem, and it was only then that he relaxed and sat down.

"This is an industrial espionage job, for Christ's sake."

"Yes, I know it is, but I thought just this once you might take it on, for old times' sake."

Sinclair knew that Hart spent most of his time on cases involving industrial counterespionage; to be the villain was basically out of character.

"If it was designs you wanted, I'd tell you to stuff it up your fawn costume; but take-overs . . . I guess they're all so bleeding shady it's not really going to amount to much anyway."

The morals might be slightly bent, but at least, Sinclair thought, he had some, of a kind.

"How will you do it?"

"Piece of cake, boy. I'll have one of my operators up there in the morning on a postal fanny."

"Fanny," Sinclair knew from experience, was the vernacular for pretext.

"We'll go through the whole project, cover the lot; the usual bugging, ventilation ducts, telephone junction boxes, flower bowls, bookshelves. Then we'll salt the blotting pads with carbon paper and flimsies underneath and switch ballpoints for pencils. Clean wastepaper baskets at every chair, of course, and a new little device, a box on the table marked 'For security reasons, please deposit all waste notes in here for destruction.' Works like a charm, that one does. Then I think just as a double precaution we do an obs on the building, and see if we can't get a man in a room opposite the boardroom windows. If this can be done, then I'll have an agent in there with a shotgun microphone; we've got a real beauty, totally directional over seven hundred feet. It ignores all the extraneous guff and just picks up the real juice. Then after the meeting in goes your fanny cleaner and there you are. You'll have a report on every bleeding word they utter. Good enough?"

Sinclair couldn't help laughing.

"Bloody marvelous. You make it sound like a Len Deighton thriller."

"Listen, boy, if we do it, then we bleeding do it. You'll get a written report—but not on my headed paper—and a bill. Don't forget to pay the bill—seven days, no discount."

Sinclair stood up. "You're on. It's a treat doing business with you, Mr. Hart."

"Right-ho, son. And you needn't bother to switch them bloody cameras of yours on. I won't nick anything on the way out. You know what you should get yourself, don't you?"

"What?"

"Get one of your furniture designer mates to build a professional bug into a really good-looking boardroom chair. It's the ultimate in radio microphones, only costs you a hundred and fifty sheets. Then you give the chair to whoever you want to check on, and there you are: Switch in, and it's just like you were by his side all the time; only he'll never know. Cheerio, son. Watch out, now."

Sinclair thought about the professional bug idea. It could come in very useful.

Freda came through on the intercom. "I'm going now. Is there anything else you want?"

"No, thanks, Freda, I'll see you in the morning. Tell Sue and Ann I want them in my office at ten for a project meeting on Jackson."

"Fine. Oh, by the way, a man called Nutting rang. He wouldn't give me any details, just said he wanted to talk to you about taking on a new account."

"Freda, you ring him back tomorrow, tell him I'm out of town for the week, and get what you can from him yourself."

"OK. See you in the morning. Good night, Dan."

He knew he was lucky to have her. She was totally loyal and devoted, and that didn't happen often, particularly in his business. He went to make himself an end-of-day drink when the phone rang. It was Mary Steward.

"Hello, stranger, how are you?"

"I'm fine, thanks, Mary. What's new?"

"Nothing special, I just rang to thank you for the flowers. Are they what you send all your accommodating press ladies?"

"No; most of them just get thank-you letters."

"Well, don't forget to keep me in mind for the next exclusive. You never know, it might turn out that we have a good arrangement. What you could call mutual benefits."

"What a good idea. I'll buzz you, Mary."

"See you, Dan."

He poured the drink and thought. To look at her, you'd never know. She had seemed like a quiet suburban mouse, not a tough, bedworthy chick. Unless of course it was a defense mechanism at work. Whichever way it was, he obviously wasn't going to be pressured into an involvement, which would have ended up badly, meaning that for him there was one less outlet for the material he needed to have published. It was ironical that it had happened that way once before, with the woman who was her boss. Tessa Drake had been very like Mary, young and new at the game but ambitious and learning fast. That time he had been just as willing, and it had all gone too far.

He had used her, she had said. What she had really meant was that he had damaged her pride. Whatever the reasons, she had never let it go. It had been a tough lesson, and since then he had been very careful never to rupture the thin protective emotional shell that separates the professional journalistic façade from the feminism that is beneath.

He must remember that with Jackson.

The morning sun was warming the large room as the three girls settled themselves in a semicircle in front of Sinclair.

He flipped the switch on the intercom. "Doris, no calls and no interruptions."

"Right you are, Mr. Sinclair."

He looked at them. Freda, wearing her glasses, notebook on her lap, looked very efficient and very proper. He wondered about her; there was never any mention or hint of a boyfriend or even a girlfriend. What did she do in her own time—think about Sinclair Enterprises? Sue Black, very attractive, short skirts, all the *Vogue* trimmings; a swinger but good, and the right image and approach with the clients. Ann, her secretary, almost a junior carbon copy but lighter, without the touch of seriousness that would turn her into an account executive. But of course there was time; she was at the age of constant change.

"Freda, are the bookings still coming in for Jackson?"

"They're heavy, Mr. Sinclair. We've already had *Harper's* on this morning—they want her for a ten-day trip to Jamaica."

"That's out. We need her in London. Would you all agree that we have to hire someone specially just to handle the dates, fees and admin?"

They were unanimous.

Sue's voice came through the hubbub. "It's getting now so that we're beginning to neglect the other clients. I've had to put off two appointments at Michael Smith's salon—not very important ones admittedly, *Vanity Fair* and *Petticoat*—but nevertheless once it starts, the clients notice they're not getting quite the same attention."

"Is everything all right with Carnel, Freda?"

"At the moment it is, because the momentum from the press party is still keeping the action going on Hometan, but they'll expect something new soon." She paused. "Could I make a suggestion?"

"Of course."

She looked at the others, and Sinclair knew she was acting as spokesman for something they had discussed and decided on between themselves.

"We think that if you could take some time off to have meetings with the major and Smith, then everything would be fine. It's not so much that we are neglecting them, but I think they are beginning to feel you're difficult to get to and maybe too preoccupied with other matters."

She was blushing faintly; it had been a difficult little speech. Sinclair knew they were basically right; the point was, did he really care?

"You're absolutely right, but we are getting to the position where they will need us more than we need them. I've just about had moaning clients and their pretty egos. This is what I think we should do. Freda, get on to that girl on Models London—what's she called?"

"You mean Janice Dearing."

"That's the girl; tell her what's happening to Jackson, and ask her if she wouldn't rather personally handle a top girl in preference to all those bitching has-beens they've got at that agency. Tell her the money'll be right; if she can leave immediately, I'll handle her notice pay. Right, now that will lift the routine work from all of you. I'll fix to see Smith and Carter. I've got enough worked out to keep them both quiet until I'm ready to do the ditching."

He opened the folder on the glass table and took some sheets of erratically typed paper from it.

"You needn't take notes. I've mapped out a schedule of projects that should build Jackson's personality image in the newspapers. If we get this lot into print, then with the genuine model bookings as well she should be well on the way to ousting the current top three."

He passed copies to each of them and kept one for himself.

"You'll see I've marked off who does what. Basically, Freda takes care of fixing the outside third-party individuals we need; she knows the background and how to persuade them. Sue, you do the contact work with the papers. How are you with the diary boys?"

"Fine. There's no problem with Hickey, Greville and the others, but Atticus might be more difficult—he's still very anti-PR. . . . You remember that farewell piece Phillip Oakes wrote?"

He'd never forgotten it. It had been the lead piece that Sunday, with one of Ralph Steadman's great cartoons as an illustration:

Atticus meets such interesting people. Most of the time, anyway. But what about the people who Atticus walks miles not to meet?

There's been plenty of them in the two years I've been editing the column, names which produce a personal reaction as violent as litmus paper doused with acid. They don't have much in common except that they're written about by all the other columnists, all the time. They're quite presentable; most likely you wouldn't mind your son/daughter marrying one.

They're industrious, ubiquitous and exceedingly available. Publicity puts roses in their cheeks. They employ good PR's or have their own built-in public relations system. They say little that's memorable, but they seem incapable of saying nothing. Silence worries them. They are—some of them—talented. They are—all of them—blisteringly overexposed . . . as a postscript, and for the record, here are eight names which this Atticus takes most pride in having a miss for the past two years.

Then, by God, he had listed the names, complete with an Atticus-type *Who's Who* biography: Simon Dee, Lady Antonia Fraser, David Frost, Patrick Lichfield, Sir Gerald Nabarro, Vanessa Redgrave, Kenneth Tynan and Mary Whitehouse.

He remembered he had had the shakes until he'd read the list through, then given thanks that none of his clients was on it. The explanation that, in spite of the apparent rebuff, Atticus had given each victim an inch of highly valuable free editorial-space publicity would not have washed.

His mind came back to the meeting. "Yes, I remember it. Here's what you do, Sue. Pick the most genuine-sounding story from the bunch I'm going to give you; then get hold of that old boyfriend of yours, the one who came down from Oxford and contributed to *Private Eye* for a spell. Take him out for a drink and casually drop it into the conversation—wouldn't Atticus love this, only they wouldn't take it from you. If my hunch is right, he'll be on the phone as soon as he's drained the dregs in the hope of a handout, and they'll be much more inclined to take it from him than from us, that's for sure.

"Ann, you're the detail girl—check that everything happens when and where it should.

"OK, then, let's go through it, item by item.

"One: Arrange a series of sittings with Pironelli, and release the story that he has picked Jackson to paint because he thinks she's the most beautiful girl in London; put out the hint that he's going to submit the finished work to the Royal Academy." He stopped, had a thought, then looked up at Sue. "You know, maybe that's the one you should feed Atticus with—Pironelli's his sort of painter." He went back to his list:

"Two: Get a shot of Jackson taking delivery of a new Monteverdi, but see the registration plates don't show, and write a caption that the car is a present from an admirer, but say that Jackson prefers to keep names out of it. You'd better get the car on a two-week hire in case we need to show it and her around.

"Three: Hire Constantine's yacht at Cowes, and take some pictures of Jackson lounging on the deck with Lord Brenson. He's a bit of a tatty peer, but the name's good enough for the *Mail*; imply there's a romance afloat. Ho, ho.

"Four: Arrange for the Indian to sit for a session with Jackson in the flat. See she's dressed appropriately. The story is that he's her personal guru and that she's having daily meditation instruction. And when you take the picture, get her sitting in the lotus pose.

"Five: Tickets have been booked for the royal film premiere. Have a photo call for the day before at Smith's; she'll be wearing a long evening skirt with a see-through top. Nothing like a bit of bare titty to make all the nationals. Prime Jackson to say that she doesn't think the particular member of the royal family attending will voice any objections to the dress.

"Six: Do an exclusive with one of the popular Sundays at the East End Settlement. Maybe have the Monteverdi in the background, but make sure the old folks are in focus. The story is that this is Jackson's one-day stint on her only day off; she feels that perhaps in a small way she is contributing something worthwhile.

"Seven: Get the newsboys over to the Revolution on the busiest night. We want pictures of our girl demonstrating the very latest in, in, dance, called the Jackson.

"Eight: Finally, get Anderson the interior decorator to check over and arrange a room-setting series of color pictures at Cadogan Square. Then we want a detailed article from him on the design motifs of the decor. I'll do a rewrite so that it reads in the first-person singular from Jackson. When that's complete, we will fix an exclusive with British and Continental magazines for publication."

He put the sheets of paper down and leaned back, trying not to look as if he were expecting them to applaud. Ann was the first one to speak.

"I don't know how you think them up, Mr. Sinclair. I mean, any one of them would make a story . . . but all of them, one after the other. I should think she'll be better known than anybody by the time they've all been published."

"Well, that's the intention, Ann. After that lot television is the next step and should be easy to arrange. What do you think, Sue?"

"No doubt about it. I think we'll make Simon Dee and Eamonn Andrews without even trying."

He stood up. "That's it. Thanks for listening; now let's get at it."

They filed out of the room, and as the door closed, he could hear them. It was all he could do to stop himself switching on the TV screen to watch the reactions. He knew it was a loaded program, but that when it had been carried through, he would be ready for the next phase. Up until now he had only been earning the flat fee, and although he was beginning to pull in extra money for his share of the model charges, it was nothing to what could be generated. Once he had established Jackson as the number one British girl personality model, they would be ready to move into the merchandizing jungle, but to do that, the right way, she had to become a symbol that every girl and woman wanted to emulate. Having created Jackson, he must now create the Jackson cult.

It took twenty-eight days for the first newspaper to use the word "cult"; then the whole of Fleet Street took it up. At that point Sinclair knew the hard press graft was over; Jackson now existed. He had taken a nobody, a myth, and in three months had made her into an accepted news commodity.

The sheer weight of published pictures and articles made it appear that a newspaper or magazine couldn't be picked up without some reference to the girl who, overnight, had taken the fashion and model business by storm, and he had made it happen. That the original material had been invented was forgotten; even the top journalists couldn't ignore what was a fact, and because it was a fact, they too joined those who interviewed the new phenomenon and so perpetuated the myth. It was a peculiar trait of journalists that they could not let it appear that they were missing out on something that their competitors were on to. Each felt it his duty to put over his particular point of view to his own readers. The *Mirror* would make it fun and sexy, the *Express* part of the supposed good life. *The Times* would analyze the success and predict its effect on current mores, and the *Telegraph* would report and try not to bore its readers.

When editors sat in conference, planning features, once they had decided on a subject, the discussion would come down to a choice of celebrities to comment on and illustrate it. Whatever the article was about—eating out in London, driving vintage cars, even the gracious-living bit—the same names would be offered up. They would be the people who had caught the imagination; a talented but unpublicized person would be rejected for that very deficiency, and so, until overexposure made their faces and opinions boring, and even in spite of this, the same names would be used over and over again.

It was a PR man's dream to get a client on this bandwagon.

The fact that the so-called celebrities in vogue did not have attributes or achievements superior to those of their lesser-known contemporaries was of no consequence; they had been taken up. What they did and said, how they dressed and lived, what their children looked like and where they went to school—all became of paramount importance. The press, with its insistence on creating personalities and then plagiarizing one another's choices, contributed to the "in" roundabout. The outcome was that the reader accepted what the new holy ones thought and did, and so patronized the same boutiques, restaurants and furniture shops, bought the same style of car, prepared the same dinner-party dishes in dining rooms that could only reflect the same influence of tastes. Thus cults were created. What was amazing was their life-span; the public was not as fickle as detractors tried to make out—on the contrary, it was loyal to the point where it was abused.

Sinclair had traded on the system and his knowledge of how it operated; he had used its weaknesses for his own ends. Yet he was only the tool and not the object fashioned; he stood aside, unaffected by the changes that being sought after often brought about. He knew that there would be changes, and he watched for the symptoms. At the beginning it had been excitement and delight, but as the press clippings gathered, the excitement wore away.

It was when the issue of *Maintenant* appeared that he noticed a definite shift in Jackson's attitude. The nude beauty pictures caused a minor uproar and major talking point for as long as copies of the magazine remained in circulation. Because he was expecting it, he could easily tolerate the new way she acted. When every newspaper and television program brought Jackson and her body into its orbit and called her "fantastic" and "beautiful" and "the best thing since the pill," it didn't take a psychologist to predict that praise at that degree must have an effect.

As with all change, it was the minor things he watched for, the telltale signs that showed a new confidence and reaction. The continual interviews, with questions ranging over subjects of which she had no knowledge and only ill-informed opinions, must have made her decide to close up. She no longer attempted justifications; she made statements and moved on. To cover the concealment, she developed nervous mannerisms, which the press reported as fey attractions: her beautiful birdlike hands that fluttered in the air before her as if they were trying to add color and shade to what she was saying.

She would look over at Sinclair at these times, knowing he must be watching the performance, and when he smiled, that still gave her confidence. She leaned on his opinions and his advice, and it made him feel a power when he heard her repeat to the journalists what he had told her in a day-old conversation. "After-shaves for men are a dead commodity; the whole scene will change. Makeup for men is coming, and the way in is through face creams."

Then the hands would flutter again, and she would look away from the interviewer. The subject had received her opinion; the matter was closed.

Sinclair was accepting overseas commitments for her now. They were always the best jobs, and he made it a condition of the booking that she was the only model used. The results were that virtually every foreign location feature in the British fashion magazines was a piece of personal publicity for Jackson.

She was on the covers of eight European glossies when the booking request came in from New York. It was from an advertising agency that wanted her as the beauty pivot for a launch campaign for its soap-manufacturing client. The agency airmailed in the rough artwork and copy; it showed a white Rolls-Royce standing in a field of corn stubble. An out-of-focus, clean-cut young man was holding open the passenger door for a girl in full evening drag. The main caption read, "Be outdoor beautiful wherever you're going." This was followed by the name of the soap: "Naturalé, nature's herbal beautifier."

Attached was a schedule that listed the various magazines in which the advertisement would appear—whole-page color, of course. It was an impressive list: *Life, Look, Vogue, Harper's Bazaar, Glamour, McCall's* and *Seventeen.* It was what Sinclair had been waiting for: prestige exposure throughout America, the top accolade in the model game. The letter which accompanied the material confirmed the fee, which by British standards was astronomical, and that all first-class expenses would be paid—for two.

Sinclair sent them a cable: ACCEPT ASSIGNMENT SUBJECT FOLLOW-

ING CREDIT ON ALL ADS: MODEL—JACKSON, LONDON, ENGLAND. They agreed by return. Sinclair played it very cool. He made a New York telephone call to the president of Prince Larsen. Prince's, as the devotees called it, was a boutique-atmosphere store around the corner from Fifth Avenue, and it was so exclusive it hurt, in the checkbook area mostly. The president was a hot-shot career woman called Aston Weiz, who was a very chic and very feminine member of the inner-circle fashion Mafia, a group of aging darlings whose jobs collectively gave them power over what happened on the American fashion scene.

"Aston? How are you? It's Dan Sinclair."

"Why, Dan, how good of you to call. How's that designer man of yours?"

"I think we would now be very happy to do the deal with you."

"That is simply marvelous. Michael Smith exclusive to Prince Larsen in all New York, right?"

"Yes, right."

"Well, here's what we do. You come on over for a presentation show as our guests, and . . . hold on while I check my diary . . ."

Sinclair waited; this could be the crunch.

"How about the third week of next month, Dan?"

He sighed. That was really very good.

"Aston, you know we handle Jackson, don't you?"

"Well, I had heard. You lucky man."

"She's due in New York in a month, and I thought it might be rather good if she modeled Smith's collection for you. Would it be too soon if we brought it forward a couple of weeks?"

"Fantastic! How clever you are. No, it'll be perfect. Now that is set. I'll have our London office issue tickets; you'll come with Smith, of course. Dan, one final point—would you confirm the exclusivity to us as of now?"

"Yes, I will. Well, that's good, Aston; so we'll see you next month."

"Oh, we're looking forward to that."

The shouting over the faint line stopped. He put down the receiver and called Freda on the house phone.

"Freda, get me Michael Smith, please."

This, he thought, was going to be very smooth.

"Michael? How's that capsule collection?"

"Bit of a stranger, aren't you? It's nearly finished. Why?"

His tone was petulant. Sinclair knew he felt neglected, and this made him come on even stronger. "Not all the work we do shows up in lights, you know, Michael. I've finished negotiations with Aston Weiz of Prince's; you're in, exclusive only to them in New York; get ready to leave in four weeks' time—you're coming with me to present the collection to the American fashion press."

"You're joking."

"Don't be a silly sod."

"My God, *Prince's!* Jesus! Dan, that's simply great, I mean tremendous—"

"Another thing, Michael; I've persuaded them to use Jackson to model the collection."

"Fantastic! Dan, I must tell the workroom. I'll talk to you later. Well, you've really done it, you really have."

Sinclair sat back and felt very satisfied. He'd been holding off the deal with Prince's until he had been ready to spring it on Smith to the greatest effect. It wasn't a question of fixing it, but of eventually agreeing to something Smith would have jumped at months ago had he known Weiz had put it up in the first place. This way he not only had combined two clients on one trip, but was using Smith and Prince's as a launch pad to introduce Jackson to the New York press in one fell prestige swoop.

There was a secondary, however minor, consideration. He called Freda in.

"I've done it, Freda—New York for Jackson, Smith and yours truly, first-class, all expenses paid."

"Oh, that's marvelous. When do you go?"

"Next month. Now, Freda, I want you to cable the ad agency and call the London office of Prince Larsen. Tell them both not to issue the air tickets; say we'll handle it this end and pick up the dollar equivalent in New York. Tell them it's better that way taxwise."

She took down the note, and while she wrote it, she knew what he was at. Apart from the undoubted tax advantage, she knew he would pick up two first-class return air fares from the advertising agency, covering Jackson and himself, and another two first-class returns from Prince's for Smith and himself. Result, a net profit of about £200 sterling, not a bad start to the trip.

When he told Jackson, she tried hard to control the excitement, but it came through loud and clear, and he knew that she was knocked out by the prospect. Ever since the Paris trip, neither of them had mentioned the conversation or the hotel-suite good-night scene, and Sinclair had felt rather pleased with himself; as far as he was concerned, she had picked up the message without any recriminations.

The way they worked together went on as before, except that he was relieved of having to watch out for the personal-involvement angle, and that suited him very well. He hadn't asked her about her private life, but as usual it came back to him and he was kept informed about the art director, hairdresser, butch male model, a young man in property and a restaurateur. So far, thank God, there had been no word of a PR man on the make, and so the only slight worry for Sinclair was that she had the beginnings of a reputation as a swinging chick.

It was something he knew must happen; as he saw it, there were few girls around that wouldn't have been affected in the same way. She was beautiful, comparatively rich, independent, on the in circle and without the acknowledged steady—it was copybook . . . and anyway, why not? As long as it didn't interfere with her professional life and looks, and provided she kept on the pill and out of the club, then he could afford to remain an observer with a vested interest. He thought it was amazing, the number of women he had known who slept around and yet managed to keep that creamy, innocent look. It wasn't fair on the righteous—you would have thought that the least nature could do was pay back, but of course it never worked out that way. They were all a bunch of female Dorian Greys, he thought.

Jackson went into training. She boned up on New York from anyone in the business who'd made a trip over the past six months; she went to the American Embassy library and read the official guides; then she bought a copy of *New York on Five and Ten Dollars a Day*—not that she was in that category, but the information was invaluable. Names came back to her from songs and old movies: Fifth Avenue, Central Park, Greenwich Village. She played Ella Fitzgerald singing "Manhattan" and longed for Mott Street in July, "Autumn in New York, that brings the promise of new life"—the lyric seemed to speak just for her. Would it be a new life or the same life in a different place?

Then she thought about her life, and where it was taking her, and how it had changed her. You get used to anything. That's what they said, and it was true; only for her it wasn't hardship—it was all play. The Maureen Stokes with dreams had ceased, and in her place there was Jackson, composed, confident and on the fast lane up.

She accepted things now that would have sent her spinning only months ago; if a man back in Chester had come up to her in a restaurant and said, "Hi, babe, do you fuck?" she would have dropped the *scampi meunière* and called for the waiter. Today she would look back and answer, "Yes, but not with you, Charlie." Everything was different; she looked out through different eyes. In a way she was like Sinclair; he had taught her well, and since Paris she chose only to see how good he was at what she was paying him to do.

There were times when she wondered if he was too clever. Nothing seemed to backfire on him, and nobody could keep on like that; sooner or later something must go wrong, and this made her wary of what he organized. There was still admiration for him, as there would have been for any man who was successful, but in the back of her mind there was a growing suspicion that one day—maybe not soon, but somewhere there on the horizon—he would become superfluous, perhaps even a drag on her.

She tried not to think that way; she still had a conscience to remind her that what he had done had put her where she was. The mind, though, plays devious tricks, finds ready justifications for changes of attitudes and opinions, and once the seed is sown, it only requires time to produce from the flow of events neatly packaged arguments that can smoothly and with clear conscience reverse those precious principles that people set such store by.

Sinclair fixed an exclusive interview with one of the Sunday papers on what Jackson would wear in New York and, when the time eventually came, arranged for the London Airport photo agency to cover both Smith and her boarding the plane out. He made it a glamor-export story: Jackson's beauty and Smith's designs. The coverage was what they now considered routine. It made the front page of every national.

9

THE Super VC 10 had settled down to its cruising speed of six hundred miles per hour; the passenger information sheet said they were traveling at forty thousand feet and that their estimated time of arrival at Kennedy International Airport was 1540 hours, local time. He had made Jackson and Smith take a Mogadon each to make them sleep for most of the journey. As well as doing them some good, it let him relax from the effort of a running conversation.

The forward, first-class compartment had twin rows of plush seats for twenty people. He thought New York must be off the list of chic places to go, because there was only one other place filled: an old lady who had squeezed herself away from the world in the farthest corner of the compartment. They had spread out and taken a whole set of seats each; both Jackson and Smith had curled up with blankets after leaving instructions that they were not to be disturbed even for the fresh Scotch salmon and champagne.

Sinclair sank back and stretched his legs—the airline advertisements were dead right so far—and sipped his whiskey and water. Even without the help of a sleeping pill he was beginning to doze.

The dark-haired hostess came and took the empty glass. She was wearing a loose, wrap-over, white cotton karate coat and flat shoes, and as she stood in the stream of sunlight coming through the forward windows, he could see the silhouette of her long legs through the coat. She saw him watching her and stood there a little longer; when she thought he had seen enough, she risked a self-smile and then walked away to the galley.

He closed his eyes and felt very pleasant; the whiskey had numbed the nervousness he had felt, in spite of having flown so often, and the warmth of the pretty, sexy-looking hostess made him quietly erotic. They had another four or five hours' flying time ahead, and he wondered how you managed to do it on a plane during the daytime. He visualized following her into the lavatory. . . .

He thought of her standing in the sun again, and that reminded him of a different girl in another place. She was standing on the corner of the main street in a village lined with smooth-barked cream-and-green-mottled trees. She looked too at ease and relaxed to be a tourist. She leaned against the tree and let the sun warm her; it was early in the evening, and if you stood in the shadows, the soft breeze was cool enough to chill you.

The place was called St.-Rémy-de-Provence, and it was in that part of the south of France that Sinclair had once loved most. He went there first because it was where Cézanne and Van Gogh had been and because he enjoyed its sensual pleasures: the countryside and the clean clear light, its Roman ruins and the wine from the lush, rolling vineyards first created by the Popes—those Popes always knew a thing or two—and everywhere the cypress and olive and fruit trees.

He had been nearly at the end of his time there and had driven down from Avignon in the dirty hired Renault, on his way to the Camargue and then to Marseilles. But he had driven too much that day, so he had decided to stay the night in St.-Rémy. He was sitting outside the hotel, Les Arts on the boulevard Victor-Hugo, when he saw the girl.

She had very long, dark hair and looked rounded in the thin dress, with her brown legs that were not quite slim enough. When he stood next to her, she seemed very short. They both smiled, and he said how pleasant the evening was, and she said for the time of year maybe a little cool. They spoke in French because her English was not very good; she had the twangy accent of the region but not its harshness. Later, after they had walked, he took her back to the hotel, and they ate trout, which the waiter first took live from the special pool, and the green salad and endives were very clean and fresh and tasting of the soil. It was all very idyllic and sentimental, and he allowed himself to feel it was very true. He knew that that was what you were supposed to feel, but he was still young enough to believe it and think that maybe going back to London and opening a public relations business was not such a good idea. But that was a long time ago, and people change, and after they change, they forget that things they experienced before are not the same twice over.

No one in the hotel minded when they went up to his room. It was on the top floor and had two beds in it but no bath. He stayed in St.-Rémy three days, and then he had to leave; but he wanted to leave, too. He was from a city, and though the country soothed him, he needed to go back now.

An old man was drinking cognac with the proprietor as he paid his bill in the morning. She waited for him by the car, and cried as he held her, and then moved away to open the car door.

It wasn't until he handed the Renault over to the Hertz man at Marseilles Airport that the enjoyment of the self-pity lifted. The need to be organized, with tickets, passport and luggage, sharpened him, and as he read his first London newspaper for a week, he was back being the other person again. St.-Rémy was an episode from the past already.

The drive from St.-Rémy to Marseilles is under an hour. . . .

The hostess was gently shaking his shoulder, and Sinclair opened his eyes. He saw that the fold of her white coat had opened as she leaned over him, and he could see her breasts and the small lace cups of her brassiere.

"I thought you might like something to eat."

He glanced over at Jackson and Smith. They were still asleep; the little old woman wasn't even visible. He sighed and wished he was somewhere less public. "That's a very good idea. I think I should have some cold roast beef and half a bottle of red wine."

The jetliner was descending at a rate of just under six hundred feet a minute. They passed the flare-out threshold, and then they were down. Jackson looked over and smiled at him.

"Well, we're here," she said. "What a super flight."

They cleared immigration and customs smoothly, except for Sinclair. He stood trying to explain to the very big customs man that the still photographs of Jackson that he had in his bag were not for commercial resale. Eventually the official decided to believe him, and he was through. They walked alongside their luggage as the porters pushed it for them on the trolley, and they saw a fat man in a navy and gray chauffeur's uniform standing in the middle of the concourse. He was wearing dark driving glasses, which made him look sinister, but when he smiled, his pudgy face became very jovial and kind.

"Why, you must be Miss Jackson." He turned to Sinclair. "And you, sir?"

"I'm Dan Sinclair, and this is Michael Smith."

He shook them by the hand. "Just call me Ed. I'm very glad to know you. Now, you just follow me."

The porters assumed a new air of respect as the big chauffeur led the way out to the large, low and seemingly endless Cadillac that stood in the restricted zone by the curb. He held the rear door open for them.

"I think you'll all be very comfortable in back, sir. We just have a quick drive to the TWA building for some pictures."

As they sank into the sitting room of the car, they looked at one another and nearly burst out laughing.

Ed's voice seemed to float mysteriously through the thick glass panel that separated them. It came over the car's intercom system, as opposed to its normal radiotelephone circuit.

"Now that building over there is the control tower. Pretty big, isn't it? Well, that's the tallest one in the world. Miss Weiz is waiting for you all; she thought she'd let you get cleared through first."

Like hell she did. Sinclair smiled to himself. He guessed they wanted the arrival pictures on home ground; no point in giving BOAC free publicity.

The building that Eero Saarinen had designed for TWA was magnificent, with its flat, distorted-saucer-shaped twin roofs. They were ushered through a side corridor and out onto the arrival bay. Aston Weiz was standing in the middle of a group of reporters and photographers. She saw them and strolled over.

"Dan, how good to see you! And, Jackson . . . well, how are you? Hello, Mr. Smith, I'm Aston Weiz. Did you have a good trip? You must have, you look so fresh and wonderful. Dan, you don't mind if we take your two protégés away from you for a minute, do you? We just would like to get a few pictures and have them meet these lovely people from the press."

Sinclair had tried to open his mouth to say something, but he conserved his energy. He knew he'd need it.

She eased off a little on the way into Manhattan but took the opportunity to outline their schedule for the next seventeen hours. It was a simple one: arrive at the hotel, clean up, dinner in their rooms alone—just to chat, of course, no visitors to tire them. Then an early night; they must pick up on the travel stress, you know. Breakfast at eight, and then a short stroll over to her office for a program meeting.

Sinclair thought that somewhere between their early night and her break in the monologue to point out LaGuardia Airport on their right, he'd missed what time he was supposed to use the bathroom. He supposed he'd have to wait to find out until he read his copy of the written schedule she said would be in the hotel suite. Jackson and Smith were transfixed at the barrage of efficient planning that issued from her. Sinclair wondered if he should put in his five cents' worth, but decided that that might throw the whole delivery off-balance.

They sped in cool, quiet comfort, now that Weiz had finished her welcome speech, along Grand Central Parkway, and got their first good look at the New York City skyline from across the East River. The Cadillac slowed to join the quick-moving queue of cars at the Triborough Bridge toll, and then they were across and onto Manhattan Island. The driver took the FDR Drive along the river frontage as far as Sixty-first Street, then cut across into Sixtieth and made his way to the St. Regis Hotel on Fifth Avenue and Fifty-fifth Street. They had arrived.

The day of Smith's presentation fashion show at Prince Larsen's was a superb piece of American efficiency, out of which came a casual, almost throwaway walk-through by Jackson. Aston Weiz sat on a chaise longue with Smith, and as Jackson strolled by with each new design, they chatted fortissimo so that the entire room could eavesdrop.

"Michael, tell me, how did you get that marvelous thirties draped look so *now?* I mean, it's as if you reoriented your intrinsic fashion feeling."

"It's in the use of the double French crepe and the cut, Aston."

"Oh, now, this one is simply out of this city! And just look at the way she wears it . . . that girl Jackson is the chic-est thing."

The deliberately overeffusive dribble went on throughout the show, with pauses every now and then for applause from an appreciative audience. Between them, the status of Prince's and Weiz had pulled in the New York fashion power. The top weight could be picked out by the number of assistants who grouped themselves around a single personage. Individuals could almost be discounted, although even they had rank over those on the lower rungs who came with a companion to give them an alter ego security blanket. The show was the smash everyone expected it to be, and circulating afterward, Sinclair could tell that he would have no need to hustle. Photo sessions were being booked, tape recorders were taking down the hallowed words of the participants, and Aston Weiz was headed his way, beaming.

"Dan, you did a fantastic job, and I want to thank you on behalf of Prince's."

"I did very little, Aston, except bring them."

"Complete nonsense! Why, even having you in the room is constructive. Now, don't you forget we have the party later."

"That's just fine, but Jackson mustn't be too late. She starts her sessions for Naturalé in the morning."

"She will look beautiful, Dan. Don't you worry about a thing." She moved closer to him as if they were in conspiracy. "You have a total success with that girl. You know that, don't you?" She didn't wait for his answer. "I mean, she is going to make the rest of them look so out."

"Well, I'm glad you think so, Aston."

"Think so! Let me tell you, three months in this city and she'd be an international fashion celebrity."

He sensed the warning signals.

"We don't want to keep her away from home too long on her first trip, Aston. Her European exposure has been fantastic. We'll consolidate and then move on. Next time she comes back it won't be as a model; she'll be a business."

"That's how I like to hear you talk, Dan. You know, you could do well here; maybe that's something to think about, too."

He'd had his allotted time, and she moved away in the direction of Diana Vreeland, the high priestess of American *Vogue*.

The crowd was thinning now, and Jackson and Smith were sitting on two of the low poufs scattered around the room, getting their breath back and having their first drink.

"Well, Daniel, how did it look?"

"You were great, Jackson. And, Michael, the clothes were a knockout. Between the two of you you've locked up the fashion pages for a week."

"Did you talk to that tall skinny woman from *Life* magazine?"

"No, Michael, I didn't. What did she say?"

Sinclair sat on the floor listening to them name-drop the top brass. Smith eventually turned to him.

"What was that about buying up my stuff from the other stores, Dan?"

"That was American promotion at its hottest. It's a lesson our fainthearted watch-the-budget stores could learn from. Look, up until today you sold dresses to any American who walked into the showroom. More than half of them bought just enough to give themselves a sampling range; then once back in New York and on to the Seventh Avenue garment market, they ran up the copies. Don't believe all you read, Michael; every British designer who's ever come back from here says he has a million dollars' worth of orders—crap, but the press prints it. Maybe Pringle, Aquascutum or Burberry's, but not your swinging designer. You know what they've done for British exports? Brought in the tourist trade. The best thing that ever happened to London's rag trade was Courrèges and the youth kick. Don't believe what anybody tells you; that Frenchman in white started it all. Maybe that's why De Gaulle was so mad at us—if Courrèges had picked up a penny on every pair of white boots we were knocking off back in 1964, he'd be a millionaire three times over. It was as crazy for him as penicillin was for us."

Smith and Jackson sat listening to him as if the room weren't there and they were back in London.

"But, to get off the hobbyhorse, when we arrived here, Michael, at least four New York stores were selling your clothes. Now Prince's was going to spend a lot of money putting this show on and taking pages of newspaper advertising to tell the city that Smith was exclusive to them. If they had let your clothes stay on the rails of the competition, not only would they have looked idiots but everyone else would have done window displays and climbed on the back of their promotion, and for free. So it was cheaper in the long term, and a damn sight smarter, to send girls out to buy up your stuff, even if it did cost them New York retail prices."

"Jesus, I've never thought they were that nervous."

"I don't think it was nerves," said Jackson. "I think they're bloody clever."

"Yes, they are. But can you imagine it in England? One, the Knightsbridge stores would know the guys in Regent Street are gentlemen and wouldn't do such a thing, and, two, nobody would think it was worth spending the money in the first place. And they couldn't upset the window dresser—after all, he must plan his windows at least three months in advance, and to throw in a quickie like that would give him hysterics. Tell me, Michael—what do you think a window display in a big store is all about?"

He looked across to Jackson as if it were a silly question and he wanted her to agree. She did, by answering for him.

"That's to sell the stuff, of course."

Sinclair had his superior look. "No, that's what the amateurs think. It should be used as a lure, just to get people through the swing doors. I remember when a big chain store here did a British Fashion Week. They had latched onto a pretty, overnight-success designer, and they went the whole hog. Policemen, London bus, everything. You know they only had twenty dresses to back up the whole operation?"

"That's bloody ridiculous, Dan. They'd hardly spend that sort of money to promote twenty dresses."

"Listen, Michael, they didn't care how many dresses they sold; in fact, they knew they were so way-out nobody would want to buy them. But the people came to see the fun, and that week the sales of refrigerators and home linen boomed. You make more money selling home appliances than dresses."

Pregnant pause.

"Dan, tell me, why are we here?"

Jackson burst out laughing; Sinclair caught the reaction, and he laughed too. By the time Aston Weiz was standing by them wondering what the hell the gas was about Smith was falling about as well.

"Well, children, do tell, so we can all have some fun too."

Jackson wiped her eyes, and in fits and starts they gradually quieted down.

"I'm sorry, Aston," said Sinclair, "it was just a stupid in thing. But before that I was telling Michael that now you've got him exclusive, he has his first solid selling base in America."

"You're so right. And you know, we must talk about manufacturing here instead of in London; save all that duty."

They were past talking business, and she felt it. The strain of putting the presentation together was showing; now it was over, and over with success, they had let the strings of tension snap. But for the formidable Aston Weiz it was just another event in a long line of events. When she had called them "children," it wasn't so much a figure of speech as a subconscious truth.

"Well, we can all relax now; the car's waiting outside. Ed will take you back to the hotel, and you can all rest up till the evening. Don't forget eight thirty P.M.—Ed'll be there to collect you."

They made the short drive in silence. Weiz was right; they needed the rest.

The party was in Weiz's brownstone—where else?—in the upper sixties off Park Avenue. The front door was open, and they could hear what sounded like a great, great time going on.

Jackson made her entrance flanked by Sinclair and Smith; she stopped the room. Vidal had sent one of his boys up to the hotel from the Madison Avenue Salon to join the makeup man from Charles of the Ritz. Three hours of concentrated preparation had produced the sort of casual look that the competition put down to lucky birthright.

For an instant they just stood and admired her; her hair was long, with a curled unruliness, and its deep bronze hit the plain brown of the long crepe dress and gave it warmth. As was routine, she wore no brassiere, and even the polite eyes stayed on her breasts before they moved up to try to isolate what it was about her neck, her face, her lips, her eyes or her expression that made them want to look and look as if it weren't quite true.

Aston Weiz broke it up, pushing through the crowd to welcome them and bring them into the depth of the party. At that point they split, Jackson moving off with Weiz and the upper echelon and Sinclair and Smith being divided out between the lower orders. Sinclair found he had mostly got the husbands who were there on escort duty and were not part of the scene. He looked quickly for a journalist, but they were all edging around Jackson, and he told himself that after all it was Weiz's operation, on her own home ground, and the main attraction had become Jackson with Smith as second billing. Sinclair was like the producer of a movie, important only on the set; his was the credit only those in the business would read, but even for them it was the star who rated highest.

The questions came thick and fast.

"How long are you staying, Jackson?"

"Oh, just for ten days."

"My, that's too, too short a time, you'll just have to come back real soon."

"I saw you at Prince's, my dear, and you were just sensational, but that must have been a guest appearance—I mean, you must photograph like a dream."

"Well, actually, I'm really here for the agency. We have to do a series of advertising shots for Naturalé."

"Now that's more like it."

"Jackson, how did you get your name?"

"We kind of thought it up ourselves, you know. It was like everybody putting names in a hat. Only we really didn't do that."

"It's enchanting, and I wouldn't mind betting who threw it to the winds."

She gave a secret sort of I'm-not-really-saying-but-you-must-know-you're-right smile. She glanced behind, just to see if Sinclair was hovering close enough to hear. He wasn't.

And so the questions went on from one to another as they complimented her and drained her attention. She was enjoying it, and why not? This was what it was all about. *This is what it must feel like when you're a star,* she thought. *Everybody clamoring to talk to you, and some to touch; the magic had happened, and they were endowing you with attributes and special things. If you spat on the floor, they would laugh and call it cute, but if they spat on the floor, they would be uncouth and crossed from the lists.* She could feel the effect of the champagne or maybe of the heady stuff of success, and it made her more bold.

"I must sit down. Why don't we all sit down?"

And so that was what they did, some on the floor and some on cushions and one each side of her on the sofa. These two were men, and she could tell they were queer, but not in an outrageous way. It was funny, she thought; with most queers you could relax because you felt they were on your side; they understood, and you knew they wouldn't grab at you all the time. The conversation with them wasn't laced with probing innuendos; it was dirty, but with a dirt you could laugh with and not one you had to play against. The blond one was very good-looking. Like all women before her, she wondered if she could bring him over to her side of the bed.

Sinclair was bored. He'd had the political scene and the economic scene and the what-do-we-do-with-New-York scene. He'd almost got to the stage where he would rather talk shop with Smith than listen to anyone else fill him in on local and national affairs. He moved away with excuses and refilled his glass.

Smith seemed to be in heavy session with a fast-looking bird from one of the teen-age magazines. It looked as if he were getting the British-designer-hero-worship stuff. Sinclair knew he didn't need any help, so he looked for Jackson. He caught the action on the sofa and wondered if he should slip over and do his protective bit—

"I wouldn't worry too much about her, they're really almost harmless."

The girl was quite tall, with very dark hair, and she must have only just come in.

"We haven't met before. I'd remember."

"No, we haven't. I only arrived two minutes ago." She laughed. "All there's been time to do is collect a drink. You're Dan Sinclair, aren't you?"

"Yes, I am, but I'm sorry, I don't know—"

"Why should you? I'm not a fashion expert. My name's Ruth Emery, I free-lance for the magazine. You'd call it social comment, I guess, pretty dreary compared to your star over there."

She had very brown eyes; the black lashes were long and curled up at the ends.

"I've got news for you; there are times, and this is one of them, when I think fashion is the most unimportant, dreary subject you could think about."

"Now you're just being kind because I'm the odd one out."

Jackson and the men were getting up; it seemed as if they were making ready to go.

"Looks like your charge is on the move. Do you have to go to work now, Mr. PR man?"

"No, I think she can manage without me. I'm what's called a back-room boy, and I'm secure. It's only your actual nervous PR's who can't let the client alone. They have to hang onto every move; it justifies their function and their existence."

Jackson was doing the rounds, kissing cheeks, shaking hands and murmuring thanks. The two men hung back waiting for her. She made her way unsteadily over to Sinclair.

"Daniel, I'm off on the town. See you at dawn."

"That's fine, love, but don't forget the session in the morning. They'll expect you on time and beautiful."

"Oh, shit to that, Daniel. You can take care of them if I'm late. Good night, everybody."

Sinclair frowned at her as she moved off toward Weiz and the door. That was the first time she had answered back. She needed stamping on, and soon, before it went to her head.

"Hardly a respectful lady, methinks."

He turned back to Ruth Emery.

"She's a little drunk, and it's been a high old day. But what about you? What's the social commentator got to say?"

"May I have another drink, please?"

"You're very funny. Look, why don't we follow suit? You haven't eaten, have you? There's a place up near the German section I used to go when the British fashion explosion was at its loudest. They have very good lasagna."

"In the German section? You have to be joking."

"No, really—it's not a German restaurant anyway. Come on, let's get out."

He moved across the room to wave to Smith, who was too engrossed looking down the bird's neckline to notice.

"Why, Miss Emery, you've met our super PR man." Weiz didn't like her, and it showed.

"Yes, I have. What a nice party. I'm sorry we have to leave so soon."

"Well, so am I. Watch yourself, Dan, Miss Emery has a reputation for not being a PR man's best friend."

Sinclair tried to laugh it away. "Oh, I'll take care, Aston. And thanks for throwing the party, it was a smash."

They were out on the street at last and hailing a cab.

"Elaine's, 1703 Second Avenue."

The restaurant was up in the mid-eighties. It was quieter there, and as they went in, a very large woman came at them from behind the bar.

"Dan! Gee, it's great to see you!" She hugged him and then turned to the girl.

"Elaine, this is Ruth Emery, and she's very nice and very hungry."

"Well, come on and sit down. What do you want? Lasagna? OK. And some drinks? Scotch, bourbon, what?"

Sinclair asked for a Scotch for the girl and the same for himself, and then Elaine left them alone at the table. There was no need for her to sit and reminisce: If you were a friend of Elaine's, you could walk out and come back four years later, and if you wanted to talk, that was fine; if not, then that was fine too. She could tell Sinclair didn't need to talk, not to her at least.

"How long has it been since you were here? In New York, I mean."

"About four years, I think. It doesn't seem to change very much."

"Why should it? There would be nothing to complain about if it did. The city without its dirt and graft and danger would throw too many people; they've become used to it. Those who hate it leave if they can; the rest stay and do the things they are supposed to do."

"Why do you stay? You don't sound like you're exactly crazy about the place."

Elaine brought the drinks over herself. "The food's on its way. Enjoy yourselves."

They toasted each other and sipped the drinks.

"Why do I stay? Because I'm like all the others. I have my work, I can make good money, an apartment I've become fond of and glamorize the rest. Do you want to hear about the theaters and concerts and the museums? Where else but in a city like New York do you get that and the people? Sure, out of town you can get the culture, but the people have different minds. Let's say it's stimulating. Now, what about you and Jackson?"

"She's a client, like Smith. I see they project the right image, get the right kind of publicity and meet all the right people in the right places."

"You don't really like doing it, do you?"

"What do you mean? Why not? Why shouldn't I? It's honest— well, almost—and like your city, it's stimulating."

"But, Dan, you're an intelligent man. What kind of satisfaction can you get out of boosting other people's egos? Surely by now any excitement has worn off—you must be treading the same ground, pushing a different person, maybe, but in the same old way."

She lowered her eyes and looked into the drink, thinking that she had gone too far and was sorry for it. Her hand went across the table and touched his and closed over it.

"What I really mean is, there can't be much more you can do. There must be other things you could move on to."

"Maybe you're right, and maybe Jackson is the last. She's the only one I've ever owned a piece of. I guess it's rather like being a pop-star manager. With all the others they only need you on the way up; they pay, but really they resent it. Then you become bored and slip a little, and all of a sudden you're only as good as your last editorial."

Elaine brought the food over herself, and Sinclair asked for some wine. The wine waiter smiled at Ruth and almost flirted with her as he poured the wine into her glass. Sinclair watched him and was surprised at himself for resenting the attention; he felt possessive, and he was almost angry that she seemed to respond. It was as if he should be the only one to wake an emotion in her.

As they ate, a party of Italians came into the restaurant, and Sinclair watched them; there were two women and two men. They stood at the bar; the women were drinking martinis and the men whiskey sours. One of the women looked over. Sinclair thought she was very attractive, and because she knew he had seen her, her movements became more studied. The man with her noticed it and smiled to himself. Maybe because he was an Italian, he knew it didn't matter, and because he was sure of her, he enjoyed other men admiring her.

Sinclair turned to Ruth. She had been watching him.

"Is she good-looking, Dan?"

His face was serious, and he knew he couldn't joke with her like the others, not about that.

"Yes, she is. Sometimes I don't think very well. Is your lasagna as good as mine?"

"Hmmm, it's marvelous. Will you be in New York all the time?"

"Yes, we stay over the weekend and then fly back Monday night. Smith goes back earlier, though; he's done what he came for. Jackson'll be tied up during the day shooting the Naturalé ads, and in the evenings we have a string of dinners, the famous

American hospitality. I have people to see, of course. The agency about Jackson's credit, lunch in the Green Room with Madam Vreeland."

"My God, you're honored! Not everyone gets that far into *Vogue*."

"It's not me they want, you know that. It's the others. I just fix things. We'll end up with a string of color pages on Smith's clothes photographed on—guess who?"

"Another scoop in the life of Dan Sinclair. I'm sorry, I didn't mean that. Weiz was right—I have a fixation about PR's."

"Don't tell me you had a bad experience with one when you were a young girl."

"Oh, *touché!*" But she laughed with him.

"What are you writing now?"

She turned away from him and seemed to be searching for someone. "Could we have some coffee?" She didn't answer until the table had been cleared and they were drinking the black coffee.

"You see, that's what I mean. Do you really care what I'm going to write about, or is it a way of finding out if there'll be another Jackson clipping to paste in the book?"

The lighting was low, from candles on the table, and he thought she looked very off-center beautiful. Her face was European, and her nose had just a slight bend in it, as if she had fallen on some ice when she was young and the bone hadn't been set properly. On another shape of face it would have been wrong, but on her it was necessary.

"Let's make a decision. I can't stop being what I am, and you can't change being a writer. But promise me you won't write a word about Jackson or Smith or Prince's or anybody connected with the operation. If you do that, then we'll both know we can say what we like without wondering all the time if it's a game."

"You mean you'd really pass up the chance of having a Jackson story that would reach God knows how many people?"

"Ruth, I mean it. I don't want you to think every time I open my mouth to talk about what I do that you'll figure I'm lining up another client plug."

"All right, it's a deal. You get nothing, period. It'll be an interesting exercise."

Sinclair thought it would be more than just an exercise. For the first time since he had started the PR business he was preparing to forgo the opportunity of taking advantage of a relationship.

He looked across the table at her. She was watching some long-haired kids in deep discussion on the other side of the room. He studied her hands and remembered that when she had touched him, they had been soft but firm. In profile she was even more European, and the dark hair against her pale olive skin made her look very Italian.

She turned and caught him staring at her, and they saw each other without embarrassment. Her dark-brown eyes seemed to grow, and he had to lean back from her because he couldn't focus properly; then he could take in the whole of her face. At that instant he wanted to give her everything, and he understood for the first time what the clichés that people sentimentalized over were about. He wanted to touch her face, to hold it, but the back years of taking and only feeling because it was expected or wanted had conditioned him too well and he could not do it.

To break the spell, he talked to her, but it didn't seem like his voice; it was without the confidence and the easy flow he remembered.

"You're right about the PR thing—it's nothing. It's a lot of talk and fixing; you live off other people, the ones who pay you to peddle and the ones you con favors from. At first it all seems very important, but then it gets easy, and you know how to do it so well you start to choose when you do do it. If they complain, you hand them a load of invective about how good you are, and to prove it, you pull a rabbit out of the hat. And they pat you and say how great and they really thought so all along. In the end you despise them all, the clients and the press and yourself. It gets out of all proportion.

"You know, you're the only person I've ever talked to like this. You've broken the image, you're looking in behind the façade, and that's dangerous. Never let yourself be wholly known, that's what the man said. You know why? Because you can't give anyone else that sort of responsibility, you can't let them in that deep. That's why marriage is a no-percentage deal; you let it all go, all the little things, the inner things, and you expect them to be treated the same way you treat them, and when they're not— smash."

She reached over and touched his hands.

"What are you trying to do, Dan, warn me off? I'm not a sixteen-year-old virgin. I've probably seen more breakups, more pretty sordid drama, than you'll ever see. But I've seen some good times that people have too, and in the end you think that maybe it's all luck. But you don't sit around sending everybody else up just because it hasn't happened to you."

"Christ, did I sound that hard? You see, that's the trouble: When people get serious, they get out the dark philosophy. Come on, let's go for a walk."

He paid the bill, and it was laughs again with Elaine, and they left.

She took his arm when they were outside and started to look for a cab.

The taxi cut across Third Avenue and Lexington and then onto Park Avenue. They drove down the long, straight avenue with the Pan Am Building as a target; then it was lost, and they were around and up and through Grand Central. They turned off at East Thirty-eighth Street, and then the driver pulled up.

Sinclair went to get out with her, but she stopped him.

"Dan, let's hold off. Say I'm superstitious or worried about the effects of candlelight. Whichever it is, sleep on it and see what it's like in the dirty gray morning. Leave a message with my answering service. I'm not in tomorrow, but I'll call them."

He didn't argue with her, and before he could move to hold her, she was out of the cab, across the sidewalk and up the steps to the door. She opened the door and looked back at him, and then the shaft of light was cut off. He told the driver to take him to the St. Regis.

10

AT eight o'clock the telephone rang in Sinclair's suite. "Good morning, sir, this is your eight A.M. call."

He grunted his thanks.

"You're welcome." The operator sounded very pert and bright. He went into the bathroom and cleaned his teeth and then put a call through to Jackson. Her voice when she answered was fresh and awake.

"Morning, Daniel. How are you? Did you have a good time after we left?"

He said it had been great, and what about her?

"Oh, we went on down to the Village, had a super meal and listened to some jazz. You know those two fellows are awfully sweet, and you'll never guess—they're in fashion too."

"Well," said Sinclair, "I kind of thought it was something in the artistic line. How are you feeling?"

"Well, fine, why shouldn't I?"

"Last night you did say you'd be out till dawn and to hell with the photo session."

"Daniel, they were just words, you know that. I wouldn't really let you down."

"Maybe, but there were other people listening, and it didn't sound the most professional piece of bravado. It was the sort of thing one would expect from a jumped-up model girl, but not from you."

He guessed that at the other end of the telephone she was pouting. He was wrong. There was a long wait then.

"OK, Daniel. You're right. I'd better go now. Mustn't keep the client waiting."

"Jackson, it's for your own good. Now, do you want me to take you over to the studio?"

"Don't worry, Daniel. I've managed to get to studios before now. I'll pick up a cab downstairs."

"That's fine, Jackson. Have a good day."

"Sure. I'll see you back here then, around seven . . . and, Daniel, you have a good day too."

Sinclair's first appointment wasn't until eleven. He rang room service for a decent breakfast and took his time getting ready.

The morning was fine and warm, and he decided to take a walk before meeting the president of Naturalé in the ad agency's Madison Avenue office. He came out of the hotel, walked up Fifty-seventh Street and stood on the corner where east and west met, trying to decide whether to turn right down East Fifty-seventh or up and across to West Fifty-seventh. He went west, past I. Miller, the shoe store, and into Henri Bendel. Bendel's he always thought of as a shop, although in fact it was a store. There was nothing like it in London; the nearest to it would be Liberty's, but without the winding corridors and antique well. He bought some token presents for the girls in his office and then went back, out of the cool air conditioning into the close New York air, which was a great way to catch a cold. A New York store was the only place in the world he knew where you should put your coat on to go in and take it off when you come out.

The lights at the junction of Fifth Avenue and West Fifty-seventh changed, and Sinclair joined that part of the herd which had detached itself into an independent group and crossed the street with them.

Smith, Prado and Collins took up four floors of the Madison Avenue skyscraper, and Sinclair took the elevator direct to the president's reception floor, the highest. As the door glided back, he stepped out onto the thick wall to wall. Immediately opposite there was a girl sitting at an ultramodern efficiency-style glass and steel desk. She was typecast: neat Doris Day hairdo and large-framed glasses. She stopped playing with the IBM electric typewriter and looked up.

"Good morning, sir. You must be Mr. Sinclair."

Oh, very smart, he thought, she's been at the appointment book and taken in the English-cut clothes. They probably didn't get many men with the hint of flare in the trouser leg, lapping over shoes without a half-inch welt around the uppers. His one recurring image of the average New Yorker was a sea of conventional-width trousers with turnups half-mast above heavy-duty shoes. He gave her his slow George-Sanders-type British delivery.

"How very perceptive of you. I imagine your leader is waiting."

She didn't quite know how to handle that one.

"If you'll take a seat, Mr. Sinclair, I'll inform Mr. Collins you've arrived."

The conference room was vast. The man who introduced himself as Clayton Collins led Sinclair past the empty boardroom table and chairs to the far end, where three other well-fed gentlemen were waiting. Sinclair repeated their names back to them as he shook hands, Dale Carnegie style—Jonas Blumenthal, William B. Trustgrove, Cedric P. Ziff—the sweetest sound in the world to any man is the sound of his own name, that's what the book had said, and it was right.

"Well, Dan—you don't mind if I call you Dan—well, Dan, our little girl is hard at it this morning, I guess, and I must say that the exposure she has had here so far has been very impressive."

Sinclair accepted the compliments with a nod and smile.

"Subject of course to the photographic layouts being what we visualize, Mr. Blumenthal here has an interesting proposition to put to you."

Sinclair turned to the head of Naturalé. "Dan." He took the large cigar from his mouth. His voice was deep and might have had Texas origins. "As you know my company is high on nationwide sales, but nevertheless we've had a problem. I say had, because I believe we've got it licked." He waited for the murmurs of assent; he didn't wait long.

"We were missing out on the junior-market level. Our image had become too static. Now, with the new campaign using your Jackson, that situation will be reversed, if you see what I mean."

"Yes, I do, Mr. Blumenthal."

"Well, that's good, Dan. We have a whole range coming out of the labs scheduled for twelve months ahead, and, ah, so far nobody's come up with a name for this great new range. I mean, there's a whole new cosmetics range here without a name."

The other men looked suitably crestfallen.

Sinclair took up his cue. "If I'm not mistaken, Mr. Blumenthal, you've come up with a name."

"You're damn right I have, boy. Jackson. You can see it, can't you? Here's a great new face with an international name and image—why, it could sweep the country."

"You're absolutely right, Mr. Blumenthal. Particularly if the campaign was backed by a tour of nationwide personal appearances."

Blumenthal stuck the now-dead cigar back in his mouth, slapped his thick thigh and beamed. "That's the kind of talk I wanted to hear, Dan boy."

The room was very pleased with itself, and Sinclair let it enjoy the euphoria. Then he dropped the bad egg.

"There is a slight problem in that area, gentlemen."

Collins leaned forward, anxious that nothing should disrupt the progress they were making.

"What slight problem, Dan?"

"I've already had a similar offer."

The cigar came out the mouth at top speed.

"Don't play games here, boy. This is serious business."

"I'm well aware of the seriousness of business, Mr. Blumenthal, which is exactly why I'm telling you that I have already received a similar offer. If I was playing at it, I would have let you make your bid before I had the grace to tell you. You all know that the person I represent happens to be in a position to help your company. That is not a unique situation, gentlemen; your competitors have similar ideas. In fact, you don't need me to tell you, I'm sure, that the cosmetics business exists on borrowed ideas."

"Now, just a minute, Sinclair—"

"Please, Blumenthal, don't get self-righteous with me. You couldn't live on the intrinsic value of your products, any of you; you have to promote, you're in the glamor trade. If what you sold was as good as you claim, if it actually did what you say, you wouldn't need me or Jackson. But it doesn't. Show me the woman who has become beautiful through using your products. At best she's given herself a psychological lift, and perhaps that's sufficient justification for the fortune you people pour away."

"Sinclair!" Collins was on his feet. "We didn''t ask you here to have a sermon thrown in our faces, no, sir. What the hell are you at?"

"Mr. Collins, you really must broaden your outlook. Just because I tell you what you must all know yourselves doesn't for a second mean that I don't want to be part of it."

That really threw them. Sinclair relaxed fractionally; this was the situation he had deliberately set out to achieve. He judged that the impression he had projected was that of the heretic who wanted to join the clan but at the same time who wasn't too particular which clan he settled for.

"OK, we get the point," said Blumenthal. "You hate the whole phony operation, but you'd rather have a piece of it than not, right?"

"Absolutely."

"How much?"

"I think it's up to you to make the offer. After all, I imagine that's what you got me here for."

They sat and looked at one another, none of them wanting to speak first. Sinclair helped them out.

"Why don't I just go down to the other end of the room and let you all have a little discussion?"

The suggestion came as a relief. Sinclair left them and went to the other end of the long boardroom.

He stood and looked out at the street below and thought what a con it was. Here they were, five intelligent men, trying to battle out a deal for the services of a little girl from the north of England, who, because of the way she photographed, backed by a load of overlaudatory publicity, had the apparent power to spearhead a vastly expensive marketing and advertising campaign that would make millions for its originators. A giant organization was prepared to stake enough money to build a small hospital on the created talents of a single person.

And where did the money really come from? From the gullible public, because the budget would be calculated by accountants and built into the unit price of each item in the cosmetic range being sold. Sinclair remembered what the marketing director of Boots Number Seven brands had once been reported as saying: "I should be marketing director of the biggest cosmetic business in Britain if women applied criteria of common sense and bought cosmetics as they do tea and sugar. But women don't, and I'm not." But what did it matter? he thought. In the end, too serious an analysis of what cosmetics actually did to a woman was beside the point. They meant luxury, relaxation and fantasy.

The cautious mumbling from the hunched quartet ceased, and Sinclair turned to look at them again. Collins was beckoning him. He went back to join the seller's market.

"Now then, Dan, we have what we think is a pretty fair deal."

"Good."

"In principle, an exclusive contract, two ways: We don't use any other girl to underwrite and advertise the product; you guarantee Jackson doesn't work for any other cosmetics manufacturer."

"Before you go on, Mr. Collins, I have no objections at all to your using other personalities. I think Jackson can hold her own. And, of course, for me to turn down beauty pictures from Revlon, Arden, Lauder and the like will cost you money."

The last point was rhetoric, but telling them they could use who else they liked negated an apparent contractual concession on their part.

Collins looked at Blumenthal; then he went on. "Well—ah—that's fine. The period of the contract to be for two years. And now, of course, you want to know about the finance."

"I think that would be a good idea, Mr. Collins."

"We think the fairest way for you to earn would be to base the whole concept on a royalty basis, with, naturally, a substantial guarantee. How does five percent of the wholesale price of all units sold with a guarantee of twenty-five thousand dollars sound to you?"

Collins sat down with the equivalent of a flourish; his colleagues were on the point of clapping but managed to hold themselves in.

Sinclair knew exactly what his answer was going to be, but the way he said it hadn't been rehearsed. So he sat and thought; he put on his serious look—a frown, a few visual contractions of the jaw muscles and a low "Hmmm." He looked up and made each of them stare straight at him as his eyes scanned them from left to right. At the point where Collins was almost forced to break the silence he answered them.

"On the face of it, gentlemen, a very good offer."

They smiled. "But"—the eyebrows lowered and the faces relaxed—"we don't enter into royalty contracts."

He held up his hands to forestall them. "Now, before you tell me it's the fairest way, and that if the campaign's a success, we stand to make a load of bread, let me say I know that argument. You'll have to excuse my cynicism, gentlemen, but I don't happen to believe the company exists that pays a true royalty return, and so the only real value of that type of contract is the guarantee, paid in advance, of course."

"See here, Dan," said Blumenthal. (It was "Dan" again, so he was on the let's-be-friends ploy.) "I don't blame you for the way you're thinking—I mean, I guess you've had some bum experiences—but you're talking to Naturalé, son, and we're a big operation, too big to worry about cheating you out of a few five percents, for God's sake."

"Mr. Blumenthal, it's because I know how big you are and how much you need a change of image that I can't accept a twenty-five-thousand guarantee. Why, your turnover last year into Britain alone amounted to twenty-five million. So if the Jackson range forms, say, five percent of your total sales, that means a potential of a million and a quarter a year, excluding America and the rest of the world. A sure twenty-five grand over two years, worldwide, doesn't seem quite so generous, does it? In fact, it comes out rather paltry."

They were getting mad, not so much because he was pushing a hard negotiation as because he appeared not to care, not to take them seriously, and for anyone not to think seriously about their company was the paramount sin.

Collins clenched his teeth and almost hissed. "What would you suggest, Mr. Sinclair?"

This was the stage he had maneuvered and waited for, and he spoke quietly but firmly.

"In exchange for the use of the name of Jackson and her services as a model on all packaging and advertising, plus a guaranteed stay, by the two of us, of one month a year in the U.S., for all promotional work and activity over a period of two years—that you pay Jackson a total fee of twenty-five thousand sterling, plus all first-class expenses. Of course, the money would be paid to a specially setup company outside the U.K., probably in Liechtenstein; we don't want to have to pay tax at the British rate, you know."

Blumenthal interrupted him. He was the calm and decisive executive, no bluff and no emotion; it was no longer a case of face-saving. While the others were reacting with their feelings, Blumenthal had assessed the economics of the offer in relation to what he was getting. At the beginning it had been he who played at business, because he had figured that Sinclair would have been eager enough to accept their first offer. He had done business with the British creative element before, and he knew that the magic of an American deal and a free trip was usually a sufficient emotive spur to make them want to accept without bothering to analyze their actual earnings too closely. But Sinclair knew the angles and knew the value of his product. Blumenthal respected him for it.

"You got a deal. I'll get our legal department to draw up the papers. I imagine this will negate any other negotiation you may have."

Sinclair took it in his stride; he knew that Blumenthal had guessed that there was no other negotiation in progress.

"There is one thing more, though, Mr. Blumenthal. I'll also require a modest fee, say, twenty thousand dollars, and the same conditions, of course."

Blumenthal grunted, considered the price and decided.

"Fifteen thousand, and we'll make it in four payments over the period—subject, naturally, to your continuing to represent the principal."

"As you say, Mr. Blumenthal, you got a deal."

Sinclair did his mental arithmetic as he sat at the bar in Schrafft's eating the hamburger lunch. He had turned down the expense-account meal on Smith, Prado and Collins because he couldn't wait to be alone, to enjoy the excitement that bringing off the Naturalé deal had given him. He jotted the figures down on his paper napkin. His 25 percent share of Jackson's fee came to £6,250, plus the additional £5,000. A total of £11,250—that couldn't be bad; and no British tax. He ordered another hamburger.

Back at the hotel he wrote the joint release that the agency would put out to the press. He had the desk send up a typist and dictated the final draft; he told the girl to type him an original and two copies. He'd leave one for Jackson to read when she came back from the studio, and on her copy he would write the actual money terms, excluding his own. He wanted her to know she wouldn't be getting the exaggerated figure that he'd put in the release. That had been the last detail agreed with the agency: how much they would announce the deal was worth to the press.

It was nearly six o'clock when he remembered that he was meant to have rung Ruth Emery.

Jackson was dead on her feet. The girls who read *Honey* and *Nineteen* would never believe it—all she had done, they would say, was sit around a studio all day having her picture taken, and what was so tiring about that? But they wouldn't know about the boredom of waiting for a perfectionist photographer to get his lighting right and having to talk for the sake of it to the people from the advertising agency who were there, nervously protecting their jobs by fussing over every minute detail. And all of that just for test shots; the real work was to come over the next few days, when the unit would go on location to Connecticut.

As she pushed the door of her suite open, she saw the hotel envelope on the floor and recognized Sinclair's writing. She didn't open it until she had taken off her street clothes and poured a drink from the supply that Sinclair had had put in the suite. She turned the television set on, more out of habit than for any special program, and stretched out on the sofa.

There were two sheets of paper. The first was a note from Sinclair; the other was headed "Draft Joint Release Naturalé Inc. Sinclair Enterprises Ltd. on behalf of Jackson." She read the release first. It was timed twelve noon and dated the following day. It was concise and to the point.

> Jonas Blumenthal, president of Naturalé, Inc., the fourth largest manufacturer of cosmetic goods in the United States, announced today that the company had secured the services of top British model Jackson. Mr. Blumenthal said that Jackson would advise the company over a two-year period on a sensational new range of cosmetics for the young market and would lend her name to a worldwide advertising and promotion campaign. Mr. Blumenthal went on to say: "We consider ourselves very fortunate to have signed Jackson, who is without doubt one of the most beautiful and talented young women of our time."
>
> Daniel Sinclair, Jackson's personal manager, added that both Jackson and himself were delighted to be associated with a company of the status of Naturalé. Although this has not been confirmed, it is believed that the contract is worth a quarter of a million dollars.

"My God." Jackson took a long swallow of the drink and then read the note from Sinclair.

> JACKSON: Don't get too stoned out of your mind. The $250,000 is for the press; the actual contract is for £25,000, including a month a year in the U.S., all expenses paid. Tell you the whole story over dinner. Love, DANIEL

Trust Sinclair, she thought. She should know him well enough by now though; he was always telling her not to believe everything she read in the papers, and the release was as good as in print.

She left the television on and took her drink into the bedroom. The suite was pleasantly warm, and she dropped the housecoat on the bed and went into the bathroom to start the bath. She unhooked the bra and then rolled down the tights and her pants in one action. She stood in front of the full-length mirror holding the drink and inspected the nude reflection.

"One of the most beautiful and talented young women of our time." It had a good sound, and she wondered just how much of it was what Sinclair really felt and how much was PR cliché. He must think she was pretty good, or he wouldn't have gone through the months of training and pushing, and in spite of his contempt for the press, they weren't all idiots, so some must have believed what they'd written. The contract with Naturalé was something of a confirmation; nobody would lay out £25,000 for nothing.

The hot steam from the bath was clouding the mirror, and she drained the last of the drink, turned the taps off and tested the water. The bath oil had made the water heavy and soft on her skin, and she breathed the scent of it as she slowly lowered herself. She ran her hands over her breasts and massaged the nipples; then she tried to pucker the flesh around her waist, but it was firm. Sinclair must be feeling very pleased with himself, she thought, and wondered how much of the deal was his doing and whether it would have happened without him.

He was a peculiar man—always trying so hard to be clever, always knowing so much more than she did, but when it really came down to it, what was there about him that made the success? There were times when she felt that he wasn't real; everything he said or did was so completely tied up with his work that she never saw any other part of him. His office, his flat, the car, the way he dressed—it was all premeditated; nothing was spontaneous. And when she really thought about it, it was difficult to remember times when he laughed freely. Even his humor was geared to the main chance or else sending somebody up. He didn't seem capable of laughing just because some stupid thing was funny, or even because he felt good. There must be something basically missing in a man who didn't have a sense of humor. The water was cooling, and she got out of the bath and sat on the stool with the large thick towel draped around her.

She was different now from the person she had been; increasingly, she was learning more from other people and events than from Sinclair, and she knew that his teaching days were over. He would handle things from now on—her publicity, deals, admin and money.

As she went into the bedroom, she made a mental note; she must remember to ask Sinclair what he was doing about *Life* magazine. Surely the deal with Naturalé would make a good story for them now?

11

THE days went quickly. Jackson commuted between the St. Regis Hotel, the studio and the location setting. The evenings were taken up with dinners she could have done without, Aston Weiz, then Jonas Blumenthal, but they were business and necessary.

They were also the only occasions when she saw Sinclair. She was becoming bored with the sameness of everything, the compliments and the predictions of success, and even he was beginning to irritate her. Each evening he would go through the day's achievements, stories he had planted, radio and television interviews to be scheduled. He was beginning to run her life, and she decided it was time for a change of emphasis.

It was their last Friday, and that evening they were having dinner with Collins from the ad agency at a place on Third Avenue. Sinclair arranged to meet them there, because, he said, he had to push cocktails with a journalist. It took her the thirty seconds she spent getting through the crush at the sawdust bar to be sure that it was a gay place. In the large and crowded restaurant part she waited for the headwaiter, but Collins beat him to it.

"Hello, there. Say, I'm sorry, I didn't know it would be this crowded. Where's Dan?"

"He's coming; he had to see a journalist or something."

"Well, if I'd known that, I'd have come right over and picked you up. Now, you just follow me and don't get lost—we're just over on the far side."

As she trailed him to the table, she looked around the room and noticed that the lighting was overbright for the usual run of restaurant. It wasn't until she had been at their table for a while that she realized why. It was—and somehow not really in the worst sense—a pickup joint. Attractive men, few of them young, were sitting alone at tables set for two; they nursed martinis and smoked white-tipped cigarettes and kept a constant watch on the entrance. When a younger man arrived on his own, he would wander among the tables, sometimes stopping to talk to couples who were having a meal, but always scanning the room. He used the brief stop not for conversation but as a weak subterfuge, to catch a stare he thought could be congenial. Then he would move on, usually to take a vacant seat. The man who had waited would order drinks, and they became like the others.

"Interesting here, isn't it?"

"I'm sorry, Mr. Collins."

"Say, call me Clay."

"Well, then, Clay . . . yes, its fascinating. Do you come here a lot?"

"Hell, no." He was embarrassed. "But I just thought that . . . well, you've probably been to so many chic places that maybe you'd enjoy something different."

"You're so right. I've had the circuit bit."

They ordered drinks and waited for Sinclair. Collins kept up a patter of business stuff about the contract and how great a deal it was. Jackson finished the drink and asked for another.

"Clay, make it a double; I feel like letting loose tonight. And let's have a pact: no more business. That's all I've had since I've been here; you're getting as bad as Sinclair."

He flagged a waiter and turned back to her. "Gee, I thought you and Dan were . . . well, you know. . . ." He was embarrassed again.

"Forget it. He's my manager, my Svengali, so I can't even say we're just good friends." She paused, realizing what she'd just said. "I didn't really mean it the way it sounded. Daniel's great, but I need more than a businessman to keep me going."

She took a large swallow of the second cocktail; the effects were beginning to show, and she was relaxing.

"Oh, shit, come on, Clay, let's play the truth game. I'll never tell a lie till midnight, and you promise to do the same. Is that a bargain?"

He was like a man deciding whether he should back the favorite or the outsider; like all novices, he went for the long shot.

"Hell, why not? OK, truthsville until the witching hour."

"All right," she said. "So let's see if you can keep the bargain. How many children have you got, Clay?"

She didn't get the reaction she had predicted. No deepening tan and nervous twitch; he smiled at her, very much at ease.

"Now you thought that would be a curvy one, didn't you?"

"What do you mean?" She was the one who had been thrown.

"Come now, remember: truthsville."

"Well, yes, I suppose I did. But you still haven't answered, have you?"

He laughed. "Atta girl, keep on coming. As a matter of fact, I've got two kids, and they're both grown up now and at college. But I don't see much of my ex-wife anymore; vacations the boys and I get together and go up to Canada for some fishing and hunting."

"Oh, I see. Well, that sounds very nice. I wonder where Dan's got to."

"Tell me, Jackson, are you a virgin?"

She sat back and roared. "Good God, Clay, that's an out-of-date question! No, of course I'm not, but I don't flash it around either. Why, have you got a fancy for me?"

He leaned forward, very intent.

"Look, this may sound stupid, but you were partly right the first time. Sure I've been here before, many times; when you get to my age and there's no real home, you try everything. I don't want to get married again, and after a while the sort of relationship you can have with a woman runs out if it doesn't have that little plum at the end of it. Yeah, I fancy you, Jackson. You're young and beautiful, and I guess maybe we're similar. No, I don't mean you're on the turn or anything, but you must be full of success, and that takes up just about most of you right now. So why not? We don't have anywhere to go, so there's no big emotional end product to worry about."

"Wow, when you make a pact, you go all the way, don't you? I don't think you're stupid, Clay. I think you're an intelligent man, maybe oversensitive, but what's wrong about that? As it happens, it's a pleasant change. For the past few months I've been closest to a man who wouldn't admit to having anything that resembled sensitivity—he couldn't afford it—so who knows, maybe you're around at a good time. As the man says, it's all in the timing."

"Why so serious, you two? Don't say the deal's off?"

They looked away from each other and saw Sinclair. He pulled up a chair and sat down.

"Jesus, I was nearly had four times on the way over. What made you choose this place, Clay? Did you think it was time we saw New York night life living the truth?"

Collins tried a smile, but it was a bad imitation; he thought Sinclair's timing was just great.

"Yes, something like that, Dan. Look, I'll get another round of drinks; then why don't we eat?"

"That's fine, Clay." Sinclair switched to Jackson. "How was the last day? Did they get what they wanted?"

She looked away, across the room at nothing, when she answered him.

"Yes, it all went very smoothly."

Sinclair got the message and wondered what the hell had upset her this time. Throughout the meal it continued; when, in the conversation, he talked to her, it would be as if he had not spoken. Collins was noticing that something was off, and he was the ad agency director again, trying to smooth a rough situation and turn its momentum. With him she was amused and vivacious; with Sinclair she could switch in mid-sentence and be sullen.

When the meal was over, Collins tried once again to jolly the atmosphere.

"Say, I know a club downtown that's a real laugh. Why don't we all pack into a cab and grab some of the action?"

"Thanks all the same, Clay," Sinclair said, "but I think I'll get an early night. Why don't you and Jackson go on without me?"

Jackson looked at him for almost the first time, and then as she smiled, she turned away before he could catch it, react and allow it to change the mood.

"Well, all right . . . but look, Dan, I was just thinking, if you two haven't got anything scheduled for the weekend, why not come out with me? I've got a small place on Long Island, and if the weather is fine, we could all just relax. It must have been a strain these past days for both of you."

"Oh, Clay, you're super," Jackson said. "That would be great with me, but I don't know about Daniel." Still she didn't look at him. It was as if she were talking about someone in another town.

"Clay, don't think I'm being pushy, but you wouldn't have room for a fourth, would you?"

Jackson spun around at him. "Who's the friend, Daniel? Don't say you're working overtime?"

He was icy with her. "No, love. This is a friend. She's not in the fashion business; she's real. What do you say, Clay—would it upset things?"

"Hell, no, it would be just fine. Why, we can have a foursome. Someone out there's bound to throw a party on Saturday. It'll work just great."

On the street Sinclair said he would walk.

"OK, Dan. Now I'll come by and pick you both up at, say, ten tomorrow morning. Don't bother to pack anything formal, will you? It's all very casual."

Sinclair watched their cab lights disappear. Then he looked for a phone booth.

"This is one extreme to the other," Jackson said, as she peered into the depths of the small clubroom. As far as she could see, there was only the typical polished wooden bar, with stools along one side and an assortment of tables, some with cloths, some without, filling the rest of the constricted area.

Clayton Collins had paid off the cab. He pushed through the doors and joined her.

"Let's sit up at the bar, and then you can watch everybody."

The barman was out of Hollywood: He was dark and big and wore a waistcoat over shirt sleeves; he was smoking a very big cigar.

"What'll you have, friends?"

Jackson expected a Texas drawl and thought it would be rather killing to slap the bar top and call for "sarsaparilla straight." She thought again: The man looked very capable of throwing her out.

"I'll have a double Scotch and soda. Clay, what do you want to drink?"

"The same. Jackson, isn't she great?"

She looked over to an alcove which was filled by a grand piano. Sitting at it was a very fat woman with long black ringlets and heavy makeup; the way the crimson lipstick had been put on, she must have been drunk at the time. She was playing Gershwin, Cole Porter-type standards, and she was singing with a low, smoke-ridden baritone voice that sounded more like a has-been vaudeville clown than a woman. But she had reached everybody in the place, and as Jackson listened to her, she too joined the silent fans. The melodies she recognized, but it took some attentive listening to catch on that the lyrics weren't being sung as written. They were being parodied; the new words were very dirty but, naturally, very funny too, and they were geared to the gay boys. It wasn't really until Jackson caught on to the lyric changes that she took in the audience properly. Apart from the pianist, she was the only woman. She whispered to Collins.

"Clay, you are rotten. It's another of your dives. I thought you'd turned over a new leaf."

She giggled but stopped short when one of the nearest group looked over and glared at her. When the woman ended her special performance, they all clapped; she left the piano, beaming, and joined a table that seemed to have the noisiest group. Once with them, she could have been a female impersonator.

"Come on, Clay, let's go now."

They finished their drinks. Out in the cool air Clay asked her if she wanted to crawl the East Village and catch the hippies.

"No, thanks, Clay. Can we go to where you live and have a nightcap? That would be nice, wouldn't it?"

He put his arm around her shoulders and kissed her forehead. "All right, baby. If that's what you want, then that's just fine with me."

He lived in an apartment house on East Fifty-ninth Street down by Second Avenue; she thought it looked like the bachelor pad of an agency man. It was designed clutter, with pieces that fitted into the overall pattern of yellow. He pointed out the things he'd picked up abroad, from Mexico and the East and Europe, and some from Capri. He obviously had a thing on lions. There were ceramic lions and wooden lions and mats with Chinese-type lions on them and even the head of a lion done in yellow paper. The rest of the apartment was brown, from the curtains and carpets to the paintwork. She sat on a leather sofa and watched him make the drinks and wondered what it was like being a homosexual.

"Clay, why didn't your marriage work?"

He gave her the drink, lit a cigarette and sat beside her.

"The usual reasons. I guess maybe you both get bored because you know each other too well. Or maybe you just can't take keeping up anymore. Women have to think about the good things that are to come—they are like children somehow; they like to get things and to look forward to surprises. It gets so that if you don't keep it up, they think you don't love them anymore. Then the things become more important than what you had together. Some women, you know, can't look back with you and say, gee, wasn't that a good time, and build on it; they can only build on the future. So when there's no good past for them anymore, and if you give up the supply, that's it. And they can get jealous, too. They start hating your work or your golf, anything that gives you satisfaction and doesn't originate from them."

He began to look sad as he talked, and she thought that made him look older.

"But don't you think, Clay, it's because of what you do to them? I mean, they have your children and stay in a house and maybe spend years having one-sided conversations with kids who can't talk back properly till they're six or seven. So they get a little jealous because you hit a little white ball around."

"Oh, you're right. And there's lots more, too. It's not done deliberately, you know; its what two people can do to each other without trying, that all."

He finished the cigarette and the drink. "Come on, Jackson, let's go to bed. We're getting too maudlin, talking about my past."

She somehow expected him to have a four-poster with drape at the head. They were very matter-of-fact about the way they undressed. She didn't look at him until she had curled against the cool sheets, waiting. Men always took longer to get undressed; it was the tie and the shirt with all those buttons. Except Reading, of course, but he always dressed as if he expected to make love anywhere, anywhere but in a bed.

The light mat of curled hair on his chest was gray, and she could see where the muscles were going loose and showing his age. He left the shorts until last, and she became excited and realized how long ago London suddenly seemed. She had been in America a whole week without anyone making a serious pass at her. It was indecent. The bloody photographer had been so concerned with his pictures and the money he was earning from the agency that he'd never gone beyond getting a rapport between himself, the camera and his model.

Clay pulled the sheets over himself, and then he held her and kissed her and touched her. He smelled good, and she wondered if that had been for her or someone else, but then she stopped thinking. It was different from what it had ever been before, because there was no panic about it. His hands were experienced, they knew how to make her feel good and warm and hungry for him.

She was losing herself until she touched him, and then it was as if the blood in her body had stopped racing. There was no hardness to caress and feel and want. He kissed her breasts and touched her and kissed her, and then he moved onto her, but still it was nothing. She knew that if she let him go, he would crack, and there would not be another time: either with her or with any other woman. She went onto her stomach on the bed and moved, and suddenly his hands became urgent and his body tighter and younger. Afterward he held her, and gradually his breathing became calmer, and she felt protected and cared for.

As she lay with him, she thought of the weekend ahead and was very pleased. She was even pleased now with Sinclair; God knew what he must think after what she had given to him that evening. She was glad he was bringing a woman; it made everything so much simpler.

They went through Queens and onto the Long Island Expressway; she sat in the front next to Clay and watched him drive. She had broken the tautness with Sinclair and had liked the woman Ruth Emery. She could tell that morning that Sinclair was prepared to be sullen with her, and it gave her a good feeling that when she smiled and was gay with him, he changed. It proved to her that she could sway his mood if she wanted to. It was like having power over him, and it meant that the relationship had changed: that he needed her and her approval. With this knowledge had come a losing of respect for him. If a man loved you, then you could understand that he would be gentle and allow you to set the emotional pace, but Sinclair didn't love anyone unless it was himself, so between them it had become a personality thing, and it would degrade him, because no matter what he had done to help and create her, she now existed and was necessary to him. The glory would never be his; he would be a follower in her reflected success.

"Now then, children," said Clay. "How about a running commentary for the tourists? Think you can stand it, Ruth?" He called the words over his right shoulder without taking his eyes from the road ahead.

"Oh, sure," she said. "Go right ahead. I'm no expert on Long Island myself, you know."

"Listen closely then, people. Long Island was originally inhabited by thirteen Indian tribes whose business was shells, and they called it Sewanhacky. It's cut off from the mainland and juts out into the Atlantic for a hundred and twenty-nine miles. Do I continue?"

They yelled, "Yes," at him in unison and laughed like children on an outing.

"The island has over a thousand miles of shoreline with coves and inlets and bays, and no matter where you come from"—he was imitating the voice of travel commentator James A. Fitzpatrick now—"the past of Long Island is part of *your* heritage, and for the benefit of our British friends let me say that the island was once occupied by their soldiers during the Revolution. Later we will show you Southampton, home of the rich in summer, where they migrate from the lush sands of their winter homes in Palm Beach. Southampton is an authentic colonial town, founded in 1640 by the English colonists. And so we say, welcome to Sewanhacky, Island of Shells."

They clapped and shouted for more, but he was done; in his normal voice he told them they were leaving the expressway and its ever-proposed extension for Montauk Highway and then Quogue, where he had his house.

The house was really an oversized cottage and looked as if its original designer had based it on an English model, although it had a raised wooden porch.

"The lumber was hand-cut from the local forests, I'll have you know," said Clay. "And I promise that's the end of the monologue."

They changed into shorts and sloppy sweaters and wore canvas shoes without socks; when they had eaten, Clay drove them to the village of Southampton, and they browsed in the small shops and enjoyed the lazy comfort of the warm afternoon. Later they sat on the porch and had early-evening drinks. Clay came back from phoning and told them there was a party that evening.

"Some of the design boys are having drinks; it should be a lot of fun. Then we can come back and I'll serve you all Collins' barbecued Long Island chicken."

The men wore open shirts with loose-knotted silk scarves under colored sweaters, the girls trousers with silk shirts and gold sandals. It was a rich, elegant casualness, and the bar was by the open swimming pool at the back of the new one-story house. The music came from hi-fi units hidden by the branches of the trees that also had lights attached to them, and the underwater spots in the pool cast a bluey-green glow.

People mingled, and some danced; but nobody fell into the pool or even dived in fully clothed, which disappointed Jackson. For an instant she thought of doing it herself, but decided it had all been done before, and why get wet anyway?

"Hi, sweetie. And how are you?"

He was big and bronzed, and he had one arm in a sling.

"I should be asking how you are, don't you think?"

"Oh my goodness, she's British—did you get that accent? Hey, Charles, have you met this cute little number?"

Charles was chunky and very smooth-faced. His fair hair was cropped very close, U.S. Army style, and he had biceps that bulged away under the short-sleeved shirt-sweater. His voice was like deep black treacle.

"Why, no, I have not . . . oh, my, but are not you a beauty one?"

Clay came back with the drinks. "I wondered when these two would get around to you," he said, smiling.

"Mary mother of you-know-who, it's that big agency president man. Now, Charles, you'll just have to watch out. If we're not careful, he'll be snapping you up for one of his tremendously prestigious advertising campaigns. Now introduce us, Clay. Be sociable."

Clay turned from them to Jackson. "Darling, these two idiot sons are Dick Racer and Charles Lowheim the Second. Gentlemen, this young lady is Jackson."

"Oh, now I know. Why, you're famous, you are. Charles, remember those beautiful pictures we saw in the newspaper . . . behold in the very lovely flesh."

Charles was beginning to sway, like a giant oak in a forest of saplings.

"Why, of course I do remember, and I considered on the occasion how superbly attractive to the human eye you were."

"I should explain, Jackson," said Clay. "Dick is a dress designer and he's very in at this time. Mr. Lowheim the Second comes, naturally, from a long-established Connecticut family, who somehow managed to build up a massive business in nuts and bolts."

"Sir," said Charles, "I will have you recognize that Lowheim superior fixtures are not an unnoticed feature on the NASA projects."

"Listen, you two, if you can still stand up at the end of this clambake, come on over to the house and have some supper. Do you think you can take them anymore, Jackson?"

She was enjoying them. "Yes, of course, that would be super."

"Oh, *super* she says—isn't that out of heaven? Charles, don't wander so. Did you hear what she said?"

"Yes, Richard, I did indeed; perfectly charming enunciation, young lady, if I may be permitted to comment."

"We'll see you later, folks. Come on, darling, let's meet some sane people."

They moved through the throng and like others stopped at the edge of the pool to gaze at the light reflections. Across the water Jackson saw Sinclair and was surprised that for once he was not holding forth to a group of women; he and Ruth Emery were standing alone.

"Looks like they're having a party all to themselves."

"Clay, you know this is the first time I've seen Sinclair actually seem interested in someone who isn't obviously going to do him some good."

"Well, maybe he's falling for her. She's an attractive, intelligent woman, you know, and she writes some damned good pieces."

"I don't believe it. That man isn't the sort to let a woman get that close to him; he'll back off sooner or later."

Clay put his hand gently on the back of her neck.

"He won't get much choice. Have you forgotten you leave for London on Monday?"

She looked up at him, and her face was gentle.

"You know, I had forgotten."

They all left the party well before it petered out. It was a warm enough night to sit on the porch, and Clay brought out the drinks before he disappeared to the kitchen to fix the chicken supper he'd prepared.

He wasn't gone long; when he came back, he was carrying an enormous tray piled with steaming legs and wings of chicken, with dishes of sweet potatoes and corn.

"Here we are, folks. Now, dig in."

"Charles, why can't you cook like this?"

Charles didn't answer. He sat very upright, staring straight in front. It happened that Jackson was directly in his line of non-sight, and somehow it disturbed her. She felt like putting up her hand and snapping her fingers.

He didn't pick up anything from the plate, and when Dick Racer put a chicken leg into his massive hands, he did nothing with it. Everyone waited for him to move, but he stayed like granite. It became almost sinister. They tried to talk around him, but nothing would work, and then at last his lips moved. He still kept the frozen look in his eyes, and he didn't turn his head. "Richard, let us go home."

"Now, Charles, live a little. Have some fun for God's sake."

"I would prefer to go home, Richard. Now."

They were all very still. Jackson put her hand out to clutch at Clay; she was frightened, and she shivered.

"Well, I'm sorry, sweeties. Looks like we got to go."

Racer wiped his hands on the otherwise apparently superfluous sling and gently went to raise his friend from the chair. He rose like a zombie, quietly said good-night to no one in particular and with an effort walked slowly and deliberately out of the circle of light cast by the house and into the darkness.

"I'd better steer the poor dear before he takes your fence with him," Racer said, and then he too was gone, with Clay following them to see them into their car.

"Oh, I'm glad he's gone," said Jackson.

"You're right. It was getting a bit much, I'm afraid," said Ruth Emery.

Clay returned out of the darkness and almost made Jackson jump.

"Gee, I'm sorry. I've never seen him like that before. Jesus, but he was out!"

"Clay, let's clear away and go up. I'm cold."

They took the things back into the kitchen, and the four of them washed and dried the dishes and glasses and put them in the pine cabinets that hung on the walls. Ruth Emery had sensed that there was a closeness between Jackson and Clay, and the ease with which Jackson had talked of "going up" confirmed it for her.

"Why don't I make nightcaps, Clay?" said Sinclair.

"No, thanks, Dan. Unless you want one, honey?"

But Jackson was already moving out of the room, "Not for me, Clay. Good night, Ruth. Good night, Daniel."

They were gone, and Ruth and Sinclair went into the low-beamed sitting room. The open fire that Clay had lit to keep the late-night chill from the room still glowed, and Sinclair threw another log onto it and kicked it until the sparks caught and made a flame. Then he went to the liquor cabinet and started searching through the bottles.

"What are you looking for, Dan?"

"Ah, here's some." He held a bottle up. "Irish whiskey. Have you ever had Irish coffee?" She shook her head. "You'll love it; just give me five minutes."

When he came back from the kitchen, he was carrying two large wineglasses of dark coffee with thick brims of cream.

He sat with her on the sofa, and they drank the coffee, taking pleasure from their silence and the feeling they had with each other.

"Well, Dan, I don't suppose I have to ask if the trip has been a success for you, do I?"

There was space between them on the sofa, and he could look at her and have her in his vision, unblurred.

"No, you could say it's been an unqualified success, I suppose—Jackson at the pinnacle, and even Michael Smith went back glowing; one tends to forget him. But there has been more than all of that, and you know it."

"What has there been, Dan? Tell me."

"You know, but you really want to hear, don't you? What is it about women that they must have it put into words?"

"It's natural insecurity; we need to be reassured. You should know that better than anyone; you're the expert in communicating the message. If you don't spell it out, how are we to know what you really think?"

He finished his drink, put the glass on the table and moved close to her. He ran his forefinger down the side of her nose.

"It's bent; doesn't that put you off?" she said.

He smiled at her; his eyes were warm, and they searched her face.

"Why don't we just follow the others?"

"What do you make of Jackson, Dan?"

"Don't change the subject."

"No, I really mean it."

He sighed and relaxed against the back of the sofa and looked into the flames of the fire.

"When we first started, it was great. I had something *new*, that was mine, that was unmolded, that I could make grow and blossom. Well, it's all happened now, and she's cocky. She'll become like all the others, demanding; only with her there's a difference —we have a three-year contract."

"She'll come to resent that, Dan. And she'll resent you. What'll happen then?"

"It won't matter how much she comes to resent it; she needs me, and I'll see it stays that way. What's the alternative? Get somebody new? She wouldn't do it—not out of loyalty, don't think I'm that naïve. I know her. It's like a marriage *sans* the conveniences but *avec* the profits."

Ruth stood up and walked across to the passage leading to the porch. "Do you think Clay bothers to lock up? I suppose he does; we're not that far from New York."

"What's the matter, Ruth?"

"It's my fault. I shouldn't have started it off. I can't seem to help having a dig every time we're alone together. It's the only thing that stops it being perfect. I have a basic disgust for PR which even knowing you can't shift. In a way knowing you makes me hate it more, because I think it degrades you, that you're maybe worth better. It's the PR man's preoccupation with the manipulation of words to create images that makes alterations in people's consciousness. Nothing he puts out can be without bias in the favor of the person who pays him, and once you recognize that, then there lies the immorality. A man blowing his own trumpet you can accept, but paying someone to do it for him, no. If something's that good, the word'll get around quickly enough without anyone's having to pay some PR man to persuade us about it." She stood behind the arm of the sofa, above him. "There, you see: lecture again. I won't do it anymore, Dan, promise. . . . Well, it's late; I guess we should close up shop."

They went around checking locks and putting out lights, and then with only the light from the hallway above they went up the stairs together. Clay had done the proper host thing and given them a room each. They reached her door, and Sinclair whispered to her, "Let me change. I'll only be a few minutes."

She laughed at him. "You make it sound like a honeymoon night."

"What's so wrong about that? And it's not so far out anyway."

When he came back to her room, she was propped up in the bed, looking through the window at the tops of the trees, black and white with the strong clear moonlight on them. He got into the bed and took his robe off, and as she turned to him and they touched, it was like the shock from static electricity, only softer. It wasn't only the abrupt realization that they were both naked. It was perhaps because they had waited until then and because they were adults and there had been an anticipation for what they had both experienced elsewhere becoming actual with them.

He smoothed her flesh, but his hand did not move into the ritual of caresses that had become a known and practiced pattern. When it closed on her breast, it touched her tenderly, and then firmly, as if for the first time it was discovering how it was to hold a rounded breast that was full but could be cupped in the palm. Their faces were together, and as they kissed, their bodies moved closer. His hand left her breast, felt the softness of her belly and then the firmer flesh of her thigh. They did not speak; their breathing became more rapid, and his hands had quickened; it was as if he wanted to feel all of her body at the same time. She moved with him now, and the grip of her hands and arms across his back and down his spine made his nerve reactions escalate. Then it was right. They were together. He could not see, and his other senses compensated. He buried his face in her and took the smell of her skin into his nostrils and sensed his own smell from her. It was a slow coming down; his mind felt in motion, like a wave washing over the inside of his head. His muscles were relaxing, and the weight of her on his arms became apparent; he moved them from under her, up over her quiet breasts, around her shoulders, to hold her gently to him. His kisses had no urgency now; he gave them not to arouse but to comfort. It seemed a long time before he could speak.

"Ruth"—the words came hoarsely from him—"I can't tell you . . ." He paused. "There should be some new words to use, words that have not been blunted by loose and careless use, words that are not lost because they are what you are supposed to say. How do you tell another person how she made you feel? I can't do it. If I said what I wanted to say, then in my language it wouldn't come out right. So I won't say it that way."

"I've always wanted to write it down, Dan, to put it into a book, to write a prose poem so that the words could tell the others how it was. I think now that even if I could do it, then it would kill what I had. After you write something down, it's finished."

In the early morning he woke and almost in the same moment turned to hold her again. This time there was no graduation; it was immediate, almost like taking her in her sleep.

Sinclair met Clay in the kitchen. He was making fresh orange juice, and the percolator was beginning to spit the hot brown coffee.

"Make enough for four, will you, Clay?"

"Sure. Did you have a good night?" He half laughed. "What I meant was—"

"Where do you keep the cups? Don't worry, I know what you meant, Clay. You've heard about Freudian slips, I guess."

"Dan, where do you think we go from here?"

Sinclair started to pour out the coffee. "I think we make a picnic lunch and we all go down to the beach and lie in the sun and go swimming. What I don't think we do is talk about it and make guesses at the future."

They had put on their swimming things before leaving the house, so when they got to the beach they could strip straightaway.

"How about opening the wine, Clay?" Jackson said.

"Let's save it till after the swim. Come on, Dan, I'll race you in."

The two men ran hard toward the sea, like young men showing off to their girls. They were slowed and nearly tripped by the water, and then they both dived into the surf.

Sinclair swam underwater for as long as his breath held out. The sudden chill shock was soon over, and his body felt clean and fresh. He came out ahead of Clay and swam back to him; then they chased each other in circles, like water polo players except that their technique wasn't so good. But from the shore they looked very competent and powerful. The sun had warmed the girls, and they too ran into the sea, making the men seem awkward with their slim, rounded bodies that were better designed for moving through the water.

They all ran up the beach to the towels. The men knew their cue, took the towels and rubbed the backs of the girls and tousled their wet hair. Then they had drinks and ate the lunch and lay in the hot sun.

They enjoyed the day all the more because they knew that the following morning it would be over, that they would go back into the city and take up the lives they had left there.

They hardly talked as they drove back toward the city on Monday morning. Clay complained about the traffic; Jackson sat mute and stared through the side window; they listened to the early-morning radio. Clay dropped Ruth at her apartment and Jackson and Sinclair at the hotel, then went straight to his offices.

They met again in the lounge at Kennedy Airport and tried the small talk of how great it had all been and how it wouldn't be long until Jackson and Sinclair were back again. Then the London flight was announced, and they walked in pairs down the corridors to customs.

"It's like the end of a shipboard romance." Ruth held Sinclair's arm, and her smile was very weak.

"Not anymore, not in the jet age."

"Don't believe it: Distance is distance. Let's not get sentimental about the future, Dan. I couldn't take that."

He stopped walking. "Listen, Ruth, you're the only real person I know. You even make me feel real; that's not something I just mark down to experience."

At the barrier that separates the travelers from those who stay behind they had kissed, and the men had shaken hands, and they all gave each other presents.

Jackson was the one who was emphatic. "I'll see you, Clay, next trip over. Now, be good and find some new clubs; the others are draggy." She smiled as if she were flirting with him for the first time. "You shouldn't need them, I don't think."

"No, you're right, honey."

Then they parted, and Ruth and Clay watched the VC10 as it surged into the air. When there was nothing else to wait for, they walked to the car and drove back into the city.

Sinclair thought about her words again on the plane, as he buckled the safety belt, and wondered how much she had meant them and how much had really been what she had said about "shipboard romance."

12

THE rat race got under way again as soon as they cleared customs. There was a whole batch of photographers waiting, and Sinclair was glad he had had Jackson change on the plane before they landed. She had put on an immaculate white tunic trouser suit and carried the copies of *The Brothers Karamazov* and *Playboy* he had given her for the occasion. A great combination, he had thought: egghead and sex. As he anticipated, the press boys loved it and made her carry the books so that the titles showed out well against the stark contrast of the suit. Sinclair had an armful of American magazines, all of which happened to carry cover shots of Jackson.

At the back of the crowd he spotted Freda, and while Jackson stood and posed, he pushed his way through.

"Hello, Freda. Are we still in business?"

"Hello, Dan. Well, yes, just about. Did you have a great time? I got your cables." She laughed. "As you can see."

"Yeah, that's marvelous, Freda. You didn't seem to have too much trouble fixing them, did you?"

"Well, not really. Particularly after your release on Naturalé arrived. I've kept the clippings, of course, mostly front-page stuff about dollar-export-business-through-beauty and things like that."

At last the press had finished with Jackson; they were free to leave. The chauffeur-driven car dropped Jackson off in Cadogan Square and then took Freda and Sinclair on to Hay Hill.

"I'll be down in an hour, Freda. You didn't tell any of the clients I was back today, did you?"

"No, of course not. They all think you'll be in tomorrow morning."

He went up to the flat. Mrs. Pond was there when he pushed open the door. "Hello, Mr. Sinclair. Have a good trip?"

"Yes, thanks, Mrs. Pond. Very successful."

"Well, I thought I'd just come in and open a few windows and see you had some food in. I expect you'd like a coffee, wouldn't you? Don't suppose they had any of that dandelion in America, did they?"

"Do you know, I didn't think to ask."

He took the bags through to the bedroom and started unpacking. It was amazing, he thought; he'd been away for only about ten days, and it seemed like months. You expected everything to have changed when you got back—like the government or something—but it was always the same, and in thirty-six hours it would be as if he'd never left. He thought of that as he slipped the gold Ken Lane links from the cuffs of his shirt. He had put them in on the plane—it was a sentimental gesture, he knew—and he took her card from his notecase: "Let me know when you give it up and I'll hotfoot it over. Love, RUTH." He put the card and the links in the drawer of his bedside unit and went to run the shower.

Exactly one hour later he walked into the office below.

"Good morning, everybody."

They smiled and replied in unison. Then he handed out the neatly wrapped boxes in Bendel's best brown-and-cream-striped paper, and they thanked him, and he went into the study.

The papers were in three neat piles on the table: one for signature, one for information and the third for action. A typed schedule lay on top of the third pile; it was a list of the personal messages that had accrued while he had been away.

He signed the checks, the orders and the letters and then sat back and went through the schedule.

Mary Steward had rung twice, no message. Major Carter once: the instruction was cryptic—"Contact immediately on return, urgent." He didn't have to think too hard to guess what that was about: Carter couldn't have missed reading about the Jackson-Naturalé tie-up. The *Evening News* and the *Express* had been on: again no message. A Mr. Nutting had telephoned for an appointment: nothing fixed. Sinclair remembered the name; he was the man Freda had told him about who had wanted to talk about the business' taking on his account. A man called Harry Brownstone had requested an interview—something he thought Sinclair Enterprises would find of great value. Freda had temporarily fixed it for eleven the next day. The rest was routine.

He buzzed the intercom for Freda. She came in, shorthand book at the ready.

"Anything else other than what's here, Freda?"

"No, you've got everything. Except that, as you suggested, I've engaged Janice Dearing from Models London to handle Jackson's bookings. She starts next Monday."

"Oh, that's great. She'll take a load of work off us. The bookings are still pouring in, I hope?"

"Yes, of course, particularly since New York. I've tentatively turned down all the beauty shots; I wasn't too sure what you'd fixed."

"You did right. As of now, Jackson's exclusive to Naturalé on all beauty. We'd better send out a release to the beauty editors telling them that from today onward they must say she uses only Naturalé products professionally. What she does actually use doesn't matter a damn, of course. It's only what they say in print that rates. . . . Anything worrying you?"

Freda hesitated.

"Well, what is it?"

"It's Sue. She's rather upset. I think you should see her as soon as you can."

"What the hell's the matter with her? Don't tell me it's Carnel."

"Yes, I think it is. Major Carter's been giving her a rough time."

"OK, Freda, tell her to come in. We'll get it over with now."

Sue Black came in looking apprehensive but nevertheless prepared to do battle for her rights. She sat on the edge of the sofa, back upright, her hands neatly folded on her crossed legs.

"What's the trouble, Sue?"

"Carnel, Mr. Sinclair. Major Carter's absolutely furious about the new deal. He wanted to ring you in New York, but I told him you had to go out of town and couldn't be reached. I didn't know what to say. I didn't know any more than he did."

She was near tears.

"Relax, Sue. I couldn't have told you anything. I didn't know myself until they made the offer late last week. By the time it was official we were just about due to come home."

"Well, all I can tell you, Mr. Sinclair, is that he thinks we've done the dirty on him. He said the least we could have done was waited and told him before signing. I think he would have made a counteroffer."

"Well, maybe he would, but I don't think so, and I don't think they would have paid the money."

She was unconvinced, and it was showing.

"Do you think you could see him today, Mr. Sinclair? I know he's going to ring again any minute, and I don't think I can stall him any longer."

Sinclair heaved a deep sigh. "All right, Sue, when he rings, tell him I'm back and fix a time for later this afternoon."

She relaxed, obviously relieved by the shift of responsibility.

"Thanks, Mr. Sinclair." She stood up. "I'll go and ring him first if you don't mind; it'll look better than waiting for him."

When she had gone, Sinclair sat and thought about it. It was just like that bloody major to browbeat Sinclair's staff; he still thought he was in charge of the troops.

Carnel Cosmetics had its offices in South Audley Street, and Sinclair arrived in its reception room at 3:30 P.M. promptly. They didn't keep him waiting long.

There were six of them ranged around the oval boardroom table. Major Carter sat at the head, and a few feet behind him was his secretary with a supply of newly sharpened pencils clasped against an open shorthand notebook. It made Sinclair think of the New York meeting; the comparison between the deliberate casualness there and the stern formality waiting to pounce in London almost made him smile. At one meeting they were prepared to offer a valuable contract; at the other they could hardly wait to spout their grievances. He strode past the seated board members and went straight up to the major. He gave him the confident smile and outstretched open hand.

"How good to see you, Major." He turned to the rest of the room and beamed. "And you, too, gentlemen; I've really been looking forward to meeting you all again."

"Yes. Well, take your place, Mr. Sinclair, and we'll get on with it."

This was Sinclair's cue to go to the opposite end of the table and sit facing the major, but he had planned that move ahead. He wasn't going to place himself in a "him-and-us" situation. Instead, he picked one of the vacant chairs next to a board member and became a part of the group. He launched the counteroffensive before the attack had time to get off the ground.

"Naturally I know why you called this meeting, and I'm very pleased you did, but before we get down to the main item on the agenda, may I just report on progress to date? Good.

"The launch and subsequent activity on the Hometan project has, I'm happy to say, produced an unprecedented volume of editorial coverage in all media, and remember, gentlemen, this is free editorial space obtained through our expertise. As you all know, it is estimated in PR circles that an editorial mention by a magazine has three times the value of the cost of the space in paid-advertising terms. This means in your case that Hometan received coverage that would have cost you half a million pounds to buy—except, of course, that you couldn't have bought that type of coverage, whatever you were willing to pay." He paused for breath, and Carter seized his chance.

"We are well aware of the Hometan results, Sinclair. That's not what we wanted to discuss."

"I know, Major. You want to talk about the American deal, and that's why I arranged to come straight here immediately after my return from New York."

As a pack they sat against the hard upright chairs and waited.

"Jackson is a client of ours; Naturalé is not. However, that company booked the services of Jackson at an extraordinary fee for a series of color advertising pictures. They were so impressed with the results that they offered her an extremely attractive on-the-spot deal, which she accepted. I was consulted about the publicity of the deal only; the contract was negotiated not with me but with my client. In fact, I advised Jackson against signing until we had had a chance to talk it over with you, but she quite rightly said that she was not in any way obligated to Carnel. We have a similar situation here, gentlemen. I have no influence over the various deals you negotiate—I'm only briefed on the results, and my advice is sought on the best means of promoting them. In any event, I take the view that the contract between Jackson and Naturalé will in no way affect the very successful working relationship we have with your company."

It was Sinclair's turn to sit back. He felt very pleased with himself. He had delivered that bunch of lies rather convincingly.

The room was silent, except for the sound the secretary's pencil made as she checked her shorthand outlines. The major avoided Sinclair's eyes as he looked around the table at the board members. His thin army face carried the kind of expression you would expect to see on the features of a commanding officer who had just pulled off a tactical coup against an enemy he despised in spite of the pessimistic predictions of his general staff.

"Sinclair, I'm afraid we do not give much credence to your oversimplified, though ingenious, explanation. Neither do we accept your conclusions."

Sinclair reacted. "Now, just a minute, Major—"

The major raised his hand. "Please. You will only give us further embarrassment." The room went still again, and he continued. "You may remember that at your meeting in the offices of Smith, Prado and Collins there was present a gentleman by the name of William B. Trustgrove."

Jesus, thought Sinclair, how the hell did they know that one? And he had hardly noticed the man.

"Well, Sinclair, Mr. Trustgrove happens to be a valuable acquaintance of mine, and I took the liberty of telephoning him after we had read about the contract in the London newspapers. Your office may have told you I did try very hard to contact you in the first instance."

Sinclair could almost feel himself turn white.

"Mr. Trustgrove was good enough to give us sufficient data for our needs, without, I might add, disclosing any information that would prejudice his company's position. Therefore I'm sure you understand, in view of what you have just told us, that our joint and unanimous decision is inevitable."

Sinclair sat up; he was damned if he would let them see he was sick to his stomach.

"As chairman of the board I am instructed to say on behalf of my colleagues that we are grateful to you and your company for the valuable services you have rendered in the past. However, we have decided to cease accepting your advice forthwith. In lieu of notice—for which may I say I personally do not feel we are liable —we have authorized as a token of good faith on our part the payment of one thousand, eight hundred and seventy-five pounds being your fee in advance for one quarter."

He passed the signed check across the table to Sinclair, who automatically took it and checked the amount and signatures. The major turned his head in the direction of the secretary. "Let it be recorded that by his acceptance of our check Mr. Sinclair demonstrates his agreement to the terms stated."

He looked at Sinclair, and the other board members followed

suit. They found it difficult to hold back their feelings of disgust.

The major stood. "Good afternoon, Mr. Sinclair."

Sinclair wanted to tell them to go stuff themselves. He almost had to prize himself loose from the chair, and as he got to his feet, he forced himself to match Carter's stare. "Good afternoon, Major, gentlemen. What a pity our association had to end on such a petty note."

The walk to the door seemed forever, and he could sense the force of their combined enmity in the center of his shoulder blades.

God, shit and *damn* them, he thought. It wasn't the money he was so mad about; it was the ignominy of being caught out. They had let him go on in front of them, knowing that every word he uttered got him in it deeper and deeper. He should have bloody well checked on the New York scene.

He went straight to the study when he got back and rang Mary Steward.

"Hello, lover boy, how are you? London missed you, Dan. It wasn't the same without your smooth-tongued stories. But even three thousand miles away you can still pull it off, can't you?"

"Mary, it's good to hear the compliments, even if you don't mean them. I see from the message pad you rang twice. It must have been urgent."

"Well, it was then, but you know newspapers. That's yesterday's garbage now."

Sinclair remembered the time before.

"Mary, I could use some home cooking after all those pre-wrapped American menus. How about taking care of a lonely bachelor tonight?"

She laughed down the phone at him. "I'd be delighted to take care of you, Dan. Make it about eight thirty."

The following morning he was late coming down from the flat. It was as if he wanted to put off telling the girls about Carnel, but there was no point in drawing it out, so he called Freda and Sue into the study. While they sat down, he walked the floor; that way he didn't have to remain static. Bending the truth somehow became more spontaneous and, he hoped, more convincing when it was delivered on the move.

"Well, I've resigned from Carnel."

"Good Lord, I didn't think you'd take it that far," said Freda. Sue didn't say anything; she just sat waiting for the rest of the story.

"There comes a point when, if there are no lines of communication open, then it's useless to keep on trying. They couldn't seem to understand that not only would there have been no conflict of interests but our association with Naturalé through Jackson would strengthen me in the beauty field and so add to our value." He leaned over the back of his chair and looked down at them. "Financially, of course, it's of no consequence; we are more than compensating for the loss of their fee by what we are now earning from Jackson, and the prospects for the future are very rosy indeed."

"Kind of off with the old, on with the new," Sue murmured. Sinclair didn't appear to hear her.

"So, basically, it's that much less work and effort for more money. Not bad economics, eh? Right now, Sue, just clear out the files and as and when you get Carnel press inquiries, the story is that it was jointly agreed that Carnel, publicity-wise, should go through a period of consolidation before embarking on a new campaign. In a month's time nobody'll even remember we handled them, so there'll be no loss of prestige for us." The speech was over, and at the door Freda turned to remind him of the eleven o'clock appointment with Brownstone.

Sue Black hovered.

"Mr. Sinclair, do you think I could have a few words with you?"

"Yes, of course, Sue. What is it?"

She was embarrassed, and then with a surge of courage she lifted her head and said, "If you don't mind, I'd like to give in my notice."

Sinclair eased into the chair. "Sit down, Sue. Let's talk this over."

"I'd rather stand, if you don't mind, and really there's nothing to talk over. I've thought about it seriously and that's my decision. I'm sorry."

He pinched the bridge of his nose between forefinger and thumb and spoke without looking at her.

"Has this got anything to do with Carnel?"

"Well—er—yes it has in a way, I suppose, but to be perfectly honest I don't think I'm cut out for PR anymore. I'm going into publishing."

"Oh? And what's so great about publishing, Sue? Hasn't it got the nasty taint of the big bad commercial world?"

"It isn't that, Mr. Sinclair. If you really want to know . . . well, I used to think you were pretty marvelous at one time, and it's just that I don't anymore, I'm afraid."

She had said much more than she had meant to, and she felt like running away, except that she doubted if her legs would move.

"Charming! It's paid you a pretty damn good living; now all of a sudden there's a big ethics problem. What's the matter, Sue, can't you take it when the going gets a little rough?"

She was glad he was getting nasty; it made the whole rotten thing that much easier.

"You know very well it's been more than a little rough. I happen to believe in playing square, and I don't like getting caught between you and a damn good client without knowing what's going on behind my back. Oh, I'm sure it's all very clever and big business, but it's the sort of business I can do without."

He jumped to his feet, and the suddenness of the movement made her flinch. She thought for a second he was going to hit her.

"Listen to me, Sue. I've taught you virtually everything you know about public relations. When you walked into this office three years ago, you didn't know the difference between an editorial and an advertisement, and now you've got the gall to tell me you don't like the way I run the business. Remember, Jackson is a client, too, and a bloody sight more valuable than Carnel. Do you think I'm supposed to sit back and let one client dictate how I act for another? So I warp the facts a little—who the hell doesn't? Everybody operates to suit his own selfish needs. If you can't take it, OK, but don't come in here with a sob story about how you suddenly don't approve of something you've been part of."

She stood very white-faced and tight-lipped.

"I think maybe I'd better leave right away, don't you?"

She stopped at the door. "I've got two weeks' holiday money owing; you can keep that in lieu of notice." As a symbol of cool restraint she closed the door gently behind her.

"In lieu of bloody notice; if I hear that again I'll go sodding spare. They make me sick. What do they think this is, the Garden of bastard Eden?"

It never changed; he should know that by now. He'd handled her badly. He should have played the cool understanding executive and not let her get him so worked up. Then she would have left feeling guilty instead of mad. Now she had a justification for her decision to leave him.

The buzz of the intercom cut across his introspection.

"What is it, Freda?"

"Mr. Brownstone's here to see you, Mr. Sinclair."

He swore again and clicked the TV switch.

"God, he must be selling carbon paper."

He was holding his hat in one hand and a battered briefcase in the other. The suit did nothing for his short, fat figure, and as he waited, he shifted the hat to his other hand, adjusted the knot in his blue striped tie and smoothed the sides of the thinning brown hair.

Sinclair wondered why the hell he had agreed to see him. He didn't even know what the man wanted. Freda must be slipping.

He turned the camera off and told her to send him in. He didn't bother to stand up as Brownstone came into the room.

"Morning, Mr. Sinclair. Good of you to give me your valuable time."

"Brownstone, isn't it?"

"That's right, Mr. Sinclair. My card, if I may."

Sinclair took the white card and brushed away the thin piece of protective tissue that clung to it. "Harold Brownstone," it said. "Music Publisher, Denmark Street, London, W.1."

"Sit down, Mr. Brownstone. Let me warn you, I don't write songs."

"Yes, very comical, Mr. Sinclair. No. Well, you see, a client of mine, very talented boy, has written some lyrics I think might interest you."

"If it's a jingle, I'm still not interested. We don't make TV commercials either."

"I'd better explain, Mr. Sinclair."

"That would be a very good idea."

Brownstone took a sheet of paper from the case and carefully placed it on the table in front of Sinclair. He noticed the type was upside down and very quickly reversed it.

"Now, I believe you have a lady client who's become very successful—due, I'm sure, to your hard work—called Miss Jackson."

"Just Jackson, Mr. Brownstone."

"Yes, quite . . . well, my client and I feel that there might be
great potential in your having a popular song on the market written, as it were, in her honor."

Sinclair suddenly took notice. He picked up the paper and read
it. It was headed "Jackson's Song."

> Listen to me: When she was young,
> She'd lie and she'd dream of charms that weren't real,
> For there was no name, no voice, that she could find
> To give to the face that she saw when she dreamed.
>
> For she is Jackson, and now you know that she's here;
> Yes, Jackson came true there in her heart.
> I knew it would happen to her
> From the day that she learned how to dream.
>
> For that is how things happen;
> You make them come true if you just try with your heart,
> Yes, you do.
> You just keep on trying,
> Don't ever give up believing that you will
> Get what you want in the end.
>
> For she is Jackson, and now you know that she's real;
> Yes, Jackson came true there in her heart.
> She's come a long, long way and now she's here to stay:
> That's so, I say.

When Sinclair had finished, he looked over at the man. Maybe
he wasn't such a quaint idiot after all. He went back to the lyrics;
yes, he thought, they were quite good.

"What do you have in mind, Mr. Brownstone?"

"I take it you like the words, then, Mr. Sinclair?" He didn't
wait for an answer. "In that case I suggest we have some music
composed, a lovely soul melody I would say, and then we try to interest one of your top recording artistes. Someone of the status of
Tom Jones or Engelbert Humperdinck would be very nice."

Sinclair's mind was racing ahead to the charts. Supposing it made number one—fantastic, and why not? Brownstone was right: A good melody, top arrangement and a great singer—it could happen.

"Mr. Brownstone, I think you might have something. What kind of deal do we do?"

"Oh, very simple: split fifty-fifty expenses and royalties."

"What sort of expenses?"

"Well, the best way to go about getting this on the road—once the music has been done, of course—is to do a demo tape which I then take round to Tom's manager and see how we go. If he doesn't like it, then we try somewhere else."

"How much to produce the tape?"

"To do it properly—and you know better than I do about presentation being half the battle—say, three hundred."

"All right, Mr. Brownstone," said Sinclair. "We'll take a chance. Although naturally I don't expect to pay our half of the session costs until I've heard the results."

Brownstone gathered up the paper and locked it away in the case; then he stood up to go. "I'll send you a letter of agreement, Mr. Sinclair. Let's hope we got a winner for ourselves."

Sinclair saw him to the door. "You'll send me a copy of the lyrics, too, won't you? Mark them joint copyright Sinclair Enterprises, Ltd." They shook hands on it, and the little man with short, quick steps made his way to the lift.

Sinclair hardly noticed Sue Black clearing out her desk drawer as he went back to the study. "Freda, get me Jackson on the phone, will you? I think she's working over at *Vogue* studios."

The excitement had cleared his mind of the Carnel and Sue Black episodes; they were things of the past now, and he was swept up in the enthusiasm of the new idea.

"Jackson? What's it like back at the grindstone? . . . Listen, we're going into the pop business . . . No, really. I didn't want to tell you until the project had advanced; well, now it's on its way . . . I'm not joking. Look, I'll send the lyrics over tomorrow morning. Do you want to know what I'm calling it? Well, get this: 'Jackson's Song' . . . I thought you'd be pleased. By the way, I've hired someone just to take care of your bookings and the detail work. She starts next Monday, so maybe we can have lunch and you can meet her; her name's Janice Dearing."

* * *

Their table at the Terrazza was downstairs. Across the room through one of the white stucco archways Sinclair could see Dudley Moore and Peter Cook lunching with a gaggle of young TV tycoons. To their left Antony King Deacon of the *Times* was listening to a man from Twentieth Century-Fox, and in the far corner Leslie Kark was tasting the Bordeaux Blanc; apparently it met his critical standards, and the wine waiter was permitted to fill his companion's glass. Sinclair nudged Janice Dearing's arm.

"Over there, Janice . . . the distinguished guy with the gray hair and the American woman, see them? Well, there sit the two top model agents in the world; he's the head of Lucie Clayton, and she and her husband, Jerry, are the Eileen Ford Agency of New York."

"You rate them as competition," said Janice Dearing.

"No, of course not. We're not in the same business. Nevertheless, I bet they'd like to get their hands on Jackson."

Janice Dearing looked over to the stairs. "If I'm not mistaken, here comes our girl."

Even in the celebrity-filled restaurant the chatter died as attention was switched to the tall redhead weaving her way between the tables. Waiters suddenly appeared, and her chair was whisked back for her.

"Hello, Daniel. Sorry I'm late."

"Jackson, this is Janice Dearing."

"Hello, how are you? My, it's crowded, isn't it? You haven't been waiting too long, have you?" Then, to the waiter: "Oh, I'll have a vodka and tonic, please."

The restaurant went back to its business, but every few minutes a head would turn, and appreciative eyes that held in them the glint of semirecognition would dwell on the face and figure that were somehow so familiar.

"How did it go this morning, Jackson?"

"Routine; you know, there are only so many ways you can photograph a fur coat." She turned to Janice Dearing. "I was doing a session for *Harper's*."

"Yes, I know. I took the booking." She smiled.

"Of course, I haven't got used to having someone in Daniel's office who just handles my stuff. I mean . . . oh, you know what I mean."

Sinclair watched them. Through the lunch it was Jackson who

did most of the talking. Janice Dearing was an attentive listener, but he could see that while she sat taking in the disconnected phrases and half-finished sentences, her eyes were searching. She would study Jackson's lips as they framed the words, then it would be her hands, then back to the face again. It gave Sinclair an opportunity to do some studying himself.

It was difficult to guess Janice Dearing's age. She could be a chic, elegant forty or even forty-five; her skin was still very good, and she had the neat, cared-for look that had stamped its mark on a particular generation of women. Maybe it was to do with the war and serving in one of the women's forces. WRENS, even he remembered, had always looked so clean and well ordered. She wore red nail polish, and her hands were beginning to take on a clawlike form. Sinclair guessed that a rinse was keeping the gray hairs from showing through the Dorothy Gray styling.

"Just coffee, please. Daniel, you'll have something, won't you?" The tête-à-tête was over, and Sinclair came back into the conversation.

"No thanks, love. You're not the only one who has to watch the scales, you know. Jackson, there's a story coming up that I think Janice could work on with you. In fact, Janice, you could give me an opinion—"

Jackson interrupted him. "We're going to sound like a sister act: Jackson and Janice, the Tuneful Strippers." They laughed, but Sinclair picked up that Janice was having to force the response.

"More like mother and daughter, I think," she said.

"Oh, come on, don't give us that routine. I might take you up on it if you're not careful. Hasn't Daniel told you Mother kind of went out of my little ol' life early on? You see before you the product of a broken home. . . . OK, Daniel, I'll be serious."

"Anyway, I've been casting around the supplements with the idea of one of them doing a feature on a day in the life of Jackson—"

"We'll have to pick the right day and skip the nights—could be embarrassing otherwise. Sorry, Daniel. I'm in the wrong mood for this type of conversation. Do go on. Janice, you can listen for me."

Sinclair was close to blowing his cool, so he took Jackson at her word. She only half heard what was said. She played with her coffee and enjoyed being looked at by the waiters and the predominantly male lunchtime audience.

"The point is that virtually every features editor I've talked to is interested. Now, who do we go for? The *Sunday Times, Impulse,* the *Mirror* or the *Observer?*"

"I don't think there's much to choose between them exposure-wise, Dan. Don't you think it's a case of which one you can trust to do the kind of story you want?"

Sinclair warmed to her. He liked the way her mind worked; most other women would have waffled on about which social strata they wanted to reach, the top end of the *Sunday Times* or the mass circulation of the *Mirror.* But her first thought had been how to get the best for their own purposes.

"What I was rather hoping was that we might make two of them."

She smiled at him. "Very crafty. But what happens when they publish, each thinking it's got an exclusive? I mean, that's hardly the thing, is it?"

"Supposing you go along with Jackson on one story and I do the other. Then when they're in print, we can plead ignorance and inefficiency."

She sat back, and one arched eyebrow lifted. "You don't honestly think they'd believe you, do you?"

"No, of course not, but it'll do as a face-saver. It gives us a case to plead, and by the time the talking's over, who the hell will really care?"

"What are you two cooking up?"

"Dan's just dreamed up a little maneuver to get you two for the price of one, that's all. I'm beginning to understand why they call him the hottest thing in PR."

Jackson took his arm and nuzzled up to him. "Is that what it is, Daniel? The hottest thing in PR? No wonder Ruth was so dreamy-eyed."

He ignored her.

"I'll get the bill. Is she working this afternoon, Janice?"

Jackson pouted. "Oh, dear, now I've made him mad. Well, you'll have to put it all down to the lunchtime *apéritifs* at the studio. Actually, I think the bloody photographer was trying to get me pissed, then he would have pounced. . . ." She put her hand on Janice Dearing's arm. Sinclair saw the slight withdrawal spasm

—it wasn't apparent to Jackson—and wondered whether she was genuinely repulsed by the physical contact or whether it was because it was what she wanted but feared most?

"I'd taken a fancy to him anyway. He didn't have to use the liquor to get me going."

They stood up to go, and Janice Dearing whispered to her, woman-to-woman style, "I wouldn't be so quick to be so free, my dear. I've always found it much more enjoyable if one takes one's time."

Sinclair sat in the study and thought about Jackson and Janice. Jackson was right: It did sound like a sister act, but it wasn't exactly a sister relationship that bothered him. Jackson, for all her flip and newly found arrogance passing for sophistication, was still an inexperienced trier, whereas Janice was the real thing and she'd been around a lot longer. In her position, with that sort of background, she was the predatory female figure, whether it was a man or woman she was after. But maybe he was wrong. It shouldn't take long to find out.

He put in a call to Michael Smith. "Hello, Michael. Did you get my letter? . . . Good; well, what do you think?" While he listened to Smith's reply, he doodled black squares connected to each other by a double track of thin lines. "Yes, that's right, a separate company; basically, it must have Jackson's name on it. . . . Look, you're on a par imagewise, Michael. It can only do you good. . . . Of course it will, the Jackson Collection designed by Michael Smith—you saw how it went in New York, it's a natural. All you have to do is design, I'll do the rest, and for that you pick up five percent of the net profit plus the publicity. . . . That's good, Michael. . . . Right, I'll send a contract letter over by hand. . . . Great. . . . Yeah, I'll see you."

He put the phone down and called Freda.

"Freda, send Smith the contract I had drawn up. He's agreed to go ahead. We'll have the first designs ready for production within the month."

He leaned back and thought that was very good: A Jackson range of dresses would do a bomb. It would be a joint company, just Jackson and himself; he could pay Smith his 5 percent for the first season, and after that he wouldn't need him; he already had a couple of fashion-design students lined up to take over where Smith left off. It was the usual rag-trade operation, but at least he was going to pay the creative element something; most of the time they were just copied outright, line for line. There was no copyright on dress designs. All you had to do was alter the length of a seam and put one less or more button on the bodice and you were off. It was getting now so that original designers wouldn't let the press photograph their new collections until they had taken the first batch of orders. Most of the boys could take one look at a photograph in a glossy magazine and have the copy in the shops within a week.

He remembered there had been a real sharp cookie once who started a delivery service for wholesale houses and the fashion press. It had seemed a godsend to them. Usually they spent a fortune on taxis to rush dresses from the showroom to the studios for photography and then back again. The quicker they got the dress back, the fewer sales they lost while it was out. With each collection costing anything from five to fifteen thousand to put together, few houses could afford to make duplicates just for the press. So when Fashion Deliveries came on the scene, offering to run a shuttle service between the rag-trade district and Fleet Street on a cheap yearly subscription rate, they couldn't move for business.

That was until someone discovered that behind the delivery service was a very efficient organization that "borrowed" the designs for half an hour, time to take enough details, even down to copying the fabric, to turn out perfect replicas at half the cost and in a fraction of the time. He thought it must have been a great business while it lasted.

Sinclair made two more calls which decided which of the color supplements would be running the "Day in the Life of Jackson" story, exclusive, of course. He went over to the Conran architect's table. He would organize *Impulse* in spite of what he knew it would cost him with Marion Cummings; Janice could take the other supplement. He headed the first sheet of paper: "A Day in the Life of Jackson—Suggested working schedule and fact sheet, magazine A." The second sheet had the same heading, "magazine B." He put them side by side and started to write, and he was laughing to himself as he worked. The girls came in to say good-night, and it was very late by the time he put the neatly stapled sheafs of paper under the bar of Freda's typewriter.

Janice Dearing sat on the thick rug in front of the imitation-coal electric fire and took the papers from the Gucci document case. She had cooked herself an *omelette fines herbes* with a green salad and served herself a small glass of brandy. The Chelsea service flat was small and comfortable, and it gave the impression of good living. The very occasional real painting hung among the uncommon prints, and the ornaments and the mantel timepiece blended well with the furniture, which was Victorian and not reproduction. She had managed to make the boxlike rooms into a well-chosen, nondeliberate expensive home for one. It had what is now thought of as an untrendy description: taste.

She sipped the brandy and set the two piles of typed paper in front of her on the floor. She thought the headings looked very efficient but unnecessarily slick. As she read each sheet and compared it with its partner, her doubts about the idea grew. Sinclair had arranged an artificial day that concertina'd what would normally have been the cream of a week's work into twelve hours. That was legitimate; an actual hour-by-hour on a typical day would be boring.

It was the occasional differences between the two schedules, which when published could make both the color supplements look idiots, that troubled her. The minor discrepancies, like showing an age difference and saying on one that she lived in Knightsbridge and on the other in Chelsea, only illustrated the perversity of their originator and were relatively unimportant. It was the items that scheduled a photograph of Jackson leaving home driving a Mercedes for magazine A and an Alfa Romeo for magazine B that started to screw the features up. She knew why he had done it that way: It fed his ego and his peculiar introverted sense of humor. Later, when he was faced with the onslaught the magazines would deliver for the double cross, it would give him shreds of slim evidence that Sinclair Enterprises' right hand might not know what its left was doing, that it was all an honest foul-up. What bothered her even more was that all the inaccuracies were listed on her assignment; the material for the *Impulse* supplement had the facts. That more than anything made her decide something had to be done about it.

She finished the brandy and took a small, slim Dutch cigar from the onyx box on the table, which also held the telephone and her private address book. She moved her finger down the index of the book and found the number she wanted. She almost prayed there would be a reply; this was not the sort of call she could make from the office. The ringing tone had the sound that seemed to tell the caller there was no one at the other end to answer, and then it stopped.

"Hello?" The voice was sleepy.

"Hello, Helen, this is Janice. You weren't asleep already, were you?"

"Well, not actually asleep, if you know what I mean."

"I'm sorry, Helen. Shall I call again later?"

"Christ, no, that'd be even worse. Don't worry, Janice, it'll be good for him. He's been getting too damn sure of himself lately. What is it?"

"Give me your word this is strictly between the two of us. It's very important you understand that, Helen."

"My God, what's wrong? You pregnant or something?"

"No, hardly. It's about the feature on Jackson that Sinclair fixed with you."

"What about it? It's still on, isn't it? I mean, it's a great idea."

"He made an exclusive deal, didn't he?"

There was a pause at the other end.

"Don't tell me the bastard's crossed me up after all this time. Christ, we've run some pretty good editorials on his clients."

Janice Dearing took a long pull on the cigar and expelled all the smoke before she answered.

"He's done a duplicate deal with *Impulse*; only for you he's changed a few of the facts."

There was even a longer pause this time, and when the other woman came back on the phone, Janice Dearing had to hold the receiver away from her ear.

"That two-timing son of a PR bitch! My God, I'll get his guts. He'll never push another story in Fleet Street. Christ, I should have listened to Tessa Drake. She told me what a con he was, and I figured it was sour grapes."

"Calm down, Helen. You can't let it out; that's what I meant in the first place. If you blow up, he'll know where it came from."

"Then I'll just cancel, for God's sake. I'm not running a

dummy exclusive and ending up looking a bloody fool in front of the editor."

"Helen, if you cancel out, he'll just take it to one of the other Sundays, and I haven't got a friend like you in every newspaper office."

"Then what do we do?"

"Go through with it as if you knew nothing, but just don't publish. Let him think he's got it all set. *Impulse* will come out with the genuine feature and you—I've got it, you do a spread on Carnel. He's just lost the account; it'll drive him crazy to see them get the space instead of Jackson."

She could hear the roars of laughter at the other end.

"Janice, you're bloody marvelous. God, if I could only be there to see his face. But what about Jackson? Does she know anything about this?"

"No, it's all Sinclair, and what he doesn't seem to realize is that if it had come off, he'd have done her a damn sight more harm than good. I don't know how the hell he's got this far without fouling her up."

"He's lucky. And, let's face it, he's good, Janice. He could talk his way out of anything. I guess he's got power-happy; he thinks with her behind him he can pull what he likes. And who knows? Maybe he's right."

She stubbed out the cigar. "Not with me around he can't, not anymore. Well, thanks, Helen, and I'm sorry for the interruption."

"Interruption? That was no interruption; that was a tonic. Ring me any time, Janice, if it's as good as that."

The two telephones were put back on their cradles, and Janice Dearing decided she deserved another brandy. As she poured the heavy liquor into the glass, she wondered how close Jackson was to Sinclair and if she should tell her what he had tried to do. She knew it was too soon, that she'd have to wait until she could judge whether the girl was as crazy for publicity as Sinclair was to create it. Then she thought about herself and where loyalty began and ended. Sinclair was paying her a very good salary to take care of Jackson, and almost the first thing she had done was turn against him. On the other hand, where should loyalty ultimately lie? With Sinclair or with Jackson?

13

THE weeks were going slowly now for Sinclair, and he had time to think and plan. He reorganized the office around the space left by Sue Black, and because Smith was more or less out of commission designing the Jackson range, there was nothing that Ann, whom he'd elevated from second-secretary status, couldn't take care of. Mansfield's secretary had rung to tell him that the big man was out of the country taking his annual vacation, and Sinclair thought he could just detect the hint of a suggestion that maybe he should travel down to the City and check the office plumbing.

Instead, he read his copy of the *Diary*, which listed every worthwhile fashion event in town, and decided it might pay off if he picked up the press show of the day. It wasn't that he wanted so much to check on the opposition as to make use of their function as an excuse to meet and chat up the journalists who'd be there.

It was the same aging routine: mediocre champagne, bits and pieces of dried toast with canned caviar and taped music with a decibel range that killed any idea of chatter. The models half walked and half danced down the runway, and the fag producer read over a tired commentary that would have done just as well for bathing suits as for the fur coats the girls were showing. "And now Natalie, doesn't she look divine, wearing what every daring trendy will have on for next spring. . . ."

Sinclair couldn't take any more. He carried his empty glass over to the low table. "You haven't any Scotch, have you?" The waiter gave him the fawning smile and brought up a bottle of Black & White.

He'd picked a bad show: Half the people there must have been friends and relations of the designer; the rest were trade and provincial agency people. By the time he was on his second Scotch he was thinking about Ruth and Long Island. It was the drink and the music; the combination made him sentimental, and every time it happened he was back with her. He'd written her one letter and so far had no reply; maybe she was out of town, or maybe he hadn't said the right things; whichever way it was, it kept him wondering about her. Not about what she felt for him but about his own feelings. This was one time when he felt unsure. With anyone else it would have been easy, and she would have been tabulated New York pleasure, but the more he thought about it, the more he realized that for once it was different.

"What the hell are you doing here?"

He was jerked out of his reverie.

"Hello, Tessa. Don't tell me there's anything for the Drake column at this excuse for a fashion event."

"It does sometimes happen, you know, that we print the odd story that's not been dreamed up by the great Sinclair. Incidentally, I heard some good news about you the other day."

Sinclair went immediately on guard. "OK, sweetheart, let me have it."

"Sue Black told me Carnel had kicked you out."

"Tessa, you really shouldn't go around putting out that kind of garbage. We parted from Carnel on very amicable terms. You make it sound as if Sue Black's putting the needle in. How did you come to meet her? I thought she'd gone into publishing."

Tessa Drake was well known for her laugh. It came from her chest deep and rich and then moved up the scale. Sinclair looked around the darkened room, but only the barman was taking any notice. All he could do was stand and try to look condescendingly amused until she stopped.

"Didn't you know? She's gone to work for Carnel as their resident PR girl."

He stared through the contrived dimness to the spotlit stage, where the models were still showing off the furs, but he did not see them. His mind was racing, trying to find an answer; he instinctively knew how to handle the situation from that minute on, but it was what to tell Tessa Drake that was giving him problems.

She saved him the trouble.

"Don't get too worked up, Dan. The dark secret's safe. You should know by now I don't spread gossip around. It's just between you and me. I have a vested interest in your downfall, if you remember, and I can wait. You don't need any help from me; you'll destroy yourself."

He could look at her again, and he knew that in spite of what she'd said, he had to make an effort.

"Tessa, that was a long time ago. Don't tell me your feminine

vindictiveness hasn't worn thin yet. Vengeance is a kind of su-
preme egotism, you know, and it betrays you. It lets people know
where you're vulnerable; it's the product of an immaturity, which
is a pity, because in every other way you're so much a woman."

"Don't give me the Sinclair potted handy pocketbook philosophy, Dan. What happened between us was just a symptom. I've
watched you operate, and after a time there's a pattern to the way
you work. I'm not an idiot. Do you think I didn't know about
Mary Steward? All the signs were there, and the same goes for the
others. Every time I see a piece of your handiwork I can pick out
the Sinclair technique, but you're starting to crumble. You must
have really slipped up with Sue Black, and that's not like you. A
few more mistakes, and not even the glamor of Jackson'll get you
out of it. I'll just stick around and watch the process."

He put the empty glass on the bar table, shrugged the eighteen-
ounce hopsack jacket on his shoulders, checked the center button
fastening and adjusted the knot in his Marmalade Weaving Company tie. "Stick around, Tessa. If you can wait that long."

He thought maybe that in the circumstances it was a pretty
good exit line. Only she was right: He had mishandled the whole
Carnel departure. But it could be fixed.

He walked out into the brightness of the hotel lobby and went
past the fountains to the row of telephone booths. He hadn't forgotten the Carnel number, and when the switchboard operator
came on the line, he asked for the public relations department.

He recognized her voice. "Hello, public relations?"

He spoke slowly and with emphasis. "Public relations as
defined by the Institute of PR is the deliberate, planned and sustained effort to establish and maintain mutual understanding between an organization and its public. I think the planning of our
relations, Sue, lacks the degree of sustained effort and understanding necessary for our mutual benefit, don't you?"

She didn't reply immediately, but neither did she put the
phone down.

"I was expecting you to call, Mr. Sinclair. I was offered the job
here after I left you. There was nothing premeditated about it."

"Sue, I'm not worried about that—in fact, it's rather a compli-
ment—but what does bother me is when I hear people like Tessa
Drake say you are going around telling Fleet Street I was chucked
out of Carnel. Now that won't do, Sue. What would be much

more diplomatic would be to say that we thought the time had come for Carnel to have an internal PR setup, and who better to run it than the executive from the firm who had done such a splendid job? That way we all come out with a nice, neat, clean image. Don't you agree that would be better for both of us, Sue?"

"It would be better for you, Mr. Sinclair, but it's not the truth."

The idealism came over the phone in waves. He could tell she wasn't going to go along with him, at least, not on that tack.

He tried to keep his voice under control, but the tough edge came through. "You've got a bad memory, kid. You seem to have forgotten that little routine document you signed when I took you on. There's a paragraph in there somewhere that says that if you ever left, then you couldn't work for any of the company's clients for a period of six months from the date of termination. Now I could make that look very sneaky; company loses account because client does a deal with the PR assistant and entices her away. As it happens, I've got a good mind to have an injunction served on you and Carnel, and I don't think, as an ex-adviser, that that would be the greatest way of starting your new association. The press loves a scandal; you should know that."

It came as no surprise to her that Sinclair had found something out of the past; her defiance had been more of a gesture than anything.

"I think I understand, Mr. Sinclair, and as I have my employer's reputation to consider as well as my own, there seems little point in taking the gamble that just as much dirt would rub off on you as on us, if you did have the gall to get legal."

"That's very sensible, Sue."

"Sensibility's got nothing to do with it. If there's nothing else you want, I'm sure you'll excuse me." The phone went dead.

He left the hotel feeling relieved. It had been worthwhile picking up the press show after all.

Sinclair reckoned it was report time again. He hadn't submitted one to Stokes since they had arrived back from the States, nor had any mention been made about the dress company or the song, all of which seemed to be progressing according to schedule.

There was nothing like a good report to keep the client happy. A public relations report is an amazing document; the trick is to submit one just as you sense the client is getting restless and wondering what the hell you are doing for your money. This didn't apply with Jackson—there was so much activity going on that it almost became a bore condensing it down—but with other clients the preparation could cause near panic, leading to frantic telephone calls and lunches that could be written up: "Results of a recent extensive and in-depth survey with the national press have lead us to the conclusion that. . . ." And so it would go on, blinding with inept and hastily contrived science.

But even with Jackson, the effort of putting results and projections on paper forced him to make a few calls, as well as hold a short conference with Janice Dearing, so that he could tie up the loose ends. He drafted the heading and then, in concise phrases, made the New York trip sound as if he'd worked his arse off being brilliant against fantastic odds. The formation of a Liechtenstein company to handle the American income would please the business mind of Stokes—no need, of course, to mention his own deal on the side.

It took him four days to work up to the finished draft. He had Freda type up an original plus one; he saw no point in giving away too many tricks of the trade to Jackson or Janice Dearing, and they might not fully endorse the way he had twisted some of the events to his own advantage. He skimmed the first half, but then even he was impressed with what followed:

Future Planning and Action
  1. We have now heard the results of the work of four leading composers in relation to the lyrics of the proposed popular record, *Jackson's Song* (lyric sheet attached). Our selection, based on the expert advice of personal contacts with E.M.I., Pye and Reprise Records, has been made, and a fully orchestrated demo acetate will now be produced.

It was always a good ploy to use the vernacular of the trade without explanation; it implied a knowledge and understanding few clients could muster. Brownstone had had to fill Sinclair in on the terms in the first place, of course: a demo acetate, he had explained, was a demonstration record, a rough pressing from the heavily spliced and doctored tape made at the recording session. A masterpiece of electronic ingenuity. As for the "personal contact" with the record companies, this was Sinclair's inspired imagination based on the opinion of the cutting-room lads at the studio. Not to be taken lightly, though: Their views were probably of at least equal value to those of the high-ranking executives with whom every pop manager in the business claimed to be on intimate terms.

On completion of the demo our associates will confirm arrangements with the managers of the foremost male singers and will ultimately conclude a contract for the commercial production and subsequent exploitation of the finished record. To our knowledge this will be the first occasion where the music industry has, as an independent endeavor, contributed to the promotion of a personality.

2. The formation of a separate limited company has now been completed for the design, manufacture and wholesale selling of a range of Jackson dresses. Premises in Margaret Street, London, W.1 (the heart of the garment-manufacturing industry), have been acquired, and the necessary staff hired. The actual making up of the dresses will be contracted out to small units of makers-up (common practice in the industry). The name of the company and the style of the business will be known as Jackson's Thing (Ltd.). In compliance with the contract between ourselves, Sinclair Enterprises, Ltd., will hold 25 percent of the equity in the new company, the balance being held on behalf of your daughter by her appointed solicitors. The first collection of designs has been produced by Michael Smith, without question one of Britain's leading designers, and certain alterations to the originals have been made by Jackson in order fully to justify the claim that the collection bears the stamp of her personality and talent. Mr. Smith will be paid 5 percent royalty on the wholesale price of all garments in which his talents have been utilized. As far as the company is concerned Mr. Smith's contribution will be treated on an anonymous basis, and all credit will accrue to Jackson.

Sinclair sensed only a slight pang of conscience as he read the sentence; he would have to prepare a convincing argument for Smith when the editorial press reviews of the collection started to appear and there was no mention of the designer's name.

A unique background method of assessing our market and promotional campaign has been used which in itself will generate a considerable volume of press coverage. Our understanding of the purpose of a dress design is that it should impart to the wearer a look which constitutes an improvement in her visual attractiveness. The designs which go farthest toward fulfilling this function have therefore the highest sales potential. What must however be taken into consideration is the age group and mental attitudes of our potential market, bearing in mind the one constant factor throughout all female age brackets and strata: that all purchases made by the female are emotionally motivated, triggered in Freudian terms, by the id as censored by an environmentally conditioned superego. In order to produce the perfect design/promotional concept, all available research data material was collated and fed into a computer programmed to produce the answers to our unique questionnaire. For your guidance, data examples were as follows: sexual awareness, varying sociological attitudes, working and recreational habits, sleep and dream patterns, shifting emphasis of female ascendancy over the male, dormant and active maternal instincts, and so forth. The findings of the computer were phenomenal and in précis form consist as under:

A. *The majority of women (within the limitations imposed by our motivational study) wish to have their nude bodies openly admired at all times, by both sexes.*

B. *Such unconscious feelings arouse guilt.*

C. *The purpose of clothes therefore becomes immediately apparent, to act as a sexual signaling barrier between the body and the inviting inquiring eye, thus satisfying the subconscious censor.*

D. *However, to meet the needs of the original impulses the clothes must be such as to titillate attention to the point where the viewer has a compulsion to remove the coverings himself, forcibly if necessary, thus satisfying both hidden urges.*

Note: The current youth as a collective unconscious (Jung) has unwittingly almost reached this conclusion. Their mode of dress screams for attention, the miniskirt giving greater exposure but the modest protective pantie tight satisfying their censor's needs.

Sinclair was loving every one of his rhetorical pseudopsychological words and particularly the heavy argument that all women, if they only had the nerve, were potential strippers. He wondered what effect typing the report had had on Freda; with luck she'd throw her censors to the winds and walk in starkers. He brought his mind back to the main purpose, impressing Stokes with his stupendous technical expertise, and read on.

Our designs therefore will comply with the computer's findings, and the promotion imply the satisfaction of the urges indicated. You will understand at this juncture why the particular company title was chosen: The clothes come under the general heading of sexual playclothes (Freudian innuendo), meaning those that are worn at home, at parties in the evening, in other words in circumstances conducive to sexual deployment and consummation. The garments will employ Velcro throughout. This material has the added psychological attraction of producing a tearing sound when it is pulled apart. The fabrics used will all be of the shiny, clinging silk type, the fashion variations from season to season being permutations in color and pattern design only. The computer's findings have therefore produced for us the perfect merchandising concept. A single idea with a basic, simple story line aimed at a properly researched and known compact section of the community. There will be no diffusion in the promotion. We will be constantly pushing the same theme. Think of the world's marketing and publicity successes, and you will find they all have this in common.

He thought it was bloody marvelous; the hours he had spent boning up on psychological terms and studying the motivational research boys' articles had been worth every minute. He had wrapped up what was a pretty ordinary, if sexy, idea in the word coatings that the professionals of the advertising and PR worlds reveled in. For some obscure reason they seemed incapable of putting their recommendations on paper in plain language. It was as if they were ashamed of the obviousness and simplicity of their conclusions.

Attached to the report was a whole wedge of press clippings, including the American coverage. He was of two minds on whether to list the proposed color supplement features on Jackson and decided against; he could squeeze more mileage out of the published results than any advance notification. He signed the report with a flourish and wondered if it would induce a greater response than Stokes' perfunctory acknowledgment note that confirmed receipt and expressed satisfaction at the progress being made.

Ruth Emery's letter arrived with the afternoon post. It was postmarked Philadelphia, and he didn't realize who it was from until he had opened the envelope. It had been typed on the air-mail paper that the Bellevue Stratford Hotel provided for its guests.

DEAR DAN,

I've been traveling again, and only just picked up your letter from the New York apartment en route to this fair city from Cape Kennedy. The astronauts' wives and families are obligatory copy, as you must know. Do you remember the W. C. Fields quote? "I went to Philadelphia once; it was closed." It happened to me. I arrived here on Sunday and got taken off to Bookbinder's on Walnut Street—doesn't that sound marvelous?—for one of their famous meals. Drawback: Philly is dry Sundays. Your letter was very spruce and full of marvelous doings. I deduce from the typing errors that, like mine, you did it yourself. There's always an odd, somehow impersonal feeling about getting typed letters from people one feels close to. It's as if you think they haven't really put all of themselves on paper. There are exceptions, of course.

There is an old friend in New York, an ex-poker-playing buddy of my father's, who retired from the magazine business some years ago but has got restless again and decided there's space for a new publication for men. *Not* the girlie-girlie stuff either, Sinclair. It'll be a sort of international traveling man's companion: business news, good writers and clean layout, something like the *New Yorker,* only for the American in Tokyo and all points west. He needs a managing editor.

You wouldn't know anyone, I suppose? He'd have to be sophisticated, well traveled, and know all the curves; nationality isn't important.

The money would be great, plus status. Currently there's no rush, so the guy could take time to make up his mind. I'll probably end up doing the odd piece for the mag myself.

It was good to read what you thought of New York; I've reread it a couple of times. How long do you think memories stay true? Do we push the routine and not-so-good away and try to improve on what was pleasant, or is it like the psychologists say—all of it's there and always ready to be recalled? A few years ago I would have played the game, but not anymore; you waste time that way, and I'm not with you on the not letting yourself be too well known idea. So I'll take my chances. What I should have done was invent a smooth new man here who was wining and dining yours truly, in the hope that you would have taken the bait and hopped a fast jet. But anyway that ploy was always a gamble and—who knows?—might only prove how resistible one was. So, so I do miss you, Dan, and I wish either you were here or I could be over there. I'm working hard, and in the short times that are free to think then you always come back again. What steams the hell out of me is that I think there's always a time for people, and if they let it go, they lose what they could have made together. Some people need closeness to grow, and if it's not there, then other things take them away. I think you're one of these, Dan; if you were here, we'd grow together, but you're not, so I worry. There hasn't been enough of us to tip the balance my way. What you were before we met is stronger again, and anything I put in a letter will seem mawkish. Where will you be when you read the words that were written maybe three, four days before? You know when lovers get each other's letters, some save them, and they wait until they are where it's right for them to read. It becomes a ritual; some girls have the letter burning in their purses all day because it has to be opened at home in the warm where they are undisturbed. But sometimes you see others in the early-morning bus or subway; for them they are alone and maybe that's their special routine too. I saw a girl weep once as she read the letter, and this made me want to share it with her and to know why.

Dan, it's very late; when I write at this hour, I overdo the soft stuff. I'll be back in New York by the time this gets to you. Will you think about the new magazine thing? You see how far we'll go to entice, don't you?

Stay well.

There is a poem, most of which I've forgotten, by Ella Wheeler Wilcox, I think; anyway, when I say it to myself, it seems a kind of justification.

> All you bestow on causes or on men,
>   Of love or hate, of malice or devotion,
> Somehow, sometime, shall be returned again—
>   There is no wasted toil, no lost emotion.

She'd signed the letter "love, Ruth." He folded it and put it in his inside jacket pocket. She had made it very plain, he thought, and it was a chance if he wanted to take it. For a little while he sat and thought about it and what it could mean to him. Maybe he could have it both ways: keep the office running in London with Janice Dearing watching over Jackson and him in New York handling the U.S. end. He could make the odd trip to London to keep control. Why not? Anyway, he was almost out of PR proper and into personal management. Mansfield wasn't paying such a big fee, and he was just about reconciled to having to give up Michael Smith, particularly after the new dress business got going.

And then of course there was Ruth. It seemed to be moving toward decision time. If he did decide to change, he knew it would mean marriage, and that was a state of affairs not scheduled in the Sinclair program. He was conditioned to categorizing people, including himself, and his own self-projected image wasn't reconciled to a shift in attitude and way of living that included a legal association which had as its base a self-indulged emotional tie. He was used to success, and the market research statistics on marriage produced poor odds.

For once Sinclair procrastinated and let the days pass without starting a return letter to Ruth. He saw little of Jackson, except for the two days he spent with her on the story for *Impulse*. It had done him good not to be so close to her, and he noticed how professional she had become. There was no need for the photographer to tell her what to do. She automatically took up the best poses in the best light, and the situation was established almost immediately; it was a Jackson sitting. He was strictly the man who pressed the shutter release. She was cool and confident, and this reflected in her face and her body and the way it moved. She was like a ballet dancer who had spent years in training and was now so controlled and so perfect that it made everything she did seem effortless and simple. Sinclair could sense her impatience if there were mistakes or long waits between setups; she liked working very fast, and when the camera was ready for her, she gave herself to it.

It was the camera and her, and the magic that went on in the space between the two of them. The ironical thing, of course, was that she could never take the camera completely to herself; there always had to be the separation that produced the sharp focus.

Janice Dearing had come on Sinclair's session, too, even though she had completed her own stint with the other color supplement. Sinclair thought she was almost too perfect; she organized, she was efficient, she took the bore of detail away from him, and Jackson obviously thought she was marvelous. It should have bothered him that Jackson would now look across at Janice when the shots were done for a sign of approval, like a child who favors only one of her parents; it didn't, though. If he had cared for her as something more than a lucrative property, he might have felt the pangs of jealousy that insecurity fosters, but he found that he was pleased and there was no sense of her slipping away from him.

As Jackson leaned against the side of the concrete upright on the building site doubling as a supposedly chic location for the make-believe fashion pictures and waited for the photographer to get his readings right, her eyes went from Sinclair to Janice Dearing and back again. For the first time she thought he looked strained; she had grown so used to visualizing him as vital that the slightest deviation became magnified. She remembered then that she meant to ask for a copy of the report he had sent her father.

It was always the same when he phoned her. "How are you, love? Just thought I'd give you a ring before you went out for the evening." That was a subtle way of saying that he wasn't checking on her and presumed she would be enjoying herself. To make it even easier he always rang at the same time on the same day—Friday evening at seven—and she made a point of being home, unless she was abroad on location, and then he would get a postcard that showed a local piece of architecture or a monument to a saint or a soldier or even a politician. "Sinclair sent me another report. Well, once you get past all the high-powered flannel, it looks very good." He was surprised she hadn't read it, and she brushed the question away and said she didn't really care about that side of things. But then she found she did care, and when Janice told her Sinclair hadn't sent her a copy either, she cared even more.

Janice had checked Jackson's makeup and hair and was satisfied. There was a soft breeze, and it had moved the long soft waves to one side of her face. Janice watched her, and as her hand brushed the hair away, her reflexes twitched, as when you are a passenger in a car and your foot moves to the brake but there is only the flat, bare floor, and the driver smiles. The photographer had caught the movement and had trapped its image on the film.

Janice thought she was exquisite and wondered if Jackson realized how beautiful she had become. Success breeds a glamor and an assurance in some people that at its best is without arrogance, almost as if they can afford to be careless. She had come to watch because the *Impulse* session was the real one, and it was important to her that Jackson was right for it.

In her own mind she had taken over from Sinclair now, although he was there, in the background, planning. She felt he was working as much for himself as for Jackson, or even more. Jackson was a property he was using and exploiting, and if it became necessary to him, he would sacrifice her for his own benefit.

Janice found herself caring for the girl, worrying about her, thinking ahead for her. She was almost at the top now, and because of Sinclair, the time it had taken had been very short. She mistrusted the speed of ascent because it hadn't given time for any consolidation. Sinclair had made it seem too easy; she was of the old school that placed high value on endeavor and overcoming obstacles; to achieve without effort was alien to her. This gave her two objects: to protect Jackson from the worst of Sinclair, and to build a foundation that would make up for the flimsy base he had constructed in his dash for success.

Two weeks before the scheduled press presentation of the Jackson dress collection, Sol Hifter came into their lives.

There is a strain of Homo sapiens which, in its immediately recognizable form, is fast on the road to extinction. The name given to this variety of species is film producer. Mr. Hifter, however, could never be confused with that group; in fact, if you were not primed, you would probably classify him as young professional. Sol Hifter was, of course, a film producer of the new school.

He arrived at Sinclair's office unannounced but not unknown; Mr. Hifter's reputation for producing motion pictures of money-making merit preceded him wherever he traveled, and he traveled extensively.

He lounged opposite Sinclair on the black leather sofa and declined the offered drink. "I seldom touch liquor, Mr. Sinclair."

The manner of delivery was such as to make Sinclair feel a traitor to the cause for permitting himself the now obviously abhorrent habit of allowing alcohol to pass his lips.

"Mr. Sinclair, I am in the process of making one of the most beautiful motion-picture experiences of our time."

Sinclair was about to respond, but Mr. Hifter was not experienced in the routines of normal conversation. He delivered statements or inquiries and expected acceptance to the former and explicit replies to the latter.

He continued. "Acknowledged fact. I am about to move location from Rome to Cannes and St.-Tropez. Through an avoidable and stupid miscalculation on the part of the studio's legal department I am without the services of an exceptionally talented British actress."

Sinclair felt the excitement pick at his stomach muscles.

"Jackson will make an adequate substitute. I need her for a month's work, starting in six days. We will pay you one thousand pounds a week for her services, plus the usual expenses. I have the contract here. If satisfactory, please sign where indicated."

There was no alternative. Sinclair took up the paper and started to read its legal terminology. It appeared to confirm Hifter's offer. He knew he should turn it over to his solicitor to check —the print was all small—but he also knew Hifter's image. The man had a reputation for paying out in overgenerous slices; every picture he made went way over budget, and more than one studio head had been known to retire for a cure until the first box-office receipts had been tabulated. Invariably they exceeded previous records, and thus Hifter could move on to even bigger and more expensive gambles.

"Do the terms have any provision for Jackson's personal advisory and publicity setup?"

"They do not. If you read paragraph thirty-five (b), you will see that it is categorically stated that no publicity of any kind is permitted without the prior authority of the producer, in writing. As a concession, however, you may provide one of your staff to accompany Jackson throughout her participation in the picture in order to gather material which may be used when filming has been completed; subject to my approval, naturally. I will sanction payment of traveling and living expenses only, to cover such a person."

"May I ask what part Jackson will play?"

Sinclair somehow felt it was an idiotic question; that the man had decided she should be cast at all was fantastic enough, and from the way the reply came, it sounded as if Hifter had the same thought in mind.

"The script calls for a beautiful incident in the story line of the main character. Jackson will fulfill that requisite. She will receive an 'introducing' screen credit."

Sinclair signed the contract.

It was only when Hifter had left that he realized he had been given no detailed matter. He needn't have worried or doubted Hifter's steamrolling efficiency. A lengthy schedule, together with two first-class open-return air tickets, arrived immediately after lunch. He called a meeting with Jackson and Janice that evening and gave them the story of his protracted negotiations with Sol Hifter and how they had culminated in the signing of a contract that would mark Jackson's emergence as a screen personality. It was the premeditated high point of his long-term planning, which would consolidate her international reputation as the girl of the era. He told them of the agreement he had made for Janice to accompany her on location and of the arrangements he had come to with Hifter that all publicity and press interviews would be held until maximum impact and coverage could be obtained. He would handle the launch of the dress collection himself, without Jackson, in such a way that they would benefit by her absence.

To an observer at both meetings, it would have been pathetic. That he should bother to fabricate his own part in what had come about naturally was verging on paranoia, but when you are a PR man, this is how it can take you. When what you have created succeeds and there is no longer any need to construct, when the product more than fulfills its promise and makes it own momentum, you start to fear that it will no longer need you in spite of the very fact that this was the situation you set out to achieve from the beginning. But you know from experience that clients very quickly become acclimatized to their press coverage. At first it is wonder, leading on to rightful acceptance, then critical analysis. Each article written about them, each photograph of their faces or products reproduced on the pages of magazines or newspapers, become a growing, demanding need, and when, because of what you have done for them, they are as familiar with the workings of the press and the people who write and photograph to fill the empty spaces as you are, then the seeds of doubt of your future necessity are sown.

And because you know the form, you recognize the symptoms, and the human response is an overjustification of your function.

In the end you say that talent burns itself out, that overexposure bores the public and that when what you made falls from favor without you in the background to cushion the shock, *then*, yes, then you can have your laughs.

Only will you be around that long?

The girls were ecstatic: a Sol Hifter movie. What a way in! Sinclair was a master, a genius; they loved him; it was the height of adulation. They left together, their enthusiasm and excitement spilling over with a tumble of words that competed with each other for expression.

Sinclair was alone, and the building at Hay Hill was silent. The double glazing at the windows insulated the rooms from the sound of cars and taxis and people. He turned out the office lights, locked the doors and went up the stairs to his flat above. It was very neat and clean and empty. He kept the level of the concealed lighting system low, made himself a drink, slid a record on to the hi-fi and sat looking out over Mayfair. Twenty-five percent of four weeks' work at a grand a week was a nice, simple, round figure piece of mathematics. Fifteen minutes with Sol Hifter, and he was £1,000 better off.

He wondered how the pay of a New York managing editor stacked up against that.

With Jackson out of the country he suddenly had to face up to his glib pronouncement that his organization of the dress presentation would paradoxically work to even greater effect without her. He was supposed to be the bright-ideas man, but even for him there were occasions when brillance did not appear to order.

He ran the mill of the ideas battery, looking for the spark that would ignite a chain of associations, back numbers of *Women's Wear Daily*, *Vogue*—the American version—and *Queen*. He rang photographers: Peter Rand, Terry Donovan and Duffy. He sat through avant-garde theater and underground cinema. He searched the windows of the King's Road boutiques. He visited the Way In, Miss Selfridge and Simpson's. Then he got it. The stream of impressions, gossip, suggestions, sights, sounds and even smells fused to a coherent stop.

He would put on the biggest load of freaked-out, turned-on, switched-in, psychedelic jazz the London fashion press had ever witnessed. By the time his show was over they would be battered into an ache of submission. It was like the old days, and he felt the adrenalin running again. He put a firm that made dummy models for window displays to work, and he combed the model hire agencies; then he booked a back-projection film unit and a stereophonic audio group. He tried to hire the Albert Hall, but what with wrestling bouts, pop shows and the Red Army Ensemble he didn't stand a chance; he settled for the Chelsea Town Hall. The final touch was a special-effects team who guaranteed to produce a foot-high layer of floor-clinging mist that gave out with the scent of Diorling.

Contrary to all the rules, he decided to throw the party in the evening. Fashion journalists resent having their free time eaten into by after-hours offers of largess and drinks. To try to persuade them to turn out in the evening is a risk. Unlike news reporters, fashion girls rarely live their jobs around the clock. Although it may seem to run counter to the glamorous image, many of them have husbands and children, who, come dusk, expect them over a hot stove rather than a hot dress designer. A party had to be something extra-special to keep them working after six o'clock. As insurance he had the invitations printed with the rider "and guest." At least that gave them the excuse to bring the boyfriend or husband with them.

The large room in the Chelsea Town Hall in the King's Road, which on Saturday nights was used for dancing, was three-quarters filled by rows of carefully spaced gilt chairs. A platform had been built in the center which gave the impression of a theater in the round—not so incongruous, because Sinclair had hired, along with all the other props real and inanimate, a director of dance, a man whose expertise ranged from seaside entertainment on the pier to television spectaculars. The lighting had been dramatically rigged, and only the stage was spotlit, leaving the rest of the room in dark shadows. There was a feeling of suspense in the atmosphere. As the journalists arrived, they were thrown by there being no one to receive them. There was no reception desk. No signing-in book, press release or handout pictures. They had to find their own way through the darkness and the rows of chairs. It was strange. They were so used to being greeted and handed a drink; there wasn't a waiter in sight. Some of them brought out their invitation cards to check that they were in the right place on the right day at the right time. The room was nearly full, and then over the restrained murmur of the intrigued mutterings of the audience came the sounds of a classical orchestra tuning up.

It was more like the prelude to a concert than a fashion show. Suddenly all the lights went out, and it was total blackness. The unseen orchestra was stilled; all attempt at conversation ceased. The uneasy silence was torn apart by a blaring cacophony of high-powered beat music. The stage was afire with flashing multicolored lights. Rising from a floor-hugging, thick mist were wax effigies of Jackson. It was almost too much for the audience to take; some of them clutched at their neighbors' arms. The men felt their muscles tense and their breathing quicken. From strategic positions three men leaped from their seats onto the platform and started to rip the clinging dresses from the static models. Then, on cue, twelve live, twisting, screaming replicas of Jackson raced through the carefully spaced corridors between the rows of chairs and joined the "happening" on stage. Each model wore a variation of a Jackson's Thing design. Other men, unrehearsed, leaped up to join the onstage party.

From his vantage point in the gallery above it all Sinclair sensed that maybe the results he had invented from the mythical computer were closer to a psychological truth than he had imagined.

The photographers were going wild. The elder, more sedate members of the audience were suitably uneasy; the younger element was impressed; everybody was positively affected. That in itself was an accomplishment. The majority of fashion shows put on for the press and the trade are variations on a boring and long-accepted theme: mildly attractive girls, sometimes accompanied by male models, parading down a center runway. They produce their false, flashing smiles, perform neat turns, then chassé back behind the scenes to change into the next uninspired dress or coat design. There was a period when dancing was the in thing. It didn't take long for that to become as much a worn-out, cliché-ridden routine as what had gone before.

Jackson's Thing was different and would stay a talked-about event until it had been overcopied. That was one trait that could be relied on in the rag trade. Anything with the slightest spark of newness or originality would be lifted.

It was Sinclair at his most flamboyant best. To have shown the fairly ordinary designs in the accepted way would have only produced a run-of-the-column fashion piece, in spite of Jackson's status. But the elaborate dressing up of the scene not only made news in itself but gathered an emotional fervor of enthusiasm for something that, on its own merits, would not have generated a quarter of the response.

There was a secondary achievement: The apparently uncontrollable nature of the show provided Sinclair with the perfect reason for the lack of credits to Michael Smith.

"It was surprising they even printed Jackson's name with that lot going on," he told him. "And why worry? The way the thing turned out, Michael, maybe it's just as well imagewise your name isn't too closely connected with it. After all, it's the loot that counts in this kind of operation; five percent of half a million dresses will turn over a very satisfactory piece of home cooking."

Smith looked convinced, and in fact, the one genuine part of Sinclair's con was that it probably would not have done Smith's image that much good. Real talent and gimmickry are a poor mixture, and seldom necessary. It didn't seem to him that it was the finest piece of PR image building for Jackson either. Sinclair had become so enthused with his own inventiveness and achievement that he overlooked one of his major dicta: "A means as a means, without a full appreciation of its effect on the end product, is shortsighted public relations policy."

14

SHE lay on the warm deck, glistening with suntan oil. The strap of her bikini top was unfastened so that there would be no lines of demarcation. The Mediterranean sun burns the flesh quickly. She was in the half-dream state that sunworshipers who live in less perfect climates long for. She could feel the heat beating in, and she seemed to take a long time to realize that she should at least turn over. *I'm just like a pig on a spit,* she thought. She let the bikini top fall and loved the freedom of not having herself enclosed, not having a hammock strung around her body. Then she had second thoughts: Perhaps it was too bold even for Cannes, and maybe one of the crew would suddenly appear, if they were not already watching. The physical business of putting her arms behind her back brought her out of the lethargy; she decided she should use the deck shower and then order a drink.

The individual high-speed streams of ice-cold water, something to do with their being routed via the ship's air-conditioning units, hit her head and splayed out to cool her skin. The muscles reacted, and she was immediately awake and sharp. She raised her arms to the water hose, and they took the force of the water.

The ship lay at anchor inside the yacht harbor—the most famous and glamorous and, for the technically minded, largest in the world. Across the beautiful Technicolor sea she could pick out the rows of colored umbrellas that sheltered the pampered tourists from the glare of the sun, and behind them the long curve of the Croisette and then the rococo magnificence of the Carlton Hôtel.

"I bet that feels great."

It was Janice; she was carrying a tray with a bottle of Campari, two tall glasses, an ice bucket and a soda siphon on it. There was also some sliced lemon and cut mint.

"Janice, you've got the most superb timing."

Jackson came out from under the shower and shook herself. They pulled up the deck furniture, and Janice made the drinks that never taste the same in London but only remind you of the sun.

Jackson raised her glass. "Sol Hifter." They touched glasses, and Janice Dearing looked very mock-solemn as she repeated the toast.

"Janice . . . I mean, just how could you imagine living any other way? This is it, the beauty of the Côte d'Azur, the sun, the sea, the wine, and all by courtesy of Mr. Hifter." She took a long swig to commemorate the announcement. They laughed together and lazed in the chairs, their legs stretched out in front of them bronzed and shiny. There is a perverse enjoyment that you get when you are in a place where everything is as you want it but you know it isn't costing you a sou. Even the rich—and particularly the new rich—get pleasure this way, and if you can do it for long enough, it can become a game that everyone plays, except one of course: the perpetual host, until another comes along to take his place.

They had both put on their sunglasses, and the dark lenses hid their eyes, so that they felt they could view each other without betraying the meanings of the questions and doubts and answers that went between them.

"How is it with Hifter?" The direct question from Janice Dearing seemed to open the way into what had been a closed area that had kept them apart. It was midafternoon, and except for a skeleton crew, they were alone on the yacht.

The unit was along the coast, in among the villas of the really rich at Cap d'Antibes, filming a section of the film that did not include Jackson. Hifter had not yet fixed on a title for his motion picture, but because it was necessary for the project to have a name, so that everyone working knew what they were working on, he had decided to call it the Film. When *Variety* and the British film-trade papers wrote about the production, that was what they used: "the Film." Hifter was very pleased with that, telling everyone that that was what the hell he was going to call it when it was finished. "It's generic. 'Have you seen the film?' 'What film?' 'Why, the Film, you stupid nut, what else?' " After the first month of shooting it was no longer a joke with the crew, and now they all accepted it and were very serious.

A slight breeze fanned across the water, but it was gentle and only took the bite out of the heat.

"I don't really know. I mean, I think he's pleased with what I'm doing in the film, but that's not what you meant, was it?"

"No, not really."

They had, without deliberately creating the situation before-hand, become confidantes. Because the time was stretching out then with the knowledge that there would be no interruptions, and because they had spent two weeks working closely together, it fused for them after they made the joke toast. Or maybe it was just that they now knew each other well enough to talk—not just to say things that people say, but to settle in and *talk*. She put the glass up against the bridge of her nose, and her eyes looked through it. Then she drew it down and clicked the rim against her teeth.

"I've learned to hold back, Janice; this one can make the running. So far I think, maybe, but I'm not sure. He could be like this with every new girl he has on a picture."

"But you don't think so, do you? You think there's something there?"

Jackson smiled. "Yes, of course I do, but I thought so once before, and I was very wrong, then."

"Was that with Sinclair?"

That made her laugh. "Yes, you're right—I suppose that was pretty obvious, wasn't it?"

"I think it was understandable," Janice said.

"Do you? Well this is a similar situation, you know. I mean, when I first met Sinclair, it was all the hero-worship bit. I was so green, and there he was aloof and so sure of everything. So I'm not green anymore, and Hifter's from the same mold; only this time there's no manipulation and changing. This time what I am is OK, and Hifter gives; have you noticed Sinclair doesn't ever give? He seems to live in a shell, and every now and then he comes out and fixes something, then goes back in again."

Janice Dearing took up the bottle of Campari and poured the cherry-colored liquid into their empty tumblers. She didn't bother to add any soda.

"How much do you know about what Sinclair has done for you and the way he's done it?"

"Well . . . not everything, of course, but a damn sight more than he thinks I know. He always thought of me as some kind of dumb puppet, that I'd learn the tricks and perform them without ever wondering what was going on behind the scenes."

She took some of the freshened drink, but it hardly inter-rupted the stream of words that she wanted to pour out.

"You have to understand that this is what I've always wanted. I wanted to be top dog; it wasn't the money, it was something inside. I don't think he's ever really understood that part of it; as far as he's concerned, I'm his product. The pupil should always be grateful to the teacher because the teacher helped make it possible, but without the will to learn, without the ability to take in and use, the pupil stays a pupil."

"What happens when the pupil graduates?" Janice asked.

Jackson paused and looked toward the beach and the people. Her voice was low, as if she didn't want the words to be heard.

"Then her time with the teacher is over, and perhaps there are new things to go for and other people to show her how."

Jackson had listened to herself, and now, like Janice, she stopped to think about what had been said. Then she turned, and if the dark sunglasses had not obscured her eyes, Janice Dearing would have seen what she could only sense: that Jackson wished it had not been necessary to say that about Sinclair but that, between them, it had to be said.

"I know what you mean," said Janice. "But surely he must understand that; he must realize that part of what he had to do is over, but it doesn't mean he's finished."

Jackson looked out to sea again. "The trouble is that I'm the one who's grown. He's just the same; he hasn't moved forward. It's like a marriage where the man suddenly makes it at last, but the woman drags. So the husband gets bored, because his wife can't contribute anymore."

"It's all very well to say that about a little housewife, Jackson, but Sinclair's in a bit of a different class. I just think he's trying too hard; he's overcompensating. That dress show, for instance; it was just too much."

Jackson jerked up in the chair. "Oh, Christ, I was livid about that! My God, and he's the image man! That's what I mean—he's pulling the same old strokes; he doesn't seem to realize I don't need that anymore. You know what Sol says; he says, 'Baby, you must cool it and let the rabble come calling.' He's so right. 'Jackson's Thing,' for Christ's sake; he won't get me inside one of those rotten dresses."

Janice Dearing knew then that she could tell her about the color-supplement trick; only it didn't seem as important any more. But Jackson was still on about the dresses.

"You know, he thinks he's so damn clever because there's no credit in any of those press clippings he sent out to us about Smith. Yeah, well, Michael phoned me after the show and said he was embarrassed to hell about it, and thank God there weren't any credits. Sinclair's had it with him, you know. That'll be the second one, won't it?"

Janice was a little startled.

"Yes, the British cosmetics company account went just after you got back from New York. I don't think it'll bother him much; he figures all he needs is you."

Jackson sighed. "Well, if he goes on like this, I wouldn't be so sure." She looked across at the other woman. "Janice, if that ever happened, what would you do? I mean, Sinclair employs you. I don't."

Janice stared down into her drink. "That's difficult to answer. You know what I feel about you. I suppose I'd wait for the first move."

Jackson stood up then, put her glass on the table, padded over to the rails of the yacht and leaned over the side. She knew what she wanted to say, but she wasn't sure how to phrase it or even whether she should come out with it. No, that wasn't really true; she had already decided about it, but like everyone, she must have a last minute of hesitation; it was an unconscious act for the other person, so that she would know you had really thought it over first; it prepared her for something important; she could feel it as if there were extrasensory perception at work. She turned from the rails and relaxed, let her arms rest along them with elbows bent and hands hanging loose.

"Janice . . . have you ever felt anything . . . lesbian?"

She had known that Jackson was going to say something like that, and she took the sunglasses off and blinked at the sudden brightness. She could see her own twin reflections as she looked directly at Jackson's hidden eyes.

"I've never had a lesbian relationship, but . . . at first I thought . . . it worried me. If you had given any sign or . . . well, you didn't, and I was glad about it." She looked away. "I think you can love someone without; I believe now in platonic love. Once you realize that it could be there but it's not necessary for it to become overt, then there is a calmness. Anyway, I've met Sam now, so everything's fine."

Jackson laughed; it was a gush, full of relief and understanding.

"I didn't know. You mean Sam the camera director. Oh, I think he's super. He's like Spencer Tracy."

They were relaxed together. It was like a mother and daughter, where the mother has watched herself and not allowed things to go slack and so does not look her age. The genuineness of their feelings could show because there was no longer any need to hold back in fear what they felt could be misunderstood; they were mates.

"It's nearly five o'clock. I'm going ashore; I promised Sam I'd buy him a new cap. He says he always has a new cap on every picture, but he's missed on this one, so I think it would be right if I got it for him."

"Get him one like Hemingway used to wear; then he can pretend he's as wise and tough as the old man was."

Janice went to change, and a little later Jackson heard the surge of the launch as the dark tanned Frenchman revved the engines. He looked very resplendent in white trousers and T-shirt and a white and navy skipper's cap. She thought that Sol did things all along the line. He had the crew parade every morning for inspection, and when he was on board, there was no question whose ship it was. The men loved him because he knew about boats and was no rich fake. She watched the launch and waved to it as it plowed toward the jetty. She thought maybe another drink, a weak one, would be all right.

She was very contented. The thing with Janice Dearing was just fine; she knew that at last there was someone close to her who was real and on whom she could rely. If she did ever split with Sinclair, she wouldn't be alone anymore.

That made her think about him again. If only she could have it out, make him see that she was grateful and that he could relax. She wanted him to stay a part of what she had; if things would only work, then it could all be perfect. There might be Hifter and then Janice and him: A great team; together they could do anything. But she didn't think he could do it that way. Sinclair was a loner and a hustler; to be part of anything and not to be in control wasn't his scene. He always had to be the big man, the unseen power, but now there was Hifter, and she felt that Sinclair would take it the wrong way.

Hifter was the coolest man she'd ever met. People knew exactly what he needed, and they bent over producing it. He got results, as Sinclair did, but unlike him, he didn't have to twist pitch; he would reckon that was wasted effort. The major difference between them was warmth. Sinclair was cold—she bet that even in bed he'd be working out the percentages. Hifter could give himself over; he could put aside the picture and the film business and become enthused about other things. There was a world outside what he had to do for himself; he recognized that other people existed as people and were not, as Sinclair saw them, there just to be used when they were needed. On the film he was in control without its being a great big deal. Occasionally if, with the director, it was not going right, then Hifter would move among them, bend his tall body and talk quietly, and then they would work again. He had their respect, and he had it without working at it; it was there because of what he was, and not because he tried.

She looked at the watch on the table. They were shooting through until dark that day. There was time for her to have a catnap, then she would change, and when Janice came back, they would go over together to the location and have wine and *fritto misto mare* with the men when they broke during scenes. Tomorrow Sinclair would arrive. She was not too happy about that; she had a feeling he would obtrude, that he would be an outsider and that, what was worse, he would act like one.

15

SINCLAIR boarded the Air France Caravelle Flight 950 at Heathrow Airport at ten twenty. Just six hundred and thirty-eight nautical miles later they were over the Mediterranean and on their approach run to the landing strip at Nice which stretched out with the water on one side and the airport terminal on the other.

As he stepped from the plane, the heat came off the tarmac and enveloped him. Unlike most of the other passengers, he had known what to expect, and the clothes that he wore were no longer as incongruous as they had appeared in London. He never understood it: People always seemed to travel in their Sunday best and arrived looking foreign, ill at ease and, purely from a practical view, wrongly dressed for their new environment. Conversely, on the return trip they clung to their tourist garb, and as they walked through the cold and usually rainswept glass corridors at London Airport, they again felt self-conscious. They did it wrong both ways.

Janice Dearing nearly passed him by. Conditioned to seeing him in his trendy town gear, she wasn't prepared for the St.-Tropez look.

"Are you sure you've come from London?" she said. "All that's missing is the Ambre Solaire smell and you'd pass for a resident!"

They went out to the open-topped car, and the driver took the bags. He looked disappointed. The film unit had nearly cleaned Avis out of drivers and hired cars, and he had grown used to transporting familiar faces as they flew in to make guest appearances in Hifter's extravaganza. Sinclair looked as if he might be somebody, but drivers of hired cars have a sixth sense about such things.

She knew Sinclear well enough to be aware that he rarely talked on a car journey, and so, like him, she enjoyed the breeze, during the times the car was able to move in the traffic, and the places, and the people. The twenty-mile stretch from Nice to Cannes is mostly flat and uninteresting, except around Cap d'Antibes, and Sinclair wished they were traveling the other way from Nice to Menton. He loved to drive the Middle Corniche, winding high along the mountains, linking the coastal places and the old hilltop villages of Eze, La Turbie and Roquebrune. The Middle Corniche is best of the three roads that link Nice to Menton, because you are near enough to the coast to pick up the detail.

Cannes, as usual in the season, was a madhouse packed with trippers, the new-rich, the pickups and the pretty boys who'd come to sell themselves to the old men with villas in the hills. He thought of the forty miles of coastline that had become the playground of the rich and those who follow them. The Riviera, once the preserve of the elite, was in the fleshy grip of a profiteers' boom, and each time he came, there would be a new monster block of flats eroding the hilly skyline. He enjoyed it best at the end of the season, when the play people had gone back to their towns and it all became calmer and more civilized.

They drew up outside the expanse of the Carlton Hôtel, which was the super palace of the Croisette. It had an ornate, dated style, a heavily jeweled guest list and hordes of flunkies. You could do everything at the Carlton. He often thought that some of the guests flew in, stayed within the lush bounds of its art gallery, terraces, private beach and beauty parlors for fourteen days and then flew out again. To them that was Cannes and their south of France vacation.

As he signed in and gave over his passport, he asked Janice for Jackson's suite number.

"Oh, we're not staying here, we're out in the harbor on Sol Hifter's yacht. He thought we might enjoy it more, but the crew and the directors are all here, so you're not alone."

He smiled at her. "Well, that sounds cozy. Let's go out on the terrace. I need a drink."

They sat, shaded from the heat of the sun, and played with their drinks.

"Tell me," he said. "How is it?"

The slight feeling of trepidation she usually felt when she answered his questions wasn't with her. She was almost uncaring about how he would react.

"Everything is fine. Jackson's loving every minute, and from what we've seen of the rough filming, the daily rushes, she's coming over beautifully. I think Hifter really thinks she's a find; he's been murmuring about exclusive contracts."

"We'll see about that." He was tight-lipped. "Exclusive film contracts are seldom on the side of the artist, you know. What about the publicity material?"

"I've been working with the unit publicist from the film company. She's a superefficient girl called Linda, Linda Sandford. Between us we've built up a great stockpile of color and black-and-white stills, and there's some marvelous story material written up. Once Mr. Hifter gives the go-ahead I'm sure the coverage'll be fantastic."

"I think I should look over all the stuff first, Janice. I don't want the usual film-publicity puff being put out. We've got a client's interest to watch out for, you know."

She understood that he had to make the effort, if only for himself, but she also knew that whatever he thought, the voice that counted was Hifter's.

"Well, I've worked out a bit of a schedule for you. This evening Mr. Hifter would like you to come out to the yacht for dinner. There'll be a launch at the quay at nine to pick you up. Then tomorrow morning we're on location, so you can either drive out with the director or, if that's too early, then come on later yourself. I'll send a car for you. Linda Sandford's expecting you, so she'll have all the material to look through, and you can watch Jackson work; she's got the tail end of a scene to shoot. Does that sound all right with you?"

"Janice, you're as efficient as ever. The only thing I'd like is some time alone with you and Jackson. There are details to discuss; a lot has been happening in London, you know."

She couldn't look at him when she answered. "Yes, well, in the afternoon Jackson's free. Would that do? You didn't say how long you intended to stay."

"No, that's fine. I'll probably stay over about three or four days, that's all. Then I'll have to get back."

She stood up and checked her watch. "Well, I'd better be going myself. We'll see you tonight, then, around nine?"

They went back to the desk together, and he got his key and then left her and walked to the lift. As she watched him go, she almost felt a little sorry for him. He seemed very much not a part of what was going on.

The dinner was served on deck, under awnings and by candle-light. It surprised Sinclair. Somehow he had thought of the meeting as a kind of confrontation; instead it was a very pleasant social occasion. Hifter was a different person from the one who had been so precise and authoritarian in his office a month ago. The man was charming, witty and, to Sinclair particularly, courteous and even attentive.

The dinner table was round. On Hifter's right was Jackson and on his left the picture's female lead. Next to Jackson was the director and on his other side Sinclair. Next to him was Sam Nolan, the director of photography; then came Janice Dearing and by her the man from the American film company whose money was backing the production. This completed the circle back to the female lead, who was considered not only a star but an actress of some accomplishment; the two seldom came together.

The conversation was light, and the subject, like a moth around the candles, flitted in and out of the urgent attraction of the film business and who was doing what, when and where. At the hub was Hifter, who seemed to guide and influence the flow of words that never became bitter but were often lifted by the thin bitch that they would call repartee. It was not until they were on brandy that out of the chattering came a direct question.

"Dan, how's your poker?" said Hifter.

Sinclair looked away from Jackson. He had been listening to her telling how the London fashion scene was evolving.

"Well, it used to be considered quite fair."

Hifter's eyes were eager, and he laughed toward the director. "How's that for British understatement, Zach?"

Zach Carson's long wrinkled face lengthened into a smile. "We will just have to see, won't we?"

"Are you two boys game?"

The man from the film company was very quick. "Sure thing, Sol."

Sam Nolan sighed. There were other things he would have preferred to do.

"Just a short game, Sol. I've got a heavy day tomorrow."

"That's fixed, then," said Hifter; and then, to the women: "Now, ladies, I don't like to break this up, so why don't you all enjoy the night air while we just adjourn to the card room."

The card room was paneled in mahogany and dominated by a green-baize-covered table at its center, above which hung a large lamp with a figured New Orleans shade that contained the circle of light within the boundaries of the table's circumference. There were five comfortable, but not too comfortable, chairs spaced at equal intervals around the table. At each end of the small room was another table; on one were a box of chips, neatly divided into color denominations, six packs of cards with seals on the coverings unbroken, and a large pad of notepaper. The notepaper was ruled vertically into five columns, and at the heads of these were written the initials of the players. The other table held an array of drinks and glasses.

"Before we take our places, Dan, I'll just explain the house rules. We all sign in for chips over here." Hifter went to the table, selected three stacks of chips and wrote their value in the column headed SH. He signed the entry. "We settle up after. Don't get the wrong idea—this is a small game. In your honor we'll play to British currency, with the whites as ten shillings, the blues a pound and the reds five, OK?"

They took turns at drawing chips and signing in. Only Zach Carson seemed in a hurry to stake his place; he sat with his back to the drinks table. When all of them were settled, Hifter made drinks for each. He took soda water for himself.

If there was an interest outside PR and fishing that came near to turning Sinclair on, it was poker. He was a devotee from way back. He hadn't missed the casual approach or his initials written in on the stake pad in advance of the probe about playing. It was a standard setup: The other men played regularly as a group. It would be an absolutely straight game, but there is always the undercurrent when a group lets in another player and the new man wonders if they are setting up to take him.

Hifter broke the seal on the first pack of cards, shuffled and dealt one, faceup, in front of each player. The jack turned its face in front of Sam Nolan, and he became the first dealer of the evening.

Sinclair played very conservatively. It was always that way with him. He took time to evaluate the betting patterns of the others in relation to the hands they held, and he watched them for physical signs that told when they were bluffing, excited or anxious.

Sam Nolan's heart wasn't really in the game, and so he could be discounted unless he suddenly got lucky. Zach Carson played as if he were directing a Mississippi gaming movie; when the cards he held were poor, his left eyebrow would rise as if he were trying to kid everyone he had all the aces. The film man from London was a sucker; he laid his money on anything just to be thought a big player. Hifter almost knew what he was doing, but like most poker players, he trusted luck and would go on betting and drawing cards where Sinclair would have folded because he played the law of averages. That made him dangerous.

The game was friendly, and for Sinclair uneventful. He was ahead on his stake money; Sam was predictably down a little; the film man was well down, Zach up and Hifter around even. After about ninety minutes there was a discreet knock, and Jackson came into the room.

"Excuse me, boys, I don't want to break things up, but we've all called it a day. The girls say good-night, and don't play late."

Sam addressed the table. "I guess that's a good idea, fellows. How about calling this the last round?"

They agreed to have one more deal each; Jackson was told she could stay and watch, provided she kept quiet. She went and stood behind Hifter's right shoulder, and he smiled up at her. At that point the game became a serious one.

Given the chance, most men will play to the gallery and particularly to a gallery from which they may expect admiration. Jackson provided the audience and an incentive other than money for the participants. All of them, except maybe Sam Nolan, wanted at least to show off their prowess. It took only the first deal to establish the main contenders.

A change in the attitude of two men can affect the atmosphere, and although there were no obviously crude physical manifestations, an observer like Jackson could easily imagine the two men alone in a deserted arena, arms outstretched and teeth bared for the fight. In fact, all that might have been noticed was that Hifter and Sinclair had changed their approach. Hifter studied each of the five facedown cards as they were dealt; then he collected them neatly in his left hand, continually fanning them as if that might change them. Sinclair sat close to the table, his elbows resting on its edge. He allowed his cards to gather on the green baize before picking them up, and he watched Hifter's face for the frown or twitch that might betray the value of what he was getting.

Sinclair had played and studied the game long enough to know that almost every player develops unconscious mannerisms which give him away. The motivating cause is excitement or insecurity. A man with a good hand will lean over it, maybe, and give a slight sniff as he bets; another will lean back and try to appear casual, just playing along to keep the boys happy. The really clever ones will assume a mannerism throughout the games that apparently signals a bluffing hand, waiting for the one real fistful of the evening when the stakes are high and the bluff becomes a double bluff.

In any game there are long periods of calm, even boring, play, with everyone waiting for the magic combination that produces the tension. Sinclair was dealing the last hand but one when his gambler's sixth sense told him the action was about to break. He watched the faces. They were intent, and his eye caught the split-second whitening of Jackson's knuckles as they tensed on Hifter's shoulder; her excitement was for him. He put what was left of the pack on the table in front of him and stared at the pattern on the backs of the five cards he had dealt himself.

Sam, to his left, checked; the film man also checked. Zach threw in one blue chip.

Hifter had said it was a small game, with chips from ten shillings to a fiver, but that was only relative to the way the players bet. Sinclair was with the poker ace of all time, Herbert O. Yardley: "The smaller the stakes, the wilder the game, the easier to win." His cards were still on the table where they had fallen, and he left them untouched until Hifter had matched Zach and thrown in one blue chip. They waited for him as he took up the cards, studied and then rearranged them in his hand. Almost without seeming to think, he threw in the chip, then another. "I'll just raise it a pound." Sam threw in his hand, the film man placed his two blues in the center and the rest added their chips to the growing pile. Sinclair picked up the depleted pack.

"Cards."

The film man threw in three. Sinclair collected them and dealt him three new ones from the top. Zach hesitated and looked around the table as if that would decide things for him.

"I'll take two."

It was Hifter's turn; he tried very hard not to look smug.

"I'll play these."

Sinclair took a good look at his hand for the first time and started to think hard. Some players will bet on anything once they sit down at a card table. Offer these same people a bet away from the poker table, even though the odds are in their favor, and they'll back down, but with cards something stimulates them and takes over. Zach, Sinclair reckoned, was one of these, the film man a straight sucker, and Hifter—what about Hifter? He was betting with his right hand, and Sinclair had remembered he only did that when he held good cards; the bluffing ploy had always shown up when he bet by throwing the chips into the pot left-handed. How clever a player was he? Sinclair checked his cards again: two kings, a four and two sevens, in mixed suits. It was a promising hand, but on form Hifter should have at least a flush or a straight, both better.

He semibluffed, throwing one card and praying the new one would be another king. He picked it up very carefully. It was the king of Spades. Full house. That beat what he hoped Hifter was holding. Sinclair allowed his lips to droop a millimeter, hoping to show disappointment. It was his bet, and he threw in a £5 chip like a loser. The film man folded; sense at last. Zach matched the bet. Hifter took out a pen and a small note pad; he wrote a figure on it, signed it and then put it on the pile of chips.

"Your five and up fifty."

Zach let a low whistle escape and threw in his hand out of turn. Sinclair sighed, and Sam sat up and took notice. They all looked at Sinclair. He placed his cards in a neat pile in front of him and stared at the pot, then at Hifter, then at Jackson. Zach didn't count; it was Hifter and Jackson against himself. He let the seconds pass.

"Sol, can I borrow your note pad?"

Hifter slid the pad across the table. Sinclair said as he wrote, "Fifty and up two hundred."

It was very still in the room. Nobody spoke; they hardly moved; they were waiting. Hifter was quick.

"OK, Dan, now let's see just how big a man you are." It was sucker-bait talk. "I'll see your two hundred and raise it another two fifty."

Jackson's face was almost triumphant.

The men were doing mental calculations. The answer was that the pot was holding more than £750.

Playing for the money was no longer the primary factor now for Sinclair. He just wanted to win, wanted to wipe that look from

Jackson's face and dismiss Hifter as an amateur in a game for pros. There was no alternative.

"I'll see you, Sol."

Hifter turned the cards over one at a time: a three, a jack, a jack, a jack . . . He held the last card for full dramatic effect; it worked. It was another jack.

"Jesus, I don't believe it!" Zach had to touch the cards to make it true.

Sinclair was cold in his stomach. He threw his cards away without showing them.

The last deal was an anticlimax, and then it was over. Sinclair played the good sport as best he could. Without Jackson there it would have been easy, but as it was, defeat became ignominy. Gamblers believe in fate and in luck, and to Sinclair, losing to Hifter seemed to put a seal on his bad run.

"Great game, Dan, just great." Hifter was smiles, and Jackson a carbon.

"We'll have to do it again, Sol," said Sinclair. "Only next time it'll be my turn."

He wrote out the check. It had been an expensive evening. As the launch pulled away from the yacht, the men turned and waved back to Hifter and Jackson.

"Great pair, those two," shouted the film man, over the roar of the outboard.

There is a small fishing village along the coast from Cannes, with a population of some five thousand souls. It is exposed to a variety of winds, and unlike other, more sheltered bays nearby, it can become quite cold in the winter months. It has no beach to speak of, and its largest single employer is a government establishment devoted to the manufacture of torpedoes. Nevertheless, the village has a great charm, and part of it had been selected for a location scene in the Film. This was not the first time the village had been featured in a motion picture. In 1957 a French pair, Roger Vadim and a young actress called Brigitte Bardot, had arrived to make *Et Dieu Créa la Femme*. The place called St.-Tropez ceased to be obscure from that time forward.

In the season the population swells to seventy thousand people, and it is these transients who create and nurture a reputation of crazy excitement. They crowd around the Café des Arts and the

Escale, journeying from Chelsea, St.-Germain-des-Prés, Greenwich Village, Stockholm and Hamburg. These nonconformists, beatniks, freethinkers suddenly become part of a ritualized society. The irony never seems to illuminate their searching, often dazed minds. Contrived outcasts in their own societies, reveling in their deeply considered differences, they become content to don the uniform of the season and enter into a recognized, if apparently disordered, way of living. In their naïveté they fail to understand the unconscious processes that produce the true individual or loner.

The chauffeur-driven car had its top up; its solo passenger was asleep across the back seat. He had decided to travel to the location alone; no doubt news of the previous night's game had been discussed in detail with all the extravagant additions that the dramatic memories of the other participants could recall. To have to face Janice Dearing so early in the morning would have been too much, so he left a message at the hotel desk that he would come alone and later. As the car braked to a standstill, Sinclair opened his eyes. God, they'd arrived.

He walked along the quay to where he could see the roped-off section that kept the would-be stars of tomorrow from the live ones of today. He was trying to explain to the imported gendarme that he was an OK person to let through when a girl wearing glasses and carrying a clipboard stacked with papers came over to them.

"You must be Dan Sinclair. It's all right; you can let him by."

"Thanks," he said. "Linda Sandford, I presume?"

"Oh, really, I thought you'd at least have an original approach line. It would have made just a helluva change in these parts."

He stopped. "Miss Sandford, you're damn lucky I'm even talking. Last night had its rough moments, as you may have heard."

Humor, that was the ploy he had decided on; disarm them with nonchalance and wry spirits.

As they walked through the groups of technicians and over the twisting lines of cables that fed the great arc lamps, he thought he could sense the stares, but it could have been his imagination. After all, people had been known to lose at poker before.

"Do you want to go over the material we have on Jackson? I brought it out specially."

"What a good idea," he said.

"The office is over here." She pointed to a Volkswagen. The sun roof was pulled back and all the windows open in an effort to reduce the boiled-beetle feeling. Someone had put towels over the front seats so as not to burn the ass off the unwary. The back seats were piled high with papers, scripts, boxes of color transparencies, sheets of black-and-white contact pictures and a portable typewriter.

"Take a seat, sir, and we won't keep you a minute. I'll just see if the managing director can see you."

"Gee, I can't wait," he said, and sat behind the wheel.

They went through the stills first, shot after shot of Jackson with the stars of the film, and Sinclair felt his first real pang of jealousy. Last night had been different, an incident in his life, but the photographs were something created without his instigation or control. It was like seeing a picture of an ex-wife with her new man. He read the written material, which at least was taken virtually verbatim from the background and story he had written himself for general handout to the press. Only the stuff on Jackson and the film was new to him. He thought it competent but uninspired.

"Well, this all looks pretty harmless, Linda."

"I'm glad you approve, Mr. Sinclair. Or may I call you Dan?"

He handed the batch of papers back to her.

"You're a very chirpy young lady."

"On the picture it's the only way to be."

"Why?" he said. "Is it tough?"

She came and sat beside him. "Any picture's tough. This one happens to be special; that makes it extra."

He searched around the car and under the seats.

"You don't happen to have a drink in this office, I suppose?"

She laughed at him. "No, we don't, but we could go to reception. That's across the road, if you don't mind stepping a few paces."

They went to a place called the Sénéquier Tea Room, and sat outside at a table with a shade. From there they could see across to the statue of Suffren, where the camera crew were setting up the next shot. He put the drink back on the table.

"Ah, that's better. I'm beginning to focus at last." He squinted over to the group of technicians. "What are they setting up for?"

"Well, you see, in this part of our story, the hero, God bless his ass, has driven over to meet the south of France incident in his life —to wit, Jackson—to deliver the old Dear John. Now, this being the picture business, we shot the tearful close-ups first, early this morning, and for some reason—you tell me—we now do the arrival by car. Zach and Sam were muttering something about the quality of the early-morning light. Sounds crazy, but when they put it all together in the cutting rooms, it'll work."

"Hifter has a great reputation, hasn't he? What's—what's he really like?"

Sinclair tried not to let the question sound too probing. Whichever way it came out, though, the answer was a response to what he really wanted to ask.

"He's not a womanizer, and he's not queer. Frighteningly normal, isn't it? But the word is that he's got something more than warm going for Jacksonbaby. The only person who's being thrown is the leading lady, naturally. She, poor cow, has to shack up in the hotel suite while Jackson lives it up on the boss' yacht. Now that is difficult for a movie queen to take; none of the pictures she's ever seen had a story line like that. I mean, even in *All About Eve* it took a couple of reels for the understudy to make home base. So naturally she has to compensate, and what does she do? Finds herself a piece of landed royalty—what else?—and has it away in the hills whenever she's not on call. Meanwhile, back at the ranch, your girl Dearing has fallen—and everyone please don't get me wrong—for Sam, Sam the cameraman. I guess the only one around here who hasn't got her own private nest going is yours truly, but there's time—what and with whom, if anyone, are you doing for starters?"

Sinclair leaned back in the seat and laughed. After a few minutes, when he had quieted down, he realized that concealed in the torrent of inside gossip that Linda Sandford had delivered with such flip expertise was the hard-core confirmation, as if he needed it, that Jackson and Hifter were, as they all say, going strong for each other.

"Linda, are you assigned to me for the whole morning?"

She sat to attention and saluted. "For the morning? Why, I'm at your command for the whole day, sir."

"In that case you can fix it for me to look at the rushes on Jackson."

She sat and thought about that one for a minute.

"Well, if you want to see them all, we have to go back to Cannes. But we do have two half scenes that Zach and the boys were going to view early this evening in the local cinema. I guess I could fix that up in about an hour. I mean like special, just for you."

He put his hand on her knee. "Linda, you're marvelous."

She put her hand over his and held it there.

"Say that again with feeling, and I'm yours."

They finished their drinks, synchronized watches and went off in opposite directions; she to find the cinema projectionist, he to watch the filming.

Hifter wasn't on the set that morning, which meant that Sinclair had only to face up to the others and to Jackson. It wasn't as difficult as he had thought; for one thing, they were all too engrossed with getting the filming done to do more than just be polite. And then it dawned on him that, to them, it had only been a game. He stood back and observed and told himself that if he went on this way, he'd end up a paranoiac. It had not always been so; with Carnel, Smith and those clients before he had ridden the rough spots and they hadn't touched him. But with Jackson he had changed. She had become a part of what he was without his being aware of it, and it made him realize how vulnerable this had made him. It was time to take stock and realize where he, where *they* were going.

He saw Janice Dearing and told her about looking at the rushes, and they arranged that he would meet her and Jackson back on the yacht at five that evening.

Linda Sandford was waiting for him outside the cinema. She had found time to change, and now that he really had a chance to look at her, he thought she was pretty good. Her legs were bare and browned by the sun, and she was wearing what seemed to be a scaled-down man's denim shirt with a short skirt in the same fabric. He guessed she'd swapped the glasses for contact lenses.

"You gotta ticket?" she cracked. "Never mind, stick with me, my boy, and go places."

There is something strange about the dark hollow space of an empty cinema, with its rows of sad seats and blank screen.

"Do you have a seating preference, sir?" she said. "As you can see we're pretty well taken up here; now if you'd made an advance reservation. . . ."

"You don't go on like this all the time, do you?" Sinclair asked her.

"Well, not really. It's an act for visiting firemen, and there hasn't been a fire around here lately."

They sat in the center of a row about halfway back from the screen. Linda Sandford turned, stuck two fingers into the sides of her mouth and let out with a young boy's piercing whistle.

"That should get 'em rolling."

The shaft of light from the projection box cut through the dark and hit the silver screen. Sinclair had viewed rushes many times before, and so the peculiarly amateurish look of them wasn't new to him.

The clapper board snapped, and the fractured English accent spoke the chalked words "Scene one-oh-five, take one." The scene was being photographed from a helicopter with a zoom lens. There was that marvelous feeling of zeroing in, as if you were eavesdropping, on the two people standing on the balcony of a villa set in the hills. It was a great opening shot of Jackson and the man. They did that five times over to get it right; each try was interrupted by the clapper board and the voice, "Scene one-oh-five, take two; scene one-oh-five, take three," and so on until they were satisfied.

The next shot was from inside a room in the villa, looking out onto the balcony. It was a medium close-up. There was one line of dialogue, spoken by Jackson: "What good is loving you going to do? It won't solve any problems, only create more." They did that one over eleven times. Twice Jackson fluffed her lines; a jet flew into the frame and killed another take; on the seventh everything was fine when the man let out a yawn. As the last take ran over, Zach's voice was recorded muttering, "Thank Christ," then, louder: "Great, you two, that was just fine."

Then the screen went blank, and the empty cinema seemed very dark and lonely. The projectionist hadn't bothered to switch the house dimmers up, so the only light came from the box as he rewound the film.

"What did you think?"

Linda's words brought him back to reality.

"Oh, she's good. But then why shouldn't she be? It's her voice, though. It comes over deeper and very sexy."

"Just what I need, great. Why don't we talk about how sexy I am?" She paused and did a piece of business that was supposed to show her in deep thought. "Hi, maybe I'm not, and *that's* what it's all about, Alfie."

She was sitting with her legs draped over the seat in front, and her skirt had ridden up her thighs. Sinclair moved closer and put his hand on her leg.

"I don't know, little one. Why we don't find out?"

She pretended to be shocked.

"What, in a public place? My goodness, think of the children."

He kissed her long and hard, and while he was doing it, his hand moved up her leg until he was holding her. She pushed him away.

"If I stay like this, you'll break my back. You'd think in France they'd know how to design cinema seats, for God's sake."

She stood up and looked around the empty place. When she was sure there were no peeping toms, she reached under her skirt and pulled her pants off. She held them up. They were minute.

"For all the good they do, I don't know why I bother."

She tipped the seats back and lay down on the floor.

"Gee, I hope they've cleaned this place. I'd hate to come out with a wedge of chewing gum attached."

Then she pulled him down, put his hand back where it had been and, while they were kissing, struggled to undo his trousers.

They came out into the sunlight a little disheveled, acting like two people who had been on a tour of a mine shaft.

"Well, I guess we can always say something good about movie houses in future."

Sinclair was trying to adjust to the bright sunlight.

"Linda, what I can say in all sincerity is that never in my life have I ever met anyone like you."

She pulled her skirt around her hips so that the zip was in the right place.

"Unique, that's it; fame at last. Say, you know that we've just created the greatest code greeting of all time."

He was checking on his trousers. They looked OK from the front.

"Tell me," he said.

"Picture this one," she said, holding both hands out flat in front of her face, the thumbs butted together to make the imaginary frame that film people use when they want to visualize their descriptions. "Married couple crouched around a hot TV screen. She's doing the knitting; he's trying not to nod off to sleep. The phone rings, he jumps and gets it. 'Hello, Sinclair's place. Who's that calling in the middle of Rowan and Martin's *Laugh-in*?' Seductive voice replies, 'It's me, Dan boy. How's about comin' to the movies?'"

They held on to each other and strolled along the narrow street. Passersby laughed at them and identified them as crazy foreigners but happy ones.

The unit was starting to pack up when they got back to the quay.

"Wonder what we missed," she said. "The statue's still standing; no news for Reuter's tonight."

He put his arm around her shoulders.

"Linda, I have to go now. There's a meeting in Cannes."

"Don't go sentimental on me, boy; remember the code word."

"Sure." He squeezed the back of her neck and walked toward the car and the waiting driver. He waved to her as they drove away, but he could not see the tears that were forming in her eyes.

The hotel got the yacht on the ship-to-shore telephone and had the launch come in to pick him up.

Jackson and Dearing were on deck waiting for him when he arrived on board. The drinks were out, and Janice poured him a large Scotch.

"How are you, Daniel?" Jackson said. "We haven't had much time to talk lately, have we?"

He sat on the rails with his back to the sea.

"Well, you have been busy and otherwise occupied."

Janice Dearing lit a cigarette.

"I saw some of the rushes today and the publicity material; it looks great. I'm beginning to put together a new program. We'll have to map out the future. You know we've achieved what we set out to do. The really important consolidation work starts as soon as you get back to London—"

She interrupted him. "Daniel, that's what I want to talk about. I mean, what happens when this is over."

He recognized the feeling that came into the pit of his stomach;

he'd had it before. The previous evening he had sensed it, and all that day, even with the girl, it was there. In the past when the symptoms had warned him—a PR man has a finely tuned psyche in that area—he had known what to do, how to pull compensation out of the bag and maneuver words and people so that the clients were drawn back from the line. They would be persuaded by the events he was suddenly able to create that they had been wrong to think badly of him. In their guilt they would lavish their congratulations, until time passed and the situation would recur. Public relations people live by the seesaw of results, and it is partly due to this that they fall into the easy habit of fabrication, first to the client, then to the press in order to appease the client. Once they're on that merry-go-round, there is only one way off.

This time, though, he couldn't diagnose the cause. There had been no letup, success all the way; it could only be Hifter.

"Jackson, now listen, we—"

She did it again. "Daniel, let me say something for a change."

He slipped down from the rails and eased himself into a chair. The air was quite cool against his flushed face.

"Go ahead, say what you want."

"You know what I think about what you've done for me. I wouldn't be here without you. But things change; people change . . . I mean, that's what this has all been about, after all."

"What are you saying, Jackson? That you want me to move over, to make way for somebody else?"

"No, I don't, for Christ's sake. I just want you to take a new look at where we are."

"I'll tell you where we are," he said. "You're currently on the cover of almost every glossy magazine printed; you're discussed on television programs; columnists quote the flimsiest piece of piffle about you they can get hold of; half the teen-agers of the Western Hemisphere copy the way you look. You have it made, Jackson. Next spring they'll be selling cosmetics that carry your name by the thousands, and right this minute the buyers are going crazy ordering the latest smash, the Jackson's Thing dress range. And now, by the grace of that slight cumulative endeavor, Mr. Sol Hifter has you in films. That, my love, is where you are. It didn't just happen, you know; the good fairy didn't wave her magic wand over Maureen Stokes—remember her?—and turn her into the biggest model sensation of all time."

He relaxed and took a long pull on his drink. Jackson glanced across to Janice Dearing, whose forehead creased as if to say, what else did you expect? Her voice was low and soft when she spoke to him this time.

"Daniel, I don't want to argue with you. Anyway, there's no argument. What you say is all true. I remember Maureen Stokes all right, but it's no use thinking I'm the same girl dressed up for the part, because I'm not; too much has happened. All I'm trying to say is, isn't it time I had a voice in what comes next?"

Janice Dearing stubbed out the cigarette and for the first time broke into the conversation.

"None of us are against you, Dan, but we're a team now. You're still the captain; some of us would like to contribute; that's all."

"That sounds fine, Janice. Who do you figure is in this team of ours?"

The answer came from Jackson.

"The three of us, and Sol."

He gave a sarcastic laugh. "Yeah, I wondered when we'd get around to Mr. Hifter."

"Oh, Jesus, don't be so touchy! Hifter's the best there is in the film business, just as you're the best PR man there is. Can't you see what that could mean?"

"The way I hear it, I'd end up being press attaché to the king, queen and lady-in-waiting."

Jackson lost her patience.

"Look, you told me once that I had to take anything you said, even if it was tearing me down. OK, well, that's just what I did; now it's your turn. You're a great PR man, Daniel, but that's all you are, and I'm the client, remember. That gives me the right to more than just an opinion about what goes on. For a start, you might as well know I don't like Jackson's Thing. Every overnight pop-star success and model has a dress range named after her. It's not the image I want. The makeup's fine, it's on the right level; but the *schmutter* business, forget it. Also, I think the time has come to play it straight. I'm not a total idiot, you know. I knew about your deal on the side with Naturalé, and this latest double cross with *Impulse* isn't very clever either. Up to now it didn't matter, it was petty stuff anyway, but the deal with Hifter could be fantastic, so from now on there'll be no tricks. We play it cool, and we play it as a team."

The two women sat there waiting for the Sinclair defense mechanism to go into action. It didn't happen. Instead, he stood up and slowly paced the deck. *What's he up to?* Janice Dearing thought. It was against character for him to take it that way. Eventually he stopped, in front of Jackson, and looking down at her, he spoke very deliberately and quietly. Janice Dearing had to concentrate on his lip movements to pick up the words.

"Maybe you're right. Sure there's a lot at stake, for all of us, and as you say, you're the client. Why don't we talk about it again when you've finished here? So—er—I'll see you back in London."

He gave Jackson the half-arm wave and nodded at Janice Dearing. Then he walked down the deck to where the launch was tied up.

"You don't think he'll go shoot himself, do you?" said Jackson.

The tension was suddenly lifted. Janice half laughed.

"Not Sinclair. He's much too tough and selfish for that. You know, I think he might even have seen the light."

Sinclair took the next plane out of Nice. The Air France PR girl fixed him on a connecting flight via Paris. That night he slept, alone, in the flat above his offices in Hay Hill, London.

16

FREDA had put the unopened envelope with "Private and Confidential" typed across it on top of the pile of papers that had gathered while he had been away. It was from Michael Smith's company, and it was short and final. He knew what it was about before he read the carefully worded paragraphs.

There had been a lack of communication, they felt, and a falling away of adequate and proper press representation. In view of this, they had decided to discontinue their association. The letter was signed by the accountant, a man Sinclair had never met. When the dirty work had to be done, they always did it by letter, never face-to-face, and Smith hadn't even had the guts to sign it himself.

Sinclair checked their account; they owed three months' fees and expenses that added up to more than £1,100—no mention of that in their communication. He knew from experience that he'd have a hell of a job trying to prize the money out of them. With luck the first and, the way it looked now, only collection of Jackson's dresses might build up enough credit on Smith's 5 percent royalty earnings to contra off what they owed. It was a gamble with all the odds in their favor, and that was the way it always was.

Sinclair couldn't bother to look at the rest of the papers, except to notice that the Nutting man had rung again. That was a great name, he thought, if you didn't mind about that sort of thing.

The lunchtime edition of each of the London papers carried a small item on the financial page. They reported in under two hundred and fifty words that City financier Cyril Mansfield had collapsed and died of a heart attack while on vacation in the Bahamas. Little was known about Mansfield, the copy ran, except his violent dislike of publicity.

Sinclair couldn't believe it. In a matter of months a thriving business had suddenly become a shell. Sure, there was still a list of clients that hired him on an *ad hoc* basis that every other PR in London would have liked to get his smooth well-cared-for hands on, but the hard core, the guts, was gone. He had watched it happen to others, those who made a business out of charging new clients a whack of a fee, knowing they would never hold the account long enough to renew. They kept moving, and while the slick sweet-talk promises lasted, there were always new suckers to believe the bait of exclusive features on themselves or their products that the *Observer* or the *People* or the *Daily Express* would fall over backward to publish.

Not hot shot Sinclair, though; he delivered. Until now. He waited until the office had closed and the girls had gone home. Then he went over and sat at the layout table. He stared at the sheaf of blank white paper in front of him, and then he started to write.

DEAR RUTH,

There's been so much happening since I got your letter that I haven't had time to stop still long enough to write to you. Now almost the whole grand empire has come to a grinding halt, so what do I do? Sit down and have a one-sided dialogue with the only person who can't interrupt or talk back. Is that why people write letters? I don't really think so, but right now I'm in a self-pitying mood. Throw the whole bundle away—don't say I didn't warn you.

When we met, I was at the top of the pile. Now two of the best clients have kicked me out, and a third has had the bad grace to die on me; this leaves Jackson, and I'm not even sure about her. I never thought I'd come around to your way of thinking—PR-wise, that is—but the way things are, it looks as if I might, even though by a different route. It's difficult to explain, but I used to enjoy all the fixing; I'd look at a piece in a magazine and think, it wouldn't have been there but for me. You can't help getting a sense of power out of that. Maybe it all went far too fast. Just think about it: A year ago there was an unknown kid called Stokes, and because of what I did to her, she's an international personality.

I've just got back from Cannes, where she has a part in Sol Hifter's picture. I guess it's the beginning of a new era for her and the end of one for me.

Naturally she's fallen for Hifter, or else she's playing it real cool. Now I think about it, that's probably what it is: When Hifter's made his contribution, she'll move on. Minor royalty would be logical; the international jet set, chalets in the Swiss Alps, private airplanes, the lot, then what? Marriage, maybe, and can you blame her?

You were right, Ruth. All a man in my position can be is second-class. Take away all the fancy trimmings, and I glow only as long as I can stand in the path of the reflected glory. But once the sun sets then I'm out in the cold like anyone else.

You know what I'd say if I was advising someone else in my position? Get out while you've still got something to show. Sounds easy, doesn't it, but what else does a man like me do? So I'll probably hang on. I'm hooked on the system.

I hired somebody you know to take care of all the detail stuff, a woman called Janice Dearing. That was the first wrong move. Not that she's done anything subversive—at least, I don't think so—but she's closer to Jackson now than I am, so what with Hifter it's three against one. To hell with it.

How are you, Ruth? I got the implication of the job. Is it true? Because it wouldn't take much to swing me. You know what would happen if I threw it over here and came to New York, don't you? I'm the guy who said that whether you stay single or get married, you're making a big mistake. Of the two blunders I'm not sure which is the least unsatisfactory. Thinking of someone else for a change, you've got more to lose than I have; all the gain would be on my side.

Enough of the introspection. I'll let you know how it goes. I guess the action will come to a head when Jackson gets back from Cannes.

Watch out for the next sizzling installment in the continuing life of Sinclair's Folly.

Love? Is that what I really feel? Or is it like all the rest, an illusion to fit the circumstances?

He signed the letter, went out to the office and typed the envelope, stamped it and then walked down to the postbox on the corner of Bruton Street. He was feeling better. There was something about getting it out of your system by writing it down on paper.

Four days later a national daily ran a half page on Jackson and Hifter. It was illustrated with stills from the film set. The newspaper girl whose byline was on the article was a close professional friend of Sinclair's.

He read the feature for the first time when he opened the pages of the paper over breakfast. Just like its four million other readers.

The yacht undulated gently on the night calm of the Mediterranean, and Jackson lay on the bed next to Hifter and wondered about him as he slept. This time she had handled the situation very well, she thought. She had made him do some of the chasing. It was peculiar that a man who was so dominant in his business life was so passive as a lover. It was as if all his drive and energy were directed to the one sphere, and there was little over for other activities. She wondered how much of what she felt for him was genuine and how much because of who he was and what he could do for her. In the end, what did it matter? Life was very easy with Hifter; he took the rough edges away.

This was her last night on board the yacht. In the morning Janice would come back from the shore and Sam, and they would get ready to leave for London. The film had another week's shooting to do before the others too packed up and moved to the Paris studios to complete the interior shots.

She thought about what Hifter had wanted to do and why she had defended Sinclair. Pay him off, he had said, there's no place for sentiment in business. Sinclair was only in it for the money, so give him the money.

She had Janice Dearing now, and she had him and the Film going for her. Sinclair's job was over; he was superfluous. She had argued for him: You don't just ditch people like that, she said. Do that and you twist yourself up inside. Let him take care of the London promotion Hifter wanted; he was probably the best person to do it anyway. Why? Hifter wanted to know. It was routine stuff: interviews, stills from the picture. There was nothing creative needed; that had all been done. Janice Dearing and the film company's publicity department could take care of it. You can't do that to someone like Sinclair, she had argued, not on his own territory, not where they all knew what he had done; it would crucify him. They had fixed on a compromise: Hifter would hire Sinclair, brief him but let him have a free hand. That way the ultimate control would lie with the film company and not Sinclair. If he did a good job, then maybe Hifter would take him on the payroll; he might be useful.

He rolled over in his sleep, away from her, so she could see his broad sunburned back. *He's tough,* she thought. What would he do when she became superfluous? Pay her off? Was that the way of it with Hifter?

It was all the same. It didn't matter what the good intentions were. You did what suited you best at the time, and if anyone else got fouled up in the process, you could always find a justification or, like Hifter, use money instead. He was right: Sinclair was in for the bread—remember Paris, she said to herself—and he wasn't the straightest operator in the business either, so what could he expect? She would let the two of them work it out between them. There was no need for her to get involved. She wasn't going to get embroiled with Sinclair in another where-would-you-be-without-me session.

She had persuaded Hifter to fly to London and talk to Sinclair. Don't make it sound like you're doing him a favor, she had said, but just pave the way.

Hifter authorized the exclusive release of a story on Jackson and himself to the newspaper in London. It'll soften him up a bit, he had said, kind of make him glad to get in on the act.

17

SINCLAIR stood outside the Mirado Building in Wardour Street and looked at the posters in their glass display cases. The one common denominator in film publicity, he thought, was the degree of naïve taste that permeated almost everything touched, like a Midas finger gone crazy. It was a long way from the hustling days of the drapery salesmen who became the czars of Hollywood, but their brash, insensitive outlook lingered on, in spite of most of the majors now being owned by oil companies or mammoth communications businesses.

It had taken a one-man revolution in the shape of Saul Bass before even the credit titles bore any resemblance to the content and form of a film. And now there was Hifter, the great white hope of the intellectuals and the moneymen. To the amazement of both he made intelligent pictures that took a fortune at the box office. So until he pulled a boner, he was the blue-eyed boy and could do no wrong.

The lift stopped at the third floor, and when Sinclair spoke the magic man's name to the receptionist, he was ushered into the boardroom without question or delay. The room was empty. At least a dozen uncomfortable-looking mahogany chairs, matching the vast table, stood waiting for occupiers capable of making earthshaking observations—"I got it, Joe, let's get Lord Snowdon to shoot a real great still spread for that supplement of his . . . what's it called?" "Harry, he ain't so available anymore." "Why not? He gone out of style or something?"

On the walls of the boardroom were framed color enlargements of the top stars who had appeared in the company's most successful productions. They were hung at discreet intervals, except that at the place of honor there was a predictably large space given over to a black-and-white photograph of the executive vice-president in charge of production—worldwide. This, as was to be expected, had its frame draped with the Stars and Stripes.

"The decor is not exactly in the style of the Italian school, I admit, but the guys around here have got to have something to worship."

Hifter came through a door cut into the heavy paneling; his office was obviously *en suite* to the room of power.

He sat at the top of the table with the large curved window at his back.

"Take a seat, Dan." He motioned to the chair three places removed to his right. Sinclair wondered where that placed him in the hierachy.

"I'm glad you were able to come. By the way, I hope you enjoyed your short stay on the set, even if it was a mite expensive."

At least there's something that makes him smile, Sinclair thought.

"Oh, I had a very interesting time, Sol. You'll have to come and play in my school one day."

"Sure. Now, about Jackson." Sinclair knew the preamble was over and this was where he learned which way the cookie was going to crumble—and crumble was the word.

"We all think you've done a fantastic, lovely job on that girl. In fact, that's why I asked you up here. As you probably know, Dan, we are going to sign her to a seven-year exclusive contract, with options, of course. Naturally, I'm sure Jackson would want to continue to have you advise her in the public relations field, but since the Mirado Company, of which I'm an executive vice-president, will have such a heavy investment in her future, we feel our involvement in that area should sustain basic control. Just a minute, Dan." He held up his hand to ward off the interruption. "That is why we have come to the conclusion that the person best suited to represent both interests would be you."

Sinclair was waiting for the catch.

"As for fees, well, I'm sure that won't present us with any problems." Sinclair's eyes widened. Was that a smile he saw before him?

"However—" That and "if" must be the words of our time, the flies in all the ointments.

"We thought it reasonable to start on an assignment basis, and as you will understand in a minute, Dan, this is going to be a pretty important assignment."

To a client every assignment was important. They both knew that.

"We would like an intensive, maximum-exposure campaign

over a split single-week period, pivoting on Jackson's signature of the contract. Basically we put ourselves in your hands; you'll have all the freedom you want, within reason."

Were they handing him rope as well as freedom?

"If"—here it came—"the company is satisfied with the results, as I'm confident they will be, then a whole new sphere of operation is open for you, Dan."

He signified that the monologue was over by unlocking his steepled fingers and folding his arms across his chest. Sinclair wondered if it was form to applaud. Hifter deserved it; it was a great performance. The high executive's ultimatum wrapped up in smoothly rehearsed rhetoric; what he could have said was, "Either you work on my terms or you don't work." But big civilized businessman Hifter couldn't bring himself down to that level. Sinclair knew he had no alternative: If he didn't fit in, they would go ahead without him, and the result would be a major promotion on what he'd considered his own personal creation, with him nowhere on the scene. He had got the obvious significance of the newspaper feature, which he knew could have appeared only with Hifter's sanction.

He tried to make his answer sound firm but nonchalant.

"Sound's fine, Sol. If you agree, I suggest I put Janice Dearing over with you people. She was responsible, under my direction, for creating a lot of the written material and ideas, and of course her familiarity with Jackson and the way we operate will be invaluable."

Hifter's right eye twitched. Very smooth, he thought; maybe Sinclair was better than he imagined. By beating him to the post on the Dearing ploy, he had asserted an authority and confidence that would have been lost if he, Hifter, had got the point over first. As it was, one of Sinclair's staff would be on the inside running their end of the operation. He had to admire the guy's guts.

"That's good thinking, Dan. We have this promotion scheduled for ten days from today. That's not too soon for you, is it?"

Sinclair shook his head. "Not at all. We work better under pressure anyway." He stood up. "I'll rough out a proposed program and send it over for you to look at."

Hifter walked him out to the reception area, and they shook hands.

The receptionist watched them and thought how absolutely super and glamorous it all was.

He was back on familiar ground, and he was grafting again. In spite of all that had happened, the excitement of scheming and working at capacity wiped it from his mind. It was what turned him on and made the adrenalin flow. For him depressions could still be reversed by the result of a single telephone call. Way underneath was the need to please, the need to be admired for what he did, and once a situation created itself where these drives could be fed, then everything else became of secondary importance.

He turned the office over to the promotion and arranged for Janice Dearing to work from the Mirado Building. Every detail was checked and every possible avenue of publicity investigated. The pure industry of the effort filtered back to Hifter, and because there had been no close personal involvement, as with Jackson, he could objectively admire Sinclair's expertise and efficiency.

The program that Sinclair had submitted was a classic of its kind; the overall conception and its pace, with each step carefully planned to culminate in a press luncheon at Claridge's, were a masterpiece of timing. He gave it immediate approval and an open budget.

Sinclair booked five hotel suites, all adjoining. The connecting doors between each pair were opened and thus formed their own private corridor. He allocated an apartment to Hifter, two to Jackson, a suite for the hairdresser, makeup and wardrobe people to use, and finally one for himself and his staff. He moved them in en masse for the period of the promotion and made Claridge's the operational headquarters.

He held the invitations to the luncheon until the last possible minute: He wanted impact. Then the noon before the scheduled day he issued a flood of one hundred and fifty telegrams, each addressed to the recipient's home. Only the cream of the journalists and photographers from his confidential card index were invited.

FLASH SIGNAL STOP TOP PRIORITY STOP
JACKSON DOES CAREER SWITCH STOP
ANNOUNCEMENT IMMINENT STOP PLEASE
ATTEND SPECIAL LUNCHEON CLARIDGES TOMORROW
STOP SINCLAIR

The usual method PR people adopt when they invite the press is to send out invitations about ten days in advance of the event they are promoting. This gives everyone time to evaluate the relative attraction of the show and to make the decision whether to go themselves or send an assistant or secretary. It also allows the opportunity for exclusives to be sought and arranged.

Sinclair aimed to catch them off-balance; he was banking on Jackson's prestige and the apparent snap decision to call a lunch conference to titillate their news-seeking sense to a point where they had no alternative but to attend. There is an urgency about a telegram that is implicit and is communicated to the message it contains, however innocuous it may really be. This more than anything appealed to Sinclair's sense of the dramatic; he nearly had one sent to himself so that he could experience the excitement and half fear that comes when you tear open the small thin envelope.

Jackson sat in front of the makeup mirror in one of her two suites and relaxed while the beauty makers went to work. The hairdresser was brushing out her long hair, and she closed her eyes and drifted into a half sleep. She had hardly spoken to Sinclair since getting back from Cannes; the details of the promotion had been routed through Hifter and Janice Dearing. She sensed that he was almost his old high-powered self again; he was in control, and it was only in the short, inactive intervals between issuing instructions to his staff that the signs of taut strain showed on his face. They both knew the unexpressed fact that for him this was the crunch. No matter how well he handled the operation, one error, one step out of line, and she and Hifter would use it as the reason for unloading him.

She thought it was amazing how people changed. You start off with somebody new, and everything is fine between you. A closeness builds up, and each admires the best in the other and overlooks or sentimentalizes the faults. But what were faults? Those that Sinclair saw in her might not appear apparent to Hifter; perhaps he would find his own in time.

She tried to analyze what it was about Sinclair that had really turned her against him. She knew it wasn't his double crossing because in a way she almost admired him for it. Everyone in business pulled strokes; honesty where money is concerned was a joke.

If you were successful, then they called it flair, acumen or brilliance. It was only when you failed that they called you a fool. She was unable to face herself and admit it was because she and Sinclair were so alike. They were both utterly selfish, and at the beginning, when it was all achievement, that was their binding asset. He, building and creating not for her, not with any of the feelings that the true master has for the protégée, but for what her success could do for himself. She, taking and climbing on his knowledge and expertise, not in the way that one who admired and respected draws on a mentor, but as one who only yearned for success and what it could give.

When she had made it to the top, then there was nothing left to hold them together. The way they had achieved what they started out to do built in its own form of personality destruction. Not once in their association had they sat together and reminisced about how it had been before, as lovers do who have built their success on their generosity and affection for each other.

It was always the way between a PR man and his client. It works at the start because of the need to climb, but there are few clients who like admitting what was done for them in the early days. They will tell others how great the PR man is, but not to his face. Perhaps they fear that he might start attributing all their talents and success to himself. Why should it be any other way? The PR man is paid for doing his thing, and he should know at the beginning where his place will always be, one or maybe two steps behind. This is not a position men who exploit for others enjoy; they too want to share in the glory.

Jackson and Sinclair were a pair brought together because one of them existed to promote and the other to be promoted. The urgency of the need and its success made a bond that was predestined to fray. It was a question of how and when, not if.

"How's that, love? Divine, isn't it?"

She came to with a start and blinked at the hairdresser.

"Been having a catnap, have you?"

"Yes, I went right off. It looks great, thanks, Michael."

The makeup man took over and cleaned the skin of her face and throat. She watched every movement, every stroke of the sable brushes as they added the soft, natural look that had been captured and put on film by the world's greatest photographers. The man was an expert, and his touch was sure and confident. He had been the makeup artist on the Film, and Hifter had flown him in specially.

When they had finished, she dressed and checked himself in the full-length mirror. The trouser suit was Yves St. Laurent, the gold bracelet and ring Andrew Grima, and the scent Joy. *What else is there?* she thought. *More of everything perhaps, and then more. Could there ever be too much? And what if it stopped?*

She walked through the rooms until she came to the closed door that led to Hifter's suite. She didn't bother to knock but walked straight in. He was standing by the windows looking down into Brook Street, and when he heard her, he turned. She stood in the center of the room, very poised, knowing how good she looked, but he enjoyed the routine of checking her over and it flattered her to let him do it.

"Is that the St. Laurent suit?"

She laughed at him. "Yes, it is. Do you think it's pretty?"

"Well, sure I do. You know you're really great, Jackson. You have that thing they all talk about."

She walked over to him and kissed him gently on the side of the mouth.

"You say very nice words to me, Sol."

"Well, just remember, baby, until they turn into actions or results, that's all they are, and anyone can learn to say words. In fact, that's all most people ever learn, and half the time the words aren't even theirs."

He broke from her. "Well, it's nearly time. Where the hell's Sinclair?"

There was a knock on the door.

"Shall I say it?"

"Don't bother," said Hifter. "Come in, Dan."

Sinclair came into the room. He was looking very suave. His suit was gray, waisted with broad lapels, and he had a deep violet-colored shirt with a tie and breast-pocket handkerchief in the same fabric.

"Well, you two are going to look great together."

Jackson was surprised.

"You're coming down with us, aren't you, Sol?"

"No, I don't do the entrance bit too well, but I'll be there. Just get the party warmed up for me, will you? Tell me, Dan," he asked Sinclair, "what sort of turnout do we have?"

Sinclair gave a confident smile. "I haven't checked, but it'll be good. Janice is down there now. I think we'd better go, Jackson."

As they walked to the lift, Sinclair told her how marvelous he thought she looked, and she thanked him. There was nothing else for them to say to each other.

At the entrance to the reception room they were met by Janice Dearing. Her face was drawn and helpless-looking. Behind her were the champagne and the rows and rows of glasses and the photographic lights and the waiters and the staff of Sinclair Enterprises and some people from the film company. There might have been a dozen other assorted people; the number of them and what they did were not important.

He looked past Dearing into the room, and the palms of his hands started to sweat. There was an icy emptiness in his stomach, and he wanted to run away. Nobody spoke. Sinclair looked at his watch. It showed twelve forty-five.

Janice Dearing was the first.

"Where are they, Dan?"

His throat was dry; he couldn't reply. The same thought kept going over and over in his mind: *not to him, not to Sinclair.* There must be a horrible mistake; maybe the taxis had gone on strike, anything. If only the room were empty. The gaggle of nobodies seemed to make an awful mockery. He searched their faces for some signs of recognition, and there was none.

He turned to Jackson and saw her fixed, beautiful profile. His mouth opened, but the words wouldn't come. She moved from him, and her large, wonderfully moist eyes seemed to devour him. Her face was flushed, and as the lips trembled, the completely irrelevant thought swamped his mind that he had never seen anyone in his life look so fantastically lovely.

He stood stunned, waiting for the verbal onslaught, but it didn't come. Instead, she turned and walked away from him, back toward the lift. She held her head high, controlled the tears that would have been a release for the pent-up fury. He had made a fool of her, and that was unforgivable. She could have taken almost anything from him, but to expose her to the insult of rejection, not that—not after the success she had tasted.

Janice Dearing walked straight past him and hurried after Jackson. He didn't seem to notice her, just continued to stand on the same spot, shoulders drooping, complete disbelief shrouding his face.

"Why didn't any of them come, Dan?" It was Freda. She was near to breaking point.

"I wish I knew," he mumbled.

"Well, I damn well know." Sol Hifter was close to losing his cool. "It's all over with you and Jackson, Sinclair. You get the message, don't you?"

Sinclair tried to interrupt him. "Let's try to find out—"

"There's nothing to find out, you dumb idiot. You just forgot the one elementary fact that any school kid would have checked."

There was a look of confusion on Sinclair's face; he didn't have to phrase the question.

"At the Savoy Hotel, London, right at this minute, they are handing the citations to the Women of the Year. That's why nobody came to your party."

It wasn't until he was on his third whiskey that he remembered how the date of the press luncheon came to be suggested. "Have it on the Monday," Hifter had said. "Monday's my lucky day."

Why hadn't he checked? Hifter was right: It was what a school kid would have done, and maybe that was what he had bet on. It was so obvious, and Jackson's status so established, that no other event could possibly be considered a rival except perhaps an annual function that in the past had honored such women as Mary Quant, Julie Driscoll and *Times* woman's page editor Susan Puddefoot. Hifter could play poker all right: He had only risked Sinclair's reputation and Jackson's pride. The one was expendable, and the other could be rebuilt. By Sol Hifter, of course.

There was a splash as the trout took the fly, and then the line went taut and the reel was screaming as the fish went up river. The end of the rod bent into a perfect arc, then relaxed because the trout was lying still in the weeds that ran up to the side of the riverbank. He walked slowly toward the spot where the line disappeared into the water, reeling in the slack as he went and keeping the line tight. Suddenly it was off again, and he saw its size as it leaped clear of the water. He bent his knees as if to soften the impact when it hit the surface of the river. It took another ten minutes before the fish had tired and he could bring it to the landing net. He weighed it on the spring balance: two and three-quarter pounds—that was a good catch.

When you fish, especially for trout, you forget everything else. Your mind is free, and you only care about the wind and the too-bright sunlight.

There had been no word from Jackson or Hifter: just a short, very businesslike letter from Ernest Stokes notifying him of the cessation of their contract.

He was away for ten days, and during that time he didn't look at one newspaper or magazine. He knew he would read about her sooner or later and that, like the public he had helped to feed in the past, he would readily believe what was served up in print.

The Porsche cruised the Winchester bypass, heading for London. He turned the radio on and listened to the endless parade of pop songs, interspersed by the inane chatter of the DJ. "Here's a new sound, night people, and you'd better believe it, 'cause this one's chartside-bound. Here we go, folks, with . . . 'Jackson's Song.' "

Sinclair came down to the office at ten o'clock that morning out of habit. Freda's last act of efficiency had only added to the stench of defeat and inactivity. There were no papers on the desks waiting for attention, everything had been cleared, and only the full wastepaper baskets showed that someone had been there. The air was stale, and as the light beamed through the shutters on the windows and onto the surfaces of the desks and the machines, the layers of dust were like decaying blankets waiting to envelop and take over. He blew at the dust and watched it rise and swirl in the shaft of light. It reminded him of his mother when she was on her knees brushing the carpet in their best front room, a long time ago. *Why disturb it?* he thought. *Let it stay there.* Like the snow, it added to the silence.

He opened the main office door and looked out into the corridor. Freda had even canceled the morning papers and the office milk. Only the postman, unaware of any change, had duty-bound continued deliveries, and there was a pathetic cluster of post waiting to be opened. But there were only the small, dull buff-colored envelopes with cellophane windows; no long white ones or lightweight blue ones with the striped, colored borders. It was like going to view an empty office that's for rent, and when you open the door, you step on post that goes on being delivered to occupants that have long ceased to live there.

There was still enough ground coffee in the pot, and he filled the percolator with water. While he waited for it to heat, he went through the drawers of Freda's desk. The unused stationery was neatly divided in sections, with carbon paper and compliments slips and newly sharpened pencils. Some drawers still had evidence that a woman had been there: discarded lipstick holders, a pair of tights and traces of powder that gave off her scent.

He heard the door open as he poured out the coffee and turned around. It was Tessa Drake.

"Hello, you come to gloat?" He went back to making the drink. "Do you fancy a coffee? It's the last one you'll get in this neck of the woods."

She walked over and sat on the edge of the desk.

"Yeah, I wouldn't mind. Black, no sugar."

He gave her the cup and then sat in the swivel chair so that he had to look up at her when he spoke.

"I guess this is a big day for you, eh? Comeuppance at last. Proves how right you were; the collapse of the big man."

"You wouldn't believe that I came to see how you were, would you?"

"Well, let's say I'd find that a little difficult."

She slid off the desk and walked around the room as if she were inspecting it. He stayed in the chair and watched her. She was wearing a tie-belted camel coat with a Hermes scarf at the neck and high brown leather boots, and she carried a Gucci handbag that had a band of red and green canvas in it.

"Well, what will you do? Clear out, go to New York? Or stick around and try something else?"

He didn't answer her for a little while. He had thought of New York, and what could be there for him, but he wasn't sure. He wasn't sure about anything.

"I don't know, Tessa. Know anyone who wants a good PR? Got a good record, you wanna see our clippings books? The only man to create something out of nothing."

"Haven't you had enough of it, Dan, for God's sake? I'd have thought even you would have got the message by now."

"What message? The only message I've got is, don't trust your friends."

She came back to the desk, and when she looked down at him, there was no malice. Neither was there pity.

"You had some friends once, Dan; only one by one you fouled them up; you took it all too far. You got so power-happy you thought you could manipulate everybody. The message is this: The day of the hot shot PR is over. And what's so ironical about it is that you started the rot. We all learned a lot from you, Dan. It's all suddenly hit us—public relations was taking over, and we were letting it happen. It was a disease of the people who needed to live by an image of themselves that the papers and television and magazines accepted and served up to a public hungry for celebrities to worship. Katherine Whitehorn warned us a long time ago, but we didn't take any notice. She said the most sinister aspect of PR was the effect on the press itself. We got flabby, and we took your stories and souped-up news instead of starting from scratch, as reporters used to do, and finding out for ourselves. You made it easy for us, Dan. You gave us the facts your masters wanted the public to know, and that's not the same as the facts they should know."

Sinclair stood up, and it seemed for a moment as if the tiredness had left him.

"Listen, you didn't have to accept anything. Don't forget that you always had the final decision. We don't print the papers, you know, you do. OK, so sometimes we fabricated a little news, but what's so wrong about that? You do it yourselves every day of the week. When Beaverbrook took a stand against the Common Market, did he print an honest, unbiased report of the facts? Of course he didn't. He picked the facts that suited him, took what helped his argument and left the rest conveniently alone. We're in it together, Tessa; we're all part of the same self-seeking group."

She was warming up to him now; the mood that brought her to his office had given over to Tessa Drake, newspaperwoman.

"The big difference you people overlook, Dan, is that everyone knew what Beaverbrook was about: He made no secret of it; but you work away hidden behind a camouflage of fake honesty. You make a flower arrangement of the facts and hide the wilted plants away behind the bright exotic blooms. No, you don't actually lie —you adapt the truth in a nice way, and unlike the advertising man who buys his space to sell his goods in the open market where everyone knows what he's at, you operate in a no-man's-land of secret infiltration where everything comes gift-wrapped in mock hospitality and flattery. You feed your warped, distorted messages into the machine of public affairs and hope they come out pure and clean and acceptable. Dan, can't you see it? If something smells, then we should *know*. It shouldn't be hidden away behind the scent of sweet perfume that public relations men spray on everything. The real motives have to be seen, or eventually we'll all become cutout cardboard images."

Now he moved around the office, and turned the leaves of the small calendar on Ann's desk until it showed the date of the day.

"You're talking as if making Jackson and pushing a dress designer were the most important things there were. Get it in proportion, Tessa. We're in the fashion world where what's trendy today is so out tomorrow it becomes a laugh. What does it matter that I played games? If it hadn't been me, it would have been someone else. You people picked the system, I didn't. I just understood how it worked. We're in the image age—nobody looks behind the façade, nobody investigates; they might not like what they'd find, it would destroy their heroes."

"Dan, it is all important. Sure, who the hell cares about the fashion business, except the people who screw a living out of it? But the methods you used are being employed by all the PR men: the drug business, the politicians, the cigarette makers. Somewhere lurking at the back of them is a PR man being paid to devise the most attractive and acceptable front he can. Look at the Biafran horror. One side was getting its story over in triplicate, and then we found that the material was coming in from Switzerland from a very efficient public relations unit. People believe what we write, and so they should. They should have the right to trust us. But what if we're got at, and got at so smoothly it almost doesn't show? The most dangerous PR's are the nice ones, . Dan, because we believe what they tell us and because we don't stop to question their motives. How can the information a man is paid to disseminate be totally unbiased? It can't be, and it's contrary to human nature to think it could be any other way."

He sank into the lush leather of the reception-area chair, and when he lifted his head, his eyes were rimmed and his long face was hollowed.

"I know. You're right, Tessa, but it's the way things are, and I'm part of it. You can analyze it all you like but it's a system now, part of the Establishment, and it won't change."

"You're wrong, Dan. Cut loose; get away from it. You're an intelligent man, for Christ's sake; you don't have to prostitute yourself. Didn't it ever hit you that what you do will always be second-rate? You're there to be used, you peddle other people's egos, and the more successful you are, the less there is of yourself. You can only be as important as the clients you represent, and so it adds up to a life of continued justification, to the clients, to the press and to yourself."

"Tessa, this is like a conversation I had before. It's funny how the two people who've ever meant anything have come up with the same set of arguments."

Her voice was low and had lost its sharp edge.

"Who was the other one, Dan?"

"It was someone in New York." He knew what she really meant, and he didn't play at it anymore. "Her name's Ruth Emery; she's a writer, and she hates PR's too. Maybe that's when the rot got going. If you once start questioning yourself and lose the drive that took you over the bumps, then perhaps the self-destruction starts, and without admitting it, you're not the same and you blame the mistakes on other people or bad luck when really it's you all the time."

He came out of the reverie and looked at his watch.

"Say, it's opening time. Let's see if I've got any booze left; we might as well celebrate the demise."

They went through the office and into the study, and he made them drinks.

"Can you think of a good toast?" he said.

She raised her glass. "What about 'the new Sinclair'?"

"Why not? It sounds good."

They drank the toast and touched glasses. His eyes moved around the room.

"You know, I nearly signed the lease on a new set of offices, skyscraper block overlooking the Thames; very chic that would have been. Do you think I could find somebody to take this lot off my hands? Maybe some up-and-coming PR consultant; yeah, it would suit him fine." He smiled at her. "Great image, designed opulence, makes them feel you're really swinging with the trendies."

She finished her drink, and she was smiling with him. "I have to go, Dan."

"Don't tell me that after all that you've got a lunch date with a PR."

She laughed. "No, it's with the editor, as it happens. I think they're going to offer me some promotion at last."

She came very close to him and reached up and kissed him on the cheek. "Let me know, Dan, won't you?"

"Sure, Tessa."

He went to the door with her and then to the lift, but she wanted to walk down. He called to her before she turned the bend in the stairs.

"Thanks for bothering, Tessa. It's a pity it took this long for us to talk to each other again."

"I'll see you, Dan."

He locked the main door behind him, went back into the study and poured himself another drink. He checked the time; it was nearly one o'clock. In New York it would be coming up to eight in the morning; if he rang now, maybe he'd catch her before she left for the day.

He got the transatlantic operator and gave her the number.

"Is there a delay on the line?"

The operator told him she didn't think there was, and she would ring him back when she was trying the call.

While he waited, he thought about her and about what he had had in London. There was a pull about London that he knew was probably illogical. It was because he knew it so well; the familiarity produced security.

The telephone shrilled, and that made him jump. He looked at the receiver and let it ring some more. Then, when he was ready, he put the drink down and lifted the arm from its cradle.

"Hello, this is Dan Sinclair."

"Good Lord, at last." The voice was strong. "You know, I was beginning to think you didn't exist. My name's Nutting, Mr. Sinclair. Your very efficient secretary has told you all about me, I'm sure."

He let the man talk, and while he listened, his fingers drummed the glass-topped table. And then he stopped the impatient drumming and took up a pencil and started to write. He had nearly covered the sheet of paper with notes by the time the man had finished.

For a moment neither of them said anything; then it was Sinclair's turn, and the adrenalin started to flow.

"Mr. Nutting, the most important thing is to get the product right. . . ."